Dark butterscotch with a creamy mane and tail, the mare was muscular and beautiful.

Sam knew she had to inspect the mare's injury if she expected to help. Without moving her head, Sam lowered her eyes.

The mare's leg was swollen. To get a better look at the wound, Sam bent her knees a fraction of an inch, then a full inch, watching the mare for reaction.

The wild horse did nothing until Ace squealed.

Sam had to look away from the mare.

Moving through a tunnel of branches laden with gold leaves, parting the pollen, shadows and sunlight, the Phantom came toward her, striding down the river like a king.

Read all the books about the

Phantom Stallion

Phantom Stallion

22
Wild Honey

TERRI FARLEY

AVON BOOKS

An Imprint of HarperCollinsPublishers

Library of Congress Catalog Card Number: 2005906567

ISBN-10: 0-06-081539-6 — ISBN-13: 978-0-06-081539-4

❖

First Avon edition, 2006

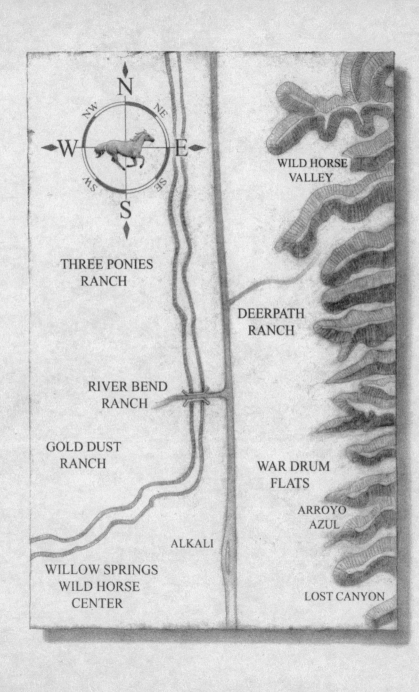

Chapter One ⚬

*L*eather creaked as Samantha Forster swung onto her horse's back and tested the saddle's position. This was no time to make a mistake.

Dawn's golden shimmer still hovered beyond the peaks of the Calico Mountains and the two-story white ranch house stood silent, with only the kitchen light glowing, but Sam was ready to ride.

Her bay mustang Ace flicked his black-edged ears forward. When she didn't urge him ahead, his ears slanted sideways, then back. He snorted plumes of vapor into the September morning, just as eager to leave as Sam was.

"Now?" Sam asked.

She did her best to sound patient, though it

wasn't like she hadn't ridden in predawn darkness plenty of times before. But her stepmother Brynna stood barefoot on the front porch, making sure Sam didn't leave without permission.

At three thirty-six A.M., Sam had heard Tempest squeal. The filly was barely three months old and she was Sam's baby. Eyes half open, Sam had lurched out of bed as if a fishing hook had lodged in the center of her chest and her filly's cry was reeling her in.

Sam had beaten Dad down the stairs but his whiplash voice had stopped her before she reached the front door.

"Samantha. You don't know what you're runnin' into."

Outside, Blaze, the ranch watchdog, had been barking. He hadn't sounded ferocious, just watchful; but Sam had known Dad wouldn't take her translation of dog talk as a guarantee of safety.

"I'll look out the window first," she'd protested loudly.

Too loudly, it turned out. Her voice kind of echoed off Dad, who'd come downstairs, too.

Sam pushed back the curtains covering the window over the kitchen sink and stared toward Tempest's corral. Dad stood just inches behind Sam, but he let her look first.

Wow. If she'd been an instant later or even blinked as she stared out the window, Sam wouldn't have caught that glimpse of waving paleness. If she hadn't dreamed of the Phantom's moonlight visit almost every night, the saddle horses' neighing and Dark Sunshine's circling hoofbeats wouldn't have made her stare past Tempest's pasture to see the silver stallion dash up the hillside, away from civilization.

"Dad, did you see —"

"I saw him. Can't think of one good thing about him lurkin' around like that, either."

Sam had stared at her father in disbelief. Even though he'd seen the Phantom, too, Dad had actually snorted when she'd insisted she had to ride after the stallion. He'd forbidden her to leave until daybreak and he hadn't been nice about it. Her disappointment didn't affect him either.

"But, Dad . . . ," Sam had moaned as he'd turned away from her and started back to his bedroom.

"Quit your sighin', Samantha," he'd said. "I can feel the draft from here."

Then he'd continued back upstairs without another word, despite the excitement that kept their saddle horses neighing and restless all night long.

Sam had stayed downstairs. She wouldn't disobey Dad, but her mind kept planning her escape — as if she would.

There'd been no chance to sneak out, anyway.

Brynna, restless herself in her last months of pregnancy, had stayed up to study maps as big as beach blankets, which she'd spread out on the kitchen table.

Just the same, Sam had gotten dressed, then saddled Ace in the darkness, making sure the latigo strap that held the saddle in place lay flat and snug. She'd taken a stupid dive out of the saddle a few days ago. Since then, Ace seemed to be waiting for another mistake.

Like the one she kept picturing right now, Sam thought. She should not be imagining herself leaning low on Ace's neck, urging him into a rash and reckless gallop up the rise, along the ridge and after the Phantom.

She should be keeping her eyes focused on Brynna, who'd appointed herself clock boss.

"I don't know what you hope to accomplish," Brynna said, finally, pulling her robe a little closer.

"There must be a reason the Phantom was here," Sam explained. "He almost never crosses over to our side of the river. Please, can I go now?"

A rooster scratched the dirt noisily, then hopped to the henhouse roof, fluttered his feathers, and gave a rusty crow.

Sam looked pointedly toward the bird. Even the chickens knew it was time to get moving.

"Okay," Brynna surrendered. "Be careful."

"Always," Sam said.

Despite Brynna's skeptical groan, Sam reined Ace, her bay mustang, away from the porch. She'd barely thought of shifting forward when the gelding set off across the ranch yard at a speedy jog that threatened to break into a lope if she'd allow it.

"Not yet," Sam told her horse, and his smooth gait turned to a pouty, hammering trot.

Sam had already opened the gates in the old pasture. She angled Ace through the first one, then let out her reins, letting Ace lope over the short, crunchy grass of the shortcut while she looked up, toward the trail head.

Other horses called after them, crowding against their fences as Ace bounded through the second gate and up the trail that ran behind River Bend Ranch. It was steep and crowded with sagebrush at first.

"Careful," Sam told her horse as the path began weaving through granite boulders. The footing disappeared between bleached drifts of cheatgrass, then turned dusty and choked with dry brush. Each time their passing cracked a twig, it gave off the smell of summer's end.

As soon as Ace reached the ridge top, Sam glanced back over her shoulder. A toy house, miniature barn, two little bunkhouses, and a bridge made up the River Bend Ranch. She was leaving it behind and riding into wild horse country. Smiling.

She and Ace were following the Phantom. The silver stallion was roaming out of his home territory and Sam had to know why.

"We would have had a better chance of finding him if we'd started an hour ago," Sam grumbled to Ace.

As if he knew and was determined to make up for lost time, Ace thrust his tongue against his snaffle. Sam shortened her reins while she decided what to do next.

Which way should she turn? The ridgeline trail stretched twelve long miles and it was mostly used by wildlife. Last fall, a cougar had roved the length of it, using downhill paths to hunt near Three Ponies Ranch, River Bend Ranch, and Gold Dust Ranch. Early that summer, Sam had seen deer standing in the last snow patches on the ridge, taking refuge from biting insects that avoided the cold. Sam had also seen New Moon, the Phantom's night-black son, on this path, and once—now twice—the Phantom himself.

Left hand steady on her reins, Sam leaned out, sighting past Ace's front hooves. One good thing about waiting until sunrise was that she might be able to see the stallion's hoofprints and figure out which way he'd headed.

But it wasn't as easy as it sounded.

Sam knew the Phantom didn't travel right down the middle of a path unless he was being pursued. Instinct kept him walking alongside the trails, through mountain mahogany, pinion pine, and other desert groves that might hide him.

Sam scanned the dusty spots between grass and brush. She saw a few pebbles, ants busy against the coming cold of autumn, and lots of different shades of brown dirt.

"I'm no good at this," Sam muttered to Ace, but she didn't tell even her horse that she could use Jake Ely's help. Her friend Jake read tracks and other natural signs as easily as she read books.

Sam cued Ace to turn right. Tracks or not, she'd never known the Phantom to head for Gold Dust Ranch. Okay, once, a long time ago, but turning right made more sense. This way would take her toward Deerpath Ranch and Aspen Creek. She'd sighted wild horses in both those places where water and forage remained through late summer and fall.

Sam drew rein at Aspen Creek about an hour later. Birds asked warbling questions as they woke. The grove around her was hazy with pollen and all the prettier because this year no cougars stalked the area.

As she'd watched for horse tracks, Sam had remembered Jake's warnings from last year. She'd checked the ground for scrapes kicked up by cougars' hind feet and tree trunks gouged by big cats that used them as scratching posts. She'd seen neither, and now she could relax.

Gold leaves swirled on blue water in a whirlpool between rocks in the creek.

The sun had risen and though most of the tracks she'd seen belonged to mule deer, every now and then Sam had seen the V-bottomed pattern of a horse's hoof. Besides, it just made sense for the Phantom to stop here. If she were a horse, Sam thought, she'd spend the morning here under the yellow canopies of white-barked aspen trees.

As Ace drank, Sam watched the fallen leaves race between the river rocks. Like valiant little canoes, they followed currents and eddies, bound for the La Charla River.

A clear hoofprint was pressed deep into the mud a few yards downstream, but it looked bigger than the Phantom's.

"It probably just filled with water and oozed out," Sam reasoned to her horse, but Ace was busy drinking.

And then he startled and shied.

Creek water splashed up, spotting Sam's dusty boots. Muzzle dripping, Ace stared and she turned to follow his gaze.

She squinted downstream, trying to make out whatever he'd seen, some form camouflaged by the aspen grove's jumble of sunbeams and shadows.

Ace's ears pointed and his nostrils opened wide. She saw nothing and heard only water tumbling over rocks. And one thing she didn't smell was the meaty, dirty laundry smell of mountain lion.

What is it, boy? Sam wondered, but she didn't ask aloud, just gave her horse enough rein that he could investigate and take her closer.

It was probably just a deer. Ace was jumpy and excited this morning. But maybe she should unbuckle her saddlebags and grab her binoculars. After her best friend Jen's accident a couple weeks ago, Sam had decided to start carrying a few emergency supplies along with her.

Except, well, making the decision was about as far as she'd progressed in stashing stuff in her saddlebags. But she knew she'd tucked her binoculars inside the leather pouch.

What was . . . ? The sound must have been wind in the dry leaves, but no.

Ace's stare had shifted to the other side of the shallow creek. Whatever he was watching must have moved, because his head lifted. When a faint neigh rumbled from him as he gazed uphill, she knew it had to be another horse.

And then she saw it.

The mustang stood all alone. It wasn't the Phantom, but Sam recognized the wild horse just the same.

The color of dark honey, the Phantom's lead mare didn't move. She didn't answer Ace or make any other sound, but something in the horse's solitude and stance told Sam the mare was in pain.

She wouldn't cry out if she was hurt, Sam thought. A prey animal in distress—even a big one like a horse—would make an easy meal for a predator.

And it didn't take Sam long to come up with a cause for the mare's discomfort.

The fight with Hotspot, Sam thought, and she could see it all over again.

The Appaloosa mare had gone missing from Gold Dust Ranch, and had been running with the Phantom's herd. Feeling threatened by the lead mare, Hotspot had lunged with teeth exposed. When her bite had missed, Hotspot had wheeled and launched a double-hooved kick at the lead mare, this dark palomino now standing on the hillside. Sam imagined the echo of those striking hooves.

Wild horses avoided serious fights because instinct told them too much was at stake. An injured horse, unable to travel with the herd, was vulnerable. But Hotspot wasn't a mustang. She hadn't known the rules and risks of being wild.

The lead mare stood off-balance, as if she were trying to keep the weight off her right front leg. Sam would bet a closer look would show her that the mare was holding her hoof off the ground. But she didn't urge Ace closer. That could spook the lonely horse into hurting herself further.

Sam's mind spun. She had to think fast. How could she help the wild horse?

She was no vet, no biologist, not even very good at roping cows. If she got close enough to rope the mare, what then? Tie her and try to examine her legs? Even a tame horse's hooves could be dangerous, she had proof of that right before her eyes.

Had the mare been left behind? How unfair was that, Sam thought, a lead mare who couldn't lead had been abandoned by those she'd protected.

The mare was watching her.

If she didn't know better, Sam would think the mare was actually appealing to her for help. Of course that was impossible. If anything, the horse was considering Sam's power as a threat.

The best thing for the horse was to be with her herd, even if she couldn't lead.

Sam's mind circled back to the reason she was out here in the first place. Where was the Phantom?

"I'm trusting you to stay ground-tied," Sam told Ace, though a squirm of uneasiness passed through her. She tried to talk herself out of it.

Why should Ace go anywhere? He had food and water right here. He was a tried and tested cowpony. He'd be just fine.

Sam lifted the saddlebags from her saddle. Without looking inside, she faced the creek. What she had, she had. It would be a waste of time to paw through her saddlebags to see what paltry supplies she carried, before crossing the water.

She took a deep breath and unfastened her rope from her saddle, too. She widened the coil and slipped it over her head and one arm, wearing it across her chest like a bandolier. Lame as she was with a lariat, Sam took all the tools she had.

Aspen Creek was low, barely covering the creek bed and rocks, and it was narrow, maybe ten feet across.

Piece of cake, Sam thought as she sat, eased off

her boots and socks, then left them on the shore.

She took four steps before the cold registered on her skin and in her brain. Then, Sam gasped. The creek sent icicle jolts between her toes. She fought the urge to curl over and grab her feet with her warm hands. If she hadn't been holding her saddlebags, she might have done it.

Piece of cake? her mind screeched. Piece of ten-million-year-old permafrozen glacier, maybe.

What had she been thinking? On an early September morning when it was barely light she was wading across a creek that would be frozen soon. How dumb was that?

Except she knew what she had been thinking, and the loose logic of it still held. She was thinking the pretty mare who'd helped the Phantom rule his wild herd needed help. And no one else was here to give it.

Sam bit her lip and took another step. How could she keep walking? Maybe counting would help. In Spanish. That would focus her mind on something besides the arctic pain.

Uno, dos . . . Oh, why couldn't her feet just go numb?

Tres . . . But not totally numb.

Quatro. Oh watch out! Not so numb that she couldn't keep her balance.

Cinco . . . Crossing the creek was tricky. Her feet must sense the difference between sand and round,

rolling rocks, or she'd fall flat on her face and . . .
Seis . . . the huge splash would send the injured mare
running.

Two more clumsy steps took Sam ashore. She
tried not to pant like a dog from relief. But she only
had to try for a minute, because close up, the mare
took Sam's breath away.

Dark butterscotch with a creamy mane and tail,
the mare was muscular and beautiful. And what Sam
had thought before was true. The mare looked
directly into Sam's eyes.

The palomino's expression was so intelligent and
expectant, Sam had to choke back the urge to talk to
her. Wild things didn't croon sweet words to calm
each other, so Sam stayed silent, but it wasn't easy.

Although the mare's eyes took in the saddlebags
and rope in a glance, she didn't bolt. She stood still,
favoring that right front hoof, holding it such a slight
distance above the ground that Sam wasn't sure she
could even slip a piece of paper under it.

But Sam knew she wasn't mistaken. The muscles
of the mare's left front leg were bunched and shaking
as if they'd held the extra load for hours. Or days.

Sam knew she had to inspect the mare's injury if
she expected to help. She let her shoulders droop.
She took slow steps, moving closer until she was only
a few feet away. Without moving her head, Sam
lowered her eyes.

The mare's leg was swollen. Just above her hoof,

a fly buzzed around a black blend of crust and goo.

To get a better look at the wound, Sam bent her knees a fraction of an inch, then a full inch, watching the mare for reaction.

The wild horse did nothing until Ace squealed.

Sam had to look away from the mare.

Ace was all right, but he was staring upstream again, and suddenly Sam knew the honey-colored mare hadn't been abandoned after all.

Moving through a tunnel of branches laden with gold leaves, parting the pollen, shadows and sunlight, the Phantom came toward her, striding down the river like a king.

Chapter Two ∾

The mare's agitated whinny rang in Sam's ear.

From her squatting position, Sam looked up to see the palomino directing all of her attention at the Phantom. The human at her feet was forgotten.

Sniffing and tossing her head, the mare tried to move forward. She made two steps before her hoof drew up. Struggling for balance, she swayed. Sun glinted off the long gentle slant of her shoulder and Sam scooted back.

The mare didn't fall, but only luck saved her. Sam reminded herself to stay alert. The horse could fall on her. She could be slammed to the earth or struck as the mare struggled to rise. And she'd be no help to the Phantom's lead mare if she was injured, too.

The attempt to go meet the Phantom had hurt the palomino. Sam saw furrows above the mare's dark-brown eyes. Pain and confusion warred in the horse's mind. Should she listen to her pain or answer her yearning to be with the herd?

The mare's second neigh soared like a scream. With her lips working and head tossing, she appealed to the Phantom for help, begging him not to leave her behind.

Poor girl, Sam thought, swallowing hard at the mare's distress.

When she looked back toward the Phantom, Sam saw he was listening. He passed through the rest of the herd as they meandered along the creek. Some drank. Others stood in the shade. Though most of the mares acted immune to the lead mare's neighs, a few stared into the rustling branches overhead and all of the foals moved with jerky, uncertain movements.

The Phantom approached with arched neck and prancing steps, his silken mane covering his neck like some kind of royal shawl, or a mantle of authority. He looked arrogant, set on taking over this shady creek-side territory, until he recognized Sam.

He gave a quick snort of inquiry.

What are you doing here? he seemed to ask, and she saw each of his senses sharpen to inspect the area again. Had she brought other humans? Ropes? Loud trucks and danger? Sensing no peril, he splashed across the creek.

Flicking his tail in annoyance, the Phantom came toward Sam. He splashed down the creek, then raised and lowered his head, telling her to back off.

In this crouch, Sam supposed she looked submissive and small as a foal and literally like an underling. But she couldn't obey the stallion's order to get lost. Any quick movements might send the lead mare shying and falling, damaging that leg even worse.

When Sam didn't move, the Phantom repeated the movements with more energy, flinging a silver profusion of mane and forelock to underline his command.

When she still didn't obey, he bolted forward. Droplets sprayed as he cut the distance between them in half and stepped from the creek to the bank.

Crouched between the stallion and the lead mare, Sam knew she was in danger. It might look to him as if she kept the mare from obeying his summons.

The stallion knew her. She'd raised him from a foal, but the accusing look he flashed her showed no hint of memory.

"Zanzibar," Sam whispered, but the stallion pawed the creekbank, tossing spatters of mud.

It was what Brynna would call an aggressive display. Infuriated by the sight of the rope slung over her shoulder and her refusal to flee, he arched his neck until muscles rippled under his silver hide and his chin bumped his chest.

Keep your silly human friendship, the stallion signaled her.

The palomino was his and Sam had no part in his life as a herd stallion.

"I can't leave," Sam whispered. "She's bleeding. You can chase off the coyotes or cougars that might smell it, but you can't help her heal, and I can. Maybe."

The Phantom drummed his front hooves, then lowered his head and snaked it in a herding movement he'd use for any mare or foal. And Sam knew what would happen if the mare or foal was slow to respond. If they were lucky, they'd see his bared teeth coming their way and get going.

Even though he'd never bitten her, Sam held her breath and then, as the Phantom's head struck toward her like something primitive and mythical, a griffin or a fire-eyed snake, she curled her arms around herself, ducked her head, and hoped.

His hooves made the ground below her shake, and Sam knew he'd divided the distance between them in half again. He must be very close because, even curled up for safety, she could smell the clover sweetness of his breath.

In tiny fractions, Sam lifted her head, letting each vertebrae in her neck align so slowly that for minutes, her eyes saw only mud, the stallion's hooves, and the wet hair curling above his fetlocks.

At last, she met his irritated gaze. His head was lowered and his eyes stared from no more than five feet away. Offended and huffing, the Phantom's expression said he wouldn't make more allowances for her simple human brain.

She'd received her last warning, so Sam stayed still though the muscles in her thighs quivered from crouching and her Achilles tendons stung. How long could her trembling toes grip the wet dirt and keep her balanced?

The creek's prattle must have covered her frightened breaths, because the stallion backed off a step with a satisfied nod, but he hadn't forgiven her. An iridescent blue-green dragonfly zipped past his nose and Ace's shod hoof struck rock, but the stallion kept one delicate ear swiveled in Sam's direction.

The Phantom was magnificent. Being this close to him was a gift, even if he was threatening her.

That's crazy talk, Sam rebuked herself.

The stallion was wild. She couldn't predict his actions. She could guess, but she'd been wrong before. She had to get out of this submissive position and beyond the reach of his hooves.

She'd be insane to risk another concussion or shattered bone on the chance that she could read the stallion's mind.

But what should she do?

The mare decided for her, lurching three steps closer to the stallion. For an instant, Sam saw dried blood cracking, opening a red fissure over the wound. Then, the Phantom wheeled, moving after the mare. His tail sung through the air like a million mosquitoes and lashed Sam's cheek.

Enough. Sam scrambled to her feet, backing off, but not running.

The Phantom cast one more look her way, rolling his eyes and jabbing his muzzle at Sam in a last command to leave the mare to him. He stalked off, assuming she'd obey.

Then, the Phantom lowered his head and sniffed his lead mare's flank as if he didn't recognize her. Next, the stallion inspected the blood running in rivulets over her hoof. The palomino shuddered and closed her eyes.

Was this the feeling people called feeling déjà vu? Sam had the sensation she'd seen this all happen before. Then, she realized it had.

The Phantom's tiger dun lead mare had cracked her hoof. She'd been found alone on the *playa* and captured by the Bureau of Land Management, but the Phantom had seen her one last time after she'd been adopted and it had been just this sad.

Sam's imagination swarmed with thousands of mustangs rounded up and jammed into trucks. One side of her mind argued she wouldn't have Ace without the BLM's adoption program, but the other half said horses like Blue, Tinkerbell, Dark Sunshine, and Jinx should still be living free.

If the BLM found this beautiful mare, she'd get the medical treatment she needed, and an adoptive home. But wasn't her real home on the range with the Phantom?

The palomino stared across the creek at the other mares and lifted her hoof higher, as if she'd rejoin the others even if she had to do it on three legs.

The two horses couldn't know what she was thinking, and Sam was grateful. As much as she wanted the mare to stay with the Phantom, she couldn't let it happen. The mare wouldn't be able to keep up with the herd. Her cries wouldn't stop them from leaving her behind, but they'd alert predators. If the wound reopened, the scent of blood would lure them to her. An adult horse was dangerous prey, but instinct would tell them they only had to wait. Eventually, she'd be weak enough to attack.

Slowly, Sam eased her rope off over her head. As Sam's fingers worked to open the loop in her rope, tears pricked at her eyes. She blinked, refusing to let them blur her vision. She had one chance to get this right.

The horses seemed to have forgotten her. The golden mare nuzzled the stallion's mane. He backed slowly to face her. Their noses were nearly touching.

As Sam watched, the Phantom finished his good-bye. With each step the stallion took away from the mare, Sam took one closer. She was only a few feet away now. Her rope couldn't miss.

The mare glanced at Sam, but her heart was following the Phantom and she hardly noticed when Sam held her breath, bit her lip, and flipped the rope over the mare's neck.

As it tightened, the stallion swung his head in reprimand. His teeth were bared, but not at Sam — at the mare.

Stay here, his gesture said. The order was cruel, but it might save the palomino's life.

He turned abruptly aside from the mare and left.

For a few hopeful seconds, Sam thought the parting was over.

Sun sifted through the leaves overhead, hunting out each silver dapple on the stallion's gleaming hide. The Phantom ignored the mare's whinny. He crossed a carpet of yellow leaves before walking into the creek and back to his band.

The mare stared after him, nostrils vibrating in a silent farewell.

And then she exploded.

With a squeal, the mare wrenched her neck sideways. The rope sizzled along Sam's palms before she grabbed and held on. The mare tried to bolt, but her foreleg pulled up in pain. Her golden shoulders heaved forward and her neck arched as she rose in a half rear, but when she came down and tried to plant her forelegs to buck and frighten off the human who held the rope, the injured leg crumpled and she slammed to the ground on her right side.

Panting and braced, Sam kept her eyes on the honey-colored lead mare and her hands on the rope.

Eyes closed, ears pinned back, the mare lay on her side, snorting through flared nostrils. Sam knew the mustang heard the clatter of wild hooves moving off, walking aimlessly, then jogging slowly. The herd hesitated without a lead mare's guidance.

The mare's muscles tightened. Her chest heaved and her eyes opened with a look so white-rimmed and agitated, it could have been madness. The mare knew she was alone. She knew she couldn't follow. Her legs thrashed briefly, running on air, and then she rested.

Sam chanced a single glance to make sure Ace had stayed ground-tied. Despite all the commotion, her loyal gelding stood only a few feet from where she'd left him.

When Sam looked back, the mare's sad brown eyes were watching her.

"Poor girl," Sam crooned. "I'll get you back to them as soon as your leg's well enough to travel. I promise."

When the mare lurched to her feet, Sam instinctively held up her hands for protection. She was standing so close, and a horse not really in control of its body seemed twice as big.

But the mare didn't hurt her. She didn't even try to walk. Her head drooped and the loop around her neck loosened. She held her hoof clear of the ground.

Without meaning to, Sam offered her hand for the mare to sniff, but the horse squealed and tossed her head up. Before the horse could hurt herself by backing away, Sam let her hand drop back to her side and looked down at the mare's wound.

Had Hotspot's hoof opened that slash from just above the center of the pale hoof, around the pastern and halfway up the fetlock?

At least she *thought* it was a slash. Beneath the coagulated blood, she made out a reddish channel. In three days, it should have scabbed over, shouldn't it? Maybe movement had kept that from happening, or the kick could have nicked a vein.

Sam gritted her teeth, realizing she didn't know enough about horse anatomy to take an educated guess.

"I know we need warm water to clean you up," Sam told the mare.

As if she realized the impossibility of that at Aspen Creek, the mare lowered her head and let her ears fall to each side.

"We'll go where we can get some," Sam said, and she could only think of one way to do that.

Sam decided she'd mount Ace. Now, while the wild horse was quiet and melancholy, was her best chance that the mare would follow him.

But where can I take her to tend that foot, then set her free? Sam wondered.

Home would be best, or Three Ponies Ranch, but Mrs. Allen's ranch was not only closest, it was part of the Phantom's territory.

Sam bit her lip, wondering if she could convince the old lady not to tell anyone about the injured palomino. After all, she was in the business of rescuing horses, not reporting them to the BLM, like Brynna.

But that cut . . .

Sam considered it, dubiously. The mare needed care, but there was no way Sam could count on Dr. Scott to keep the mare a secret. He was on a monthly salary from BLM to care for the captive mustangs.

But wait! Jen wanted to be a vet. And if Sam could trust Jen with her life—and she knew she could—she could trust her with this mare's freedom, too.

That was the best she could do: get the mare to Deerpath Ranch and call Jen.

With that decision made and the rope resting in her fingers, Sam hurried. An infection could be spreading up the mare's leg and into her system while Sam put off her next move. She knew a shortcut to Deerpath Ranch, but it meant crossing the creek here, then back across in about half an hour.

Sam took a bold step closer. The mare's eyes opened wider, but she barely flinched when Sam pulled the loop snug. The horse tossed her creamy forelock back from her eyes and yanked against the rope.

Digging her bare heels into the dirt, Sam braced herself. Any minute, the mare could take off. Sam pictured herself skiing through the mud at the end of her own lariat.

She tightened her fingers into fists around the rope, but nothing happened. The mare was no more skittish than Dark Sunshine.

The mare not only tolerated the rope, she didn't startle or spook at a human voice.

What was going on? Was the mare sicker than she looked? Had she simply lost the will to fight?

A breeze blew and dry aspen leaves applauded overhead, reminding Sam that it was autumn. Soon, the Phantom and his herd would leave for their wintering spot and this mare should go with them, even if she couldn't lead, because there was no way in the world she could keep this mustang secret until next spring.

She didn't have time to puzzle everything out right here and now.

"Okay baby, let's take a few easy steps."

The mare responded to the rope's pressure by walking gingerly, then taking a three-legged hop.

"We'll just go over and get Ace," she explained, "and you can follow him downhill to Mrs. Allen's."

As she walked after Sam, the mare's head bobbed downward on the left side, as if that would help her balance.

"There you go. No need to giddy up too fast," Sam said.

She couldn't help thinking how weird it was that the Phantom's lead mare acted almost domesticated.

Forget about it, Sam ordered herself. She didn't have to touch the mare's swollen leg to know it was hot and painful. The sooner she got it washed, treated, and bandaged, the sooner the mare could catch up with the Phantom. Then she'd be herself again.

"And I promise you, beauty," Sam said, "if you want to go back to the wild, you're going."

Sam and the honey-colored mare were halfway across the creek when the horse stopped, nearly jerking Sam off her freezing feet.

The mare gave a loud, relieved sigh. Her shoulders shifted forward and her head sagged almost to the water's surface.

"Does that cold water feel good?" Sam asked through nearly chattering teeth.

If the creek flow cooled the horse's wounded flesh, Sam guessed she could just stand here and shiver for a little while.

After all, she remembered the times she'd applied ice packs or even a plastic bag of frozen vegetables to her basketball injuries. She couldn't help sympathizing with the mare, even though her own feet felt like blocks of ice and then, after a few minutes, like big numb lumps where her shins entered the water.

"It's getting cleaner," Sam said as the water swirled around the mare's legs. But it would just get dirty again by the time she reached Mrs. Allen's barn and the first aide kit she kept inside. Mentally, Sam sorted through the things she'd brought with her. What could she use to pad and protect the mare's injury?

"Socks!" Sam said, and when the mare shied, she

resolved to stop talking.

Along with her binoculars and a granola bar, she had a pair of fresh socks in her saddlebag. They were wool, and they might be scratchy against the open wound, but not if she ripped a piece off her shirt and tied it over the wound before she wrapped the sock on.

Suddenly, the mare lurched toward shore and Sam hurried to keep up.

"Careful, careful," Sam cautioned the horse. One slip caused by that weak front leg and they could both go down. It was unlikely they'd drown, but it sure wouldn't be much fun.

The mare stopped beside Ace. While the two horses sniffed each other all over, Sam took the opportunity to put her boots back on. She didn't need them to ride Ace, and it would put her in a vulnerable position for a few minutes, but she felt safe here, and pretty sure she could keep hold of the rope and tug on her boots at the same time.

"Thank goodness," she moaned when she managed to stand and stomp her cold toes down into her boots.

But it wasn't her stamping that made both horses recoil. They heard rustling in the leaves overhead. It wasn't a morning breeze or a crow hopping on a branch, either.

Sam's right hand clamped onto her rope while her left snagged Ace's reins.

Looking up, she searched for whatever was

moving. And she walked backward. So what if she was clumsy? There was no way in the world that she'd turn around and expose her spine to whatever was jouncing those tree branches.

A cougar had swept her from the back of a horse once before. She refused to let it happen again.

"C'mon!" Sam hissed, but neither horse followed. She flung her weight against the rope and reins, knowing she wasn't hurting the animals half as much as a cougar would.

The horses seemed mesmerized. Of course, they weren't remembering that smell, or the sight of a cougar gnawing a deer long-frozen in a snow bank not far from here.

She had to scare the cat off, but how? If she bent over to pick up a rock to throw, she'd look like four-legged prey. That was out. She could yell, maybe, but would she be safer in the saddle? Sure, if she was riding Ace. He'd hightail it out of here like the mustang he was, but what about the injured horse?

Sam drew a breath, determined to make a commotion. She hoped the honey-colored mare was terrified enough to outdistance a predator before it identified her as lame.

What was that? Ace snorted and both horses' ears pointed as something struck the ground across the creek. Sam whirled to look, too.

Good. Whatever it was had moved to the other side of the water.

Sam's shoulders sagged with relief an instant before her brain reminded her cats didn't like to swim, and she would have seen it pounce. Before she could make sense of those facts a dark shadow blocked the sun, and something landed heavily behind her.

Chapter Three ∾

Reeling with panic, Sam turned to face her attacker.

"Next time you steal a horse you might pick one with four good legs."

Jake Ely wore running clothes. He leaned forward with his hands on his thighs to stare at the palomino's front hoof, then used the back of one hand to brush at a twig caught in his black hair.

He looked pretty casual for a guy who'd practically given her a heart attack, a guy who was about to pay for it big-time.

Sam's thoughts vanished under an avalanche of outrage. She didn't mean to drop the end of her rope. It just happened. One second she was picturing herself gripping his shoulders and shaking him until his teeth clacked together and the next second she'd pushed off from the ground and launched herself right at him.

Of course it didn't work out the way she'd pictured it.

She charged.

Jake sidestepped.

She whirled around to take another run at him. He bent, grabbed her rope as it trailed past, and caught the palomino. Then he rolled his eyes sympathetically at Ace as if they were both so used to Sam's dramatics.

How could she punish him, but not traumatize the horses?

Sam knew she probably shouldn't waste time wondering. The wild mare fidgeted at the end of the rope, looking more fascinated by Jake than frightened.

In that moment of quiet, Sam heard her own quick, shallow breaths. Jake studied her like she was an amoeba under a microscope. She couldn't put together a sentence to tell him to stop.

"You look pale."

"What I look is homicidal," Sam managed, but then she wrecked her sarcasm by feeling so dizzy she had to grab an aspen trunk for support. How could he have scared her so badly?

"Sit down before you fall down," Jake insisted.

Something about that order made Sam's weakness vanish, and she was pretty sure her voice sounded calm as she said, "I'm not going to faint. I'm going to wipe that grin off your stupid face."

Totally on its own, her right arm swung through the air, hand fisted.

He grabbed her wrist.

"Not like that, you won't," Jake said. Instantly he released her wrist and took a step back.

"I know you're not giving me advice on how to beat you up." Sam rubbed her wrist as if it hurt, but it didn't.

"Punchin's a useful skill for a horse thief," Jake said, then tilted his head toward the palomino mare. "Where'd ya get this one?"

Sam thought about Jake's choice of words. *This one,* as if she were forever stealing horses. The only horse she'd ever stolen was Dark Sunshine, and that awful Flick had deserved to lose her. That's why he was in jail.

Sure, she'd been accused of stealing the Slocums' Appaloosas, but she really hadn't.

"She's wild," Sam said.

"I can see that," Jake said sarcastically as the mare glanced between them, following their conversation.

While she tried to figure out what was going on with the Phantom's lead mare, Sam realized she was almost smiling. Even though Jake had scared her half to death, his leap from the aspen trees was just the sort of prank he used to play on her.

Since he'd cut off his long hair for his college

visits and scholarship interviews, then cranked up his academic and athletic efforts for his last year in high school, he'd been different from the Jake who'd been her friend ever since she could remember.

She'd missed him.

It made her happy to see him acting like a kid. As usual, though, he was a patient kid. While her mind had veered off on a tangent, he stood waiting for her to explain the way-too-tame mustang.

"She's been running with the Phantom's herd for a long time," Sam said, and it took little effort to recall the first time she'd spotted the mare. "Remember on Dad and Brynna's wedding day how you shampooed my hair in the horse trough?"

Jake nodded, with a satisfied smile.

"That was because she knocked Ace off his feet and jumped over us."

"Hmm," Jake said. He reached a hand toward the mare and she backed clumsily, head swinging from side to side, to avoid his touch. When her right front hoof brushed the ground, the weak leg wobbled and she gave a pained squeal.

Jake made a comforting sound to the horse, but the look he flashed Sam was stern.

"Better bandage her up and get her to a vet."

"I have a plan," Sam protested, then told him how she wanted to wrap the wound with a piece of her shirt and the sock, then lead the mare to Mrs. Allen's ranch.

She took Jake's shrug to mean her idea was barely better than nothing, so Sam didn't swear him to silence. She didn't insist the Phantom's lead mare had to return to the herd. Right now, she needed Jake's help. She could browbeat him into agreeing with her later.

They picked a spot of shade and tied Ace to a tree, then brought the mare alongside him.

Sam lifted her saddlebags off Ace. She'd just started to crouch beside the mare, as she had across the creek, when Jake said, "You want to hold her and I'll do that?"

Was he saying he could do a better job or taking on the risk of getting kicked? Sam didn't bother asking. She knew he wouldn't give her a straight answer.

"I'll do it. You hold her," Sam said.

Then, maybe because he didn't like her answer, Jake started being a jerk.

"Didn't Sheriff Ballard talk to you about admirin' other folks' horses a little too much?"

"Jake, you know I've never—"

"And how could you not know I was here? The tread on these running shoes makes distinctive tracks and that wild bunch had me spotted from a mile away."

"Distinctive—" Sam cut off her outburst because of the horses, then muttered, "Pardon me for not having the instincts of a wild animal."

"You need to concentrate on something besides that stallion," Jake insisted.

Sam wanted to yell in frustration, but she didn't. She couldn't help going stiff, though.

Both Jake and Dad thought she lost her good sense where the Phantom was concerned. They were wrong, but she didn't want to have that argument right now, either.

For the first time in maybe a thousand conversations, Jake filled the silence between them.

Expressionless, with his lids half lowered, he said, "You did good over there" — Jake nodded to the far side of the creek where she'd roped the mare — "but she's not wild."

Sam could barely believe it. Jake had seen her pinned between the two horses and hadn't rushed to her rescue. That had to be another first. Either he trusted her judgement, or he thought she'd be in greater danger if he swooped in heroically. But he didn't believe the mare was wild.

"Whatever," Sam said. "You be the expert. I don't care. But she's the Phantom's lead mare and she has to get back to the herd before they go —" Where would the herd head? Certainly to a lower altitude, where they'd be warmer and have more food. Maybe the Phantom's secret valley? "Wherever they winter," she finished lamely, then added, "And she's really hurt, Jake, so why don't you help, instead of harassing me?"

Jake's only response was to stare down at the

wound again. The bleeding seemed to have stopped. Had the cold water helped? Sam glanced away from the wound to see if Jake's expression told her what he thought of the mare's condition.

He didn't meet her eyes.

"Jake?"

"Settle down. Cut's a long way from her heart." Jake's typical cowboy understatement didn't soothe her until he added, "Let's see what we can do."

After doing the best they could without disinfectant and gauze, Sam rode Ace and led the mare, while Jake walked alongside. It had taken double the usual time to reach the border of Deerpath Ranch, but either the cold water or the soft sock covering must have eased the tenderness around the mare's injury, because she kept walking.

Their gait was so slow and uneven. Ace stopped several times and might have napped if Sam hadn't kept him moving. But the mare seemed more cautious than miserable.

Jake had insisted on walking beside the horse to watch her for any danger signs, but he hadn't spoken since they'd left the shade of Aspen Creek.

Now they were moving down a path flanked with horse-high weeds. Ace and the palomino were wary as they approached the Blind Faith Mustang Sanctuary, but Sam spotted the pointed roofline of Mrs. Allen's lavender house with relief.

As they entered Mrs. Allen's ranch yard, Jake stayed near the mare, but in all this time he hadn't touched her.

He is so patient, Sam thought as she watched him observe the mare's ears, eyes, and nostrils inspect this new place.

Deerpath Ranch was strangely silent. Out of habit, Sam's eyes wandered to the iron gate barring the path through the garden to Mrs. Allen's house. It still had spear-shaped uprights and they looked as dangerous to Sam now as they had when she was a little kid.

The Boston bull terriers must be shut up in the house, because they weren't yapping at the arrival of company. Mrs. Allen's three old saddle horses, Calico, Ginger, and Judge, dozed in the midday shade at the far end of their pasture. The captive mustangs were probably down by the stream that spurred off the La Charla River.

Sam tightened her grip on the rope leading to the mare as the sound of a rake scraping over dry ground tipped Sam off to the old lady's location.

Dressed in jeans and a faded denim vest slapped on in place of a shirt, hair stuffed under a maroon baseball cap her teenage grandson had left behind two weeks ago, Mrs. Allen worked in the big pasture.

With robotic movements, she raked then shoveled sun-dried manure into a wheelbarrow. Had she even noticed she had company?

She's exhausted, Sam thought. Though Trudy Allen wasn't the shuffling, out-of-focus woman she'd been last year, before she'd taken in more than a dozen "unadoptable" mustangs, she looked burned out.

Why wouldn't she? Mrs. Allen ran Deerpath Ranch all alone, though it was about the same size as River Bend.

Sam did a quick count, tapping fingers down on her saddle horn. Pepper, Ross, Dad, Dallas, Gram—she had to go to her other hand and tapped her fingers on her jeaned leg—Brynna, and her. Sam counted again and shook her head. They had seven people to share the chores at River Bend Ranch, and though Mrs. Allen didn't run cattle anymore, just taking care of the horses, fences, and house was more than one person could handle.

"Ride on in," Jake said. His glance told Sam it would be bad news to be standing at the ranch entrance if a car or truck drove up.

"Right," Sam said.

Cautious as if her hooves were treading on a sheet of glass, the mare followed Ace and Sam couldn't help looking back once more. Mrs. Allen had grown so thin that she looked taller, and her arms were like sticks. Mrs. Allen was a talented artist, but she wasn't much of a cook. Was she eating right?

Sam was telling herself she sounded like Gram, when she saw Mrs. Allen become aware of them. The old lady lifted her head and Sam just had time to take in the hollows beneath her cheekbones before Mrs. Allen threw down the rake. The clash of metal striking the wheelbarrow made both horses shy.

"Just what I need," Mrs. Allen shouted as she came toward them. "Another broken-down nag to add to my collection."

Sam met Jake's eyes. Was he remembering their childhood fears that Mrs. Allen was really a cackling witch who lived behind the spike-tipped iron fence in her purple house?

"Bad time?" Jake muttered.

Maybe, but they couldn't hide the horse while they waited for Mrs. Allen's mood to improve.

"What are we going to do?" Sam asked, and her voice must have carried.

"Don't mind my crummy disposition," Mrs. Allen said, "but don't expect any lunch, either. I haven't been to the store for weeks and I'm pretty much down to canned soup and stale crackers." She yanked the cap off her gray-threaded black hair and wiped the back of her hand across her sweaty brow. "And heaven knows it's too hot for that kind of lunch."

Mrs. Allen's tone said she was joking, but Sam noticed her hands were shaking.

"What if I go in and make some iced tea?" Sam asked.

Mrs. Allen gave a self-mocking grunt. "As if I remembered to fill the ice cube trays this morning. Or last night." She pulled the cap back on her head and smiled. "Although I will say you're getting more like your grandmother every day, trying to fix what's wrong with something to eat or drink."

Sam shrugged, then she looked pointedly at the mare.

"I can't take on another horse. Don't even tell me the story on this one," Mrs. Allen said flatly. "Do you know, day before yesterday I got a call from a vet over in some neighborhood outside Reno? I turned down a horse he wanted me to take. A wild one, just a yearling, he said." Mrs. Allen's feisty voice began fading. ". . . wandered into town and was hit by a car."

Sam leaned forward against Ace's neck, trying to hear. At her movement, the palomino gave a nervous nicker. Surely Mrs. Allen would comment on the beautiful horse now.

But she didn't.

"Thing that's been bothering me, is I forgot to ask what would become of the yearling when I said no. I've been going over the possibilities ever since. Could hardly sleep last night for wondering how they'll do it." Mrs. Allen squinted at the sun behind Sam's head. "You know they'll put him down."

Mrs. Allen closed her eyes, clearly aching for someone to contradict her. Sam knew Jake wouldn't. He just stood there, wordless as the two horses.

"No they won't," Sam said, and when Mrs. Allen opened her eyes, Sam added, "They'll find some city horse-lover to take him in."

"I hope so," Mrs. Allen said. "But I'll tell you the truth, I'm at my wits' end trying to keep this place running. It's falling apart faster than I can fix it. Why, can you believe a quail crashed through my kitchen window this morning? It did. Being chased by a hawk, I guess, and the poor stupid thing didn't know it couldn't fly through glass. Course, that's shattered on the floor, now."

Mrs. Allen gave such a heavy sigh, Sam didn't ask if the quail had died. She knew it must have.

"Let me take care of that," Jake said.

Sam felt as surprised as Mrs. Allen looked.

Her lips, wearing old, cracked lipstick, opened and closed a couple times before she said, "It's a mess. I—well, I didn't have the energy to sweep up the glass and bury the poor bird." She ducked her head in embarrassment. "I just put the dogs in my studio and came outside."

"No problem," Jake said, and he strode away to do what had to be done.

Chapter Four ∞

"He's a nice boy, Samantha," Mrs. Allen said, staring after Jake.

The iron gate creaked as he opened it, then clanged shut behind him.

"Uh-huh," Sam said. She knew it was true, though her pulse disagreed. It had just finally settled down after thinking Jake was a pouncing cougar.

"I'm glad he offered to help with the window. Winter will be here before you know it, but I probably would have just taped something over the broken glass." Mrs. Allen rubbed her hands on her tanned arms as if she already felt goose bumps. "Do you think he knows how?"

"Probably," Sam said. "Ranch boys have to do a

little bit of everything." Then she drew a breath.
"About this horse—"

"Can you believe your grandmother called to
invite me to a church social tonight?"

Sam could believe it. Gram and Mrs. Allen had
been friends when they were girls, and they'd
recently rekindled their friendship. Sam also believed
Mrs. Allen had decided the best way to keep from
taking on a new horse was not hearing its sad story.

"A senior citizens mixer, Grace said." Mrs.
Allen pronounced the words as if they were a newly
discovered virus. "Can you imagine anything more
depressing?"

"It might be fun," Sam encouraged her.

"Maybe it would start out that way, but Grace
and my daughter both seem to think I need rescuing.
They don't like me living out here all by myself." Mrs.
Allen flashed an accusing stare at Sam, as if she'd
agree.

"You have all the animals," Sam said.

"Right," Mrs. Allen snapped. "I don't need a
white knight galloping in to take me away from all
this. I like where I am just fine." Mrs. Allen gave a
nod so sharp, the palomino sidestepped away.

"Not that I'd turn down a couple strong backs
and some hands that aren't afraid to get dirty doing
something worthwhile," Mrs. Allen added.

"I just know there are kids—adults, too, I bet—all
over the country who love horses and would work to

save them if they could," Sam said, but she refused to be led off the subject of the Phantom's injured lead mare. "This horse—"

"If those dedicated folks lived next door and worked as hard for the horses as you do, I wouldn't have any problems at all," Mrs. Allen mused.

Delight buzzed through Sam. Mrs. Allen couldn't have given her a greater compliment. And she meant it. She wasn't throwing praise around to get Sam to do something for her. In fact, Mrs. Allen wasn't even looking at Sam.

Her hands were on her hips as she glared toward the road leading into the ranch. "Can you believe someone filed a complaint against me with the Humane Society?"

"What?"

"That's right. Someone said I wasn't caring for the horses properly and my sanctuary should be shut down."

"But who?" Sam asked as images of the rescued horses flashed through her mind.

She thought of Faith, a Medicine Hat filly blind from birth, of the pretty young mare with crippled front legs, and the black horse with bumps scarring its body from an untreated allergy. Where would these horses go without Mrs. Allen?

"The Humane Society wouldn't tell me who reported me, but that's another thing I went to thinkin' about late last night. It could have been these tourists who stopped in and wanted to see wild horses. They were disappointed because I didn't have a chuck wagon breakfast waiting for them. Then they decided the horses must be sick because they weren't running around." Mrs. Allen tsked her tongue. "In this heat? I ask you, what kind of dumb animal would be galloping just for fun?

"And then there's Linc Slocum. He still wants to get his hands on about sixty of my acres, to make a dude ranch or some such nonsense."

Mrs. Allen's eyes wandered to the honey-colored mare. Sam held her breath, waiting. If Mrs. Allen really looked at the palomino, she'd be hooked.

Sam watched Mrs. Allen's eyes dart from the mare's flaxen forelock to her glossy muscled shoulders, to her injury, then back up to the mare's brown eyes. Mrs. Allen took a deep breath, not as if she'd speak, but wistfully, as if she imagined the mare free.

When Mrs. Allen sighed, crossed her arms in surrender, and nodded, Sam knew she had a partner in crime. She didn't dare dance in delight, but she felt like it.

"My, she's a beauty," Mrs. Allen said. Her eyes skimmed over the horse with reluctant admiration once more. "A mustang, you say? She looks mighty fit. Must have wintered well and had plenty to eat this summer."

"She's been running with the Phantom's herd.

She's his lead mare," Sam said.

Mrs. Allen gave a faint hum of interest. The Phantom's herd often crossed onto Deerpath Ranch. "What happened to her leg?"

"I'm not sure. I think she got kicked by another horse. I just found her at Aspen Creek, and then Jake came along, and your ranch was the closest, safest place for her."

"She can stay 'til you've called Brynna to trailer her up to Willow Springs," Mrs. Allen consented. She glanced south, toward BLM's Wild Horse Center. Then, noticing that Sam didn't respond, Mrs. Allen used the edge of her hand to shade her eyes and studied her. "You do want to call Brynna?"

Sam had dreaded the question, and now that Mrs. Allen had asked it, she wasn't sure how to answer. If she called Brynna, her stepmother would bring in Dr. Scott to tend to the mare. That would be great, except that Brynna would have little choice about what happened next. Even if she let Mrs. Allen foster the mare for a few weeks—something Mrs. Allen didn't seem eager to do—the horse would soon be turned over to BLM for freeze-branding, vaccination, and, eventually, adoption.

"No, I don't want to call her," Sam said. She swallowed hard. Hoping she could trust Mrs. Allen to understand, she explained, "What I'd really like is to patch her up and keep her here until she's well enough to turn back out."

"Ah, Sam." Mrs. Allen rubbed her fingertips against her eyelids.

"You're right at the edge of wild horse country." Sam talked as fast as she could, so that Mrs. Allen couldn't protest. "I'll do everything I can to help. You said I was a good worker," Sam reminded her. "And then, before the horses go hole up somewhere for winter, we'll set her free. I know she'll find her way back to the Phantom's herd."

Mrs. Allen's wrinkled hands dropped from her eyes.

"I'll tell you a secret, Samantha. I don't know how to keep this whole operation afloat. If the Humane Society decides I need to make a lot of improvements—" She broke off, unwilling to spell out what would happen next.

"We'll help," Sam said.

"We?" Mrs. Allen asked wearily.

"I know I can get Jake and his brothers, probably Callie, and Jen, of course—"

"Sam, doesn't the Kenworthy girl have a broken rib?" Mrs. Allen demanded.

"Well, yeah, but she's getting better, and Jen's my best friend—"

"Still," Mrs. Allen said dubiously, and then she laughed. "She's the little bookworm, isn't she?"

"And a math genius," Sam insisted.

At that, Mrs. Allen looked faintly hopeful. "Even though she's young—"

"She's brilliant," Sam finished for her.

"That may be, but I was thinking her fresh eyes might look over my finances and see if I've overlooked any buried treasure."

"She'll find something worth noticing. I just know it," Sam said, though she had no idea what she was talking about.

"You're whistling in the dark, Sam," Mrs. Allen said. Then, before Sam could ask exactly what that meant, she added, "For now, we need to treat that injury. If you don't want to call Brynna, I suppose you won't phone Dr. Scott."

Disapproval lowered Mrs. Allen's brows and the corners of her mouth.

"No, but if I can use your phone to call Jen, she's got lots of books on—"

"This will cause me grief, I just know it, but go ahead. First, get the mare into the box stall where I had Belle and Faith, if you can. You know the one. Then skedaddle in and call your friend. I'll help you, Samantha, but I won't let the horse suffer for your fantasy of how grand it is to be free."

Sam gritted her molars together to keep from arguing that freedom, the way the golden mare had enjoyed it, *had* been grand.

"All right," Sam said. She firmed her legs against Ace. As he stepped out, Sam ignored the nagging suspicion that she wasn't doing the right thing.

"And speaking of dreams," Mrs. Allen said with a lopsided smile, "if I'm going to pursue my dream of having a wild horse sanctuary, I'd better keep shoveling."

The honey-colored mare didn't seem to mind the stall.

What does that mean? Sam wondered as she walked toward Mrs. Allen's house and saw Jake coming toward her.

Sweat sheened his face. With both hands full, he couldn't push back the black hair that was falling over his brow, so he tossed his head like a restless horse, reminding her that when she'd been a child, she'd thought Jake had mustang eyes.

Then Sam noticed the garbage bags he carried. One tinkled and the other looked empty, except for a single lump in the bottom.

Sam didn't ask if the broken window had been as much of a mess as Mrs. Allen had said, because Jake's expression warned her that it had. She still had to ask him something.

Quickly, before he strode on past her, Sam asked, "Are Mrs. Allen's horses in bad condition?"

Jake stopped and blinked. Standing there in his running shorts and school jersey, with a bag full of broken glass in one hand and a sack of dead quail in the other, he considered her question. Sam guessed he was mentally reviewing the horses they'd seen as they rode in.

"The old ones," he began.

"Not Ginger, Calico, and Judge," Sam interrupted. "The mustangs."

Jake's head tilted to one side. "They shoulda had their hooves trimmed. And a coupla them need wormin', I'd say."

He waited a minute in silence while Sam chewed on her lip. Suddenly she remembered Brynna saying she hoped Mrs. Allen had given the mare Belle some kind of supplements because blind foals like Faith tended to nurse longer than sighted ones.

Would the Humane Society be able to tell if Mrs. Allen hadn't done that?

"That all?" Jake asked.

"Someone reported Mrs. Allen to the Humane Society and she's afraid they'll ask her to do something expensive."

Jake waited as Sam stared toward the house, but he was beginning to look impatient.

"I'll go call Jen, and then will you help me with her?"

"Can't nobody help you with her," Jake said, and it took Sam a second to realize he wasn't talking about the palomino.

"I was talking about the mare," Sam explained.

"Why didn't ya say so," Jake said, lifting the bags. "That, I can do."

* * *

Sam had told Jen everything she knew about the palomino mare, but Jen's first remark had nothing to do with equine medicine.

"You're about to get in trouble again. You know that, right?" Jen asked.

"I don't think so," Sam began.

"The queen of denial," Jen muttered.

Sam took a breath, squinted in confusion toward the open space where Mrs. Allen's window used to be, and asked, "Cleopatra? I don't get it."

"Not Cleopatra. Not the Nile. You are the queen of *denial*. Every time you're on the verge of getting in trouble, you assume other people will understand why and just line up on your side."

As Sam mulled that over, she heard Jen rummaging through books. Sam pictured her friend, with crazy-colored clothes and swinging braids, searching like an alchemist in a chaotic tower for the right formula to change a wild mare into a healthy horse.

"I'm not saying they shouldn't be on your side," Jen went on, "it's just that they don't always get what you're doing. And it's not because—here it is! Uh, no," Jen said, and Sam heard a book slam closed, then the rustling of more pages. "It's not because you're irrational or anything. It's just that your solutions are creative and people . . ."

Sam let Jen babble as she searched.

". . . don't pay attention, and they should, because you have a good heart and you're my friend and I'll defend you to the death—though I hope it doesn't come to that—but remind me how many horses you've stolen?"

"Jen!"

"Just checking to see if you're listening," Jen chirped. "Anyway, here's what you do."

Minutes later, Sam had taken a full page of notes on the back of a big brown envelope she hoped Mrs. Allen didn't need.

"So, you don't think one of her veins has been nicked?" Sam asked.

"Without looking, and without a degree in veterinary medicine—" Jen began.

"I know, but you think it's okay for us to treat it ourselves?" Sam repeated.

"Sam, this is what happens when you spend your formative years in San Francisco. Yes, I think it's okay to treat her yourself. My dad rarely calls the vet. Ranchers have been nursing their own stock for generations. Besides, if it happened more than twenty-four hours ago . . ."

"Lots more," Sam said. "It was the day before Ryan brought Hotspot home."

"Why are you so convinced it happened then?" Jen asked.

"Because I saw her get kicked," Sam said.

"But are you sure that's what caused this injury?" Jen asked. "You just told me when Hotspot kicked her, you heard a meaty thump."

"That's right," Sam agreed.

"Legs are bony. A meaty sound doesn't seem right," Jen mused. "There's all kinds of things she could've scuffed up against, anything from a branch to downed wire."

"Would that be better?" Sam asked.

"I don't know," Jen admitted. "We're already past the golden hours."

"Whoa! The what?" Sam asked.

"It's what they call the first three hours after an injury," Jen explained. "After that, the chance of complete recovery starts declining."

Sam had no trouble understanding that, and hope wilted.

"So, here's what you do," Jen said. "Clean it up. Trim back the hair. Remove any dead tissue—"

"Remove it how?"

"Just clip it off with scissors and—What's that sound?"

"Nothing."

"Are you moaning?"

"A little," Sam admitted.

"Maybe Jake or Mrs. Allen can do it without being sick," Jen teased.

"I won't be sick. I just feel sorry for her. She's been through a lot," Sam said.

"If you don't want her to have to go through any more, take care of her. And don't be fatalistic. Just because it's been more than three hours doesn't mean there can't be a complete recovery. Mustangs are tough. You tell me so all the time. Now hustle on out there and get started and I'll try to work out a way to come see her tomorrow, unless you give in and let Dr. Scott check her out."

"I won't," Sam said, but she wasn't as sure as she sounded.

Sam took about two minutes to rinse the empty ice cube trays Mrs. Allen had left in her sink. She refilled them with water and stuck them in her freezer. Then she headed for the door and the decision waiting for her in the box stall.

She felt like a human scale, and imagined herself standing with arms outstretched. In one hand, she held the lead mare's freedom. In the other, the mare's physical well-being. In Sam's imagination, her arms were exactly level.

Maybe, she thought grimly, when they cleaned up the mare's wound, they'd see she was in danger and needed a vet's care to survive. Survival outweighed freedom, didn't it?

Or maybe, under all that dirt and old blood, they'd see the mare's injury was no big deal.

"Sure, she's just been faking," Sam grumbled as she closed Mrs. Allen's door and walked past flowerbeds where limp stalks had replaced the straight stems of orange day lilies. "And any minute now, she'll suddenly burst into the wild horse boogie and just dance right on out of here. That'd tip the scales, all right."

But with my luck, Sam thought, *neither of those things will happen.*

The horse couldn't choose for herself, and so far no one had stepped forward and wrested the choice away from Sam.

Right then, she almost wished someone would.

Chapter Five ⁊

"Not one of us is going to crouch down inside that box stall with a wild mare," Mrs. Allen warned as she dropped an armload of alfalfa in the corner.

Sam nodded in grudging agreement. Being next to those hooves on the hillside above the creek, where she could roll away if she had to, had been risky enough.

Mrs. Allen formulated a plan as she watched the mare. The palomino sniffed the alfalfa, then sidestepped away, as if it were unsafe to do even that much.

"Now what was it we did when we worked on Belle right after we got her?" Mrs. Allen mused. "Oh yes, we improvised a squeeze chute by using an air mattress. You know, the kind you slip under your sleeping bag so that your back won't kink up while you're camping?" Mrs. Allen shrugged when Jake looked skeptical. "We brought Belle out of the stall and led her next to the barn wall, then used the air mattress against her body to give the impression of being contained."

Jake's hands rested on his hips and Sam could tell that if he'd been wearing jeans instead of shorts from Darton High's green and white cross-country uniform, he'd be hanging his thumbs in his pockets. He wasn't sold on Mrs. Allen's plan.

"Do you have any other ideas, Jake?" Sam asked, and it must not have sounded sarcastic, because he thought for a few seconds, then shook his head.

"Not a one," he said.

The mare seemed to go on tiptoe as they led her out of the box stall and tied her to a ring in the barn wall.

"I know you're not supposed to tie a wild horse," Mrs. Allen said, "but how else are we going to get this done?"

The mare didn't shy or bolt, just remained cautious as Mrs. Allen sorted through her first aid box and Sam and Jake took turns blowing up the air mattress.

The mare's curiosity was a sign the doctoring could be accomplished, but it didn't do anything to bolster Sam's insistence that the horse was wild.

Even though their hands and brains were busy, Sam caught Mrs. Allen and Jake giving her confused looks. It made her feel weird because their expressions were really easy to read and said they couldn't believe someone with her horse savvy really thought the mare was wild. But she'd seen it with her own eyes!

When the air mattress was inflated and the mare had been given a chance to sniff it and bump it with her nose, Sam suggested drawing straws for the task of working on the wound. Mrs. Allen and Jake believed Jake should do it.

"I've known her longer. I don't see why it should be you," Sam said.

"If anyone's gonna squat down there and get his brains kicked out, it might as well be me," Jake said in a long-suffering tone.

"Oh, all right." Sam pretended to go along. "I guess that makes sense. No one will notice the difference afterward."

"Samantha!" Mrs. Allen's voice soared on the middle syllable just like Gram's did when she was acting appalled.

"Don't feel sorry for him," Sam said. "Believe me, you don't know what he's capable of, Mrs. Allen. Jake Ely is not all good deeds and helping hands."

From the corner of her eye, Sam saw that though Jake's expression stayed cool, humor sparked in his eyes as he got down to work.

The palomino pretended to ignore the air mattress as Sam and Mrs. Allen closed in on her. She looked up, down, past them, then jerked her muzzle toward the rafters.

"Yes, girl, I'm afraid it is coming at you," Sam crooned to the horse. "But it won't hurt, I promise."

Sam's voice must have comforted the mare. As they gently pressed the air mattress to hold her in place against the barn wall, she stayed put.

The only thing wrong with their arrangement was that Sam had agreed that since Mrs. Allen knew more about doctoring animals, she could stand closest to Jake, get a better view of the injury, and offer advice if she thought he could do something differently.

But Mrs. Allen only nodded in approval and Sam had to crane her neck to see past the old lady as Jake's hands moved gently over the horse before he began washing her.

Even though he was crouched in an exposed position that could be tough to scramble out of if the horse acted up, Sam saw Jake paid attention to the mare's face, not the path his hands were taking.

"Shouldn't you watch her hooves? Or look where you're touching her?" Sam whispered, finally.

"If her eyelid twitches, her lips jerk back from her teeth, or she gives me any other sign it hurts, I'll check where I am," Jake said.

Once, when his hands pressed the swelling high on the mare's injured leg, she bucked back against the rope and Jake had to scuttle out of the way. Jake nodded to himself a few times. It was then that he lowered his gaze to stare at his hands as if his fingers had memories and could report where the mare was sore.

Finally he squeezed spongefuls of warm water over the dirt and blood, turning the palomino's leg clean and butterscotch gold again.

"Look at that," Mrs. Allen said approvingly. "He's gentle as he'd be with a newborn babe."

Jake sucked in a breath as if the description were sissified, but he didn't contradict Mrs. Allen, even when Sam added, "Oh Jake, that's so sweet."

By the time he'd finished sponging the dirt and caked blood away, the cut didn't look so bad.

Jake sat back on his bootheels for a few quiet seconds and stared at the cut. Then he gave a quiet laugh of surprise. When Sam leaned to get a better view around Mrs. Allen, she was in time to see Jake looking up at her.

"It's already healing," Jake said with a shrug. "I don't think the cut's bothering her much. She did something up here between her forearm and chest. That's where it's swollen."

"Does it feel hot?" Mrs. Allen asked.

Jake shook his head "no."

"It would if there was an infection," Mrs. Allen said, then shrugged. "It could be that she has a bruise from the kick and that, plus the cut, have combined to make her favor that leg. How does that sound to you?"

Sam didn't bother answering, since Mrs. Allen was obviously talking to Jake.

He nodded, as if that was exactly what his gentle exploration of the mare's legs had told him.

"Maybe Jen was right," Sam said, nodding slowly.

"About what, Samantha?" Mrs. Allen asked. The lines around her lips made a drawstring effect. Clearly she doubted that Jen could have made a diagnosis over the phone.

"By my description, Jen wasn't convinced the cut came from Hotspot's kick, because when I heard it, it sounded meaty."

"Meaty," Jake muttered, under his breath. "How poetic."

As it turned out, the bandages, scissors, gauze, adhesive wrap, and antibacterial ointment in the first aid kit were all Jake needed to tend the horse.

At last he stood, holding all the supplies his arms would carry, and stepped back from the horse. The mare's head swung around as far as the rope would allow, to watch him. Jake nodded that Mrs. Allen and Sam could remove the air mattress.

They stepped back and the mare blew through her lips in relief as they led her back into the stall.

"I think she deserves a snack," Sam said.

"You know where I keep the feed," Mrs. Allen said, then turned the watch on her wrist so that she could read it. "It's after noon. I'll go up to the house and see if I can get us a little something."

"No need," Jake said.

"I'm not hungry, either," Sam said, remembering Mrs. Allen had greeted them with a warning that they shouldn't expect lunch.

"Nonsense," Mrs. Allen snapped. "Come up when you're ready and I will have found something to feed us. For the first time in days, I'm feeling a bit peckish, myself."

Together, Sam and Jake watched the palomino lower her head to the clean straw bedding. She lipped at it, snorted, then nosed the alfalfa with more interest than she had before.

Don't get too comfy, girl, Sam thought.

"So all she needs is to rest, and then I can turn her out," Sam said. For some reason she didn't feel satisfied. It had to be Jake's fault, but she wasn't sure why. "Right?"

Jake shrugged.

Then, centering his weight between his running shoes so he could bolt if he had to, Jake laid one palm against the mare's withers. Her golden hide shivered, but she didn't move away. Even when he leaned against his hand, like Sam would if she were trying to move Ace, the mare just shifted her weight instead of shying or snapping at him.

Without lecturing, Jake was telling Sam she was about to break the law. If this mare belonged to someone else, she wasn't allowed to roam free on the public lands.

"You think she's been domesticated," Sam said.

Jake shrugged, but he kept looking at the mare as if her gentleness spoke for itself.

"What's so wrong with letting her go back to the herd? No one will even know she's been away. No humans, I mean, except for you, me, and Mrs. Allen," Sam said, but Jake still didn't look convinced.

"She's the Phantom's lead mare. You know a lead mare picks good grazing, and disciplines the young bachelor stallions who get too uppity, and . . ." Her voice trailed off, but then she thought of something Brynna had said. "More wild horses die during winter than any other time. They die of exposure, or get so cold they don't paw snow off the brush underneath and eat it. And there's a harsh winter coming. Everyone says so. If the lead mare's not there to find shelter they could wander into a blind canyon and get snowed in."

Sam stopped talking.

The Phantom was an experienced herd stallion now. He could think for his herd. And there were few enough that he could watch out for them. Besides, he'd probably lead them back to his hidden valley, where there was shelter and food year-round.

Sam swallowed. Then she gritted her teeth in frustration. Why was her brain refuting its own arguments?

"I'm not sayin' it's wrong . . ." Jake began.

"What *are* you saying, Jake?" Sam snapped. She could have bitten her tongue off. Her tone was sarcastic, and that never worked with him. "No, really, I want to know."

But Jake's warm, brown eyes had turned as blank as the barn wall.

"Nothin'," he said, and then he left.

As he walked away, Jake's form was silhouetted in the barn door. He moved like a cowboy even when he wasn't dressed like one.

Sam kicked at the straw in frustration. After fourteen years, she should have learned how to handle Jake Ely.

Then, for just the slightest second, his footsteps paused.

Turn around and tell me I'm doing the right thing, Sam begged silently.

But he didn't. Jake kept walking.

Sam sighed and turned her attention back to the mare.

The palomino had a mouthful of alfalfa. She chewed loudly, taking such pleasure in it, her lips were covered with greenish foam. She was probably comparing the hay to the dry, end-of-summer cheatgrass and weeds the wild horses had been living on.

"Well, shoot, girl," Sam whispered to the mare. "No one makes this easy, do they?"

Sam caught up with Jake before he went inside.

Or maybe he'd waited for her because he was about to be set upon by Mrs. Allen's Boston bull terriers. When they'd been little kids, she and Jake had called them devil dogs.

They probably weren't the original devil dogs, Sam thought, as Imp and Angel announced them as intruders even before they touched the doorknob, but their yapping pandemonium was the same.

"Go," Sam said. She led the quick entrance into the house and slipped through the barely opened door, careful to not let the dogs escape.

The two little black-and-white dogs bounced off the floor as if it were a hot griddle.

It was crazy, loud, and annoying. Jake stood redwood-tree still, thinking this would discourage them. Sam let the dogs ricochet off her legs and take flying licks at her fingers, but neither strategy really worked. Imp and Angel acted like jumping beans until they were good and ready to stop.

Usually, Mrs. Allen gave them totally ineffectual orders to behave, but now she sat as if she didn't hear the dogs' racket.

For a second, noticing the way Mrs. Allen's hands sat, fingertips touching, atop the kitchen table, Sam thought that the old lady was praying. Sam squirmed in embarrassment at the rude way they'd crashed Mrs. Allen's devotions.

But maybe not. Mrs. Allen's hands were cupped, as though she'd caught something delicate.

Sam heard Jake swallow. He rubbed the back of his neck in discomfort, and Sam agreed with his unspoken embarrassment. She was less at ease with this quiet Mrs. Allen than the cranky one.

"The phone was ringing when I got up here," Mrs. Allen said.

"Not Gabe—" Sam blurted.

"No, Gabe's fine. In fact, everything's fine. Out of the blue, I just got an offer to make a nice little chunk of money."

"That's great!" Sam said. Again, though, she felt too loud. "Isn't it?"

"It is if I can get you kids to help me," Mrs. Allen said.

Sam hesitated for a minute. Since school had started, she had tons of homework. She hadn't done a single one of her Saturday chores before riding out at dawn, either, and Gram wanted her to clean the oven. Sam shuddered. She didn't know why she had to do it. It wasn't like she'd let an apricot pie boil over, or a pork roast spatter, but Gram pointed out that since she had no trouble eating what came out of the oven, she could help clean it.

So, yeah, she had a lot to do, but if Mrs. Allen needed her . . .

"'Course," Jake said.

"Of course," Sam echoed, wishing he hadn't beaten her to agreeing. "What do you need?"

Mrs. Allen opened her hands and smoothed out a

page from a tablet. It was covered in her erratic hand-writing. Since she'd had it rolled into a tight tube, it took a couple tries to make it lay flat.

"Well, to start out with, we'll need a fire truck," Mrs. Allen said, "and a nine-by-twelve-foot tarp, a baby stroller, an umbrella, enough scrap wood to make something like railroad tracks—that's no problem—" Mrs. Allen interrupted herself, then went on, "I'm not sure where we'll get one of those big foam 'we're number one' fingers people wave around at sports events, but—" Mrs. Allen broke off again and gave Jake an appraising look. "I don't suppose you'd be willing to dress up as a clown and ride a unicycle if I could find one?"

"Ma'am?" Jake choked the word out.

"Just a bicycle, then, I suppose, and maybe one of my big hats." Mrs. Allen sighed, nodded, and looked back at her list. "I guess that's all, since they'll be bringing their own guns loaded with blanks."

Chapter Six ❧

Sam wondered if this was how life unrolled around you when you were crazy. People spouted weird, unrelated words and no matter how hard you listened, they still sounded loony.

Sam eased away from the kitchen table. She'd spent enough time in Mrs. Allen's house that she felt at home, so she opened the freezer to see if the ice cubes had frozen yet. They hadn't, but she couldn't help thinking one person in this room definitely needed a cool drink to soothe a heat-fevered brain.

"Sheriff Ballard called," Mrs. Allen began.

"Oh. Got it," Jake said.

Sheriff Ballard. Bicycles. Tarps. Guns.

That all made sense to Jake?

Luckily, Mrs. Allen saw Sam's confusion and explained.

"It seems Sheriff Ballard has gathered some local riders for a mounted posse he can call out for emergencies," Mrs. Allen said. "He mentioned search and rescue, which I understand, and riots, which I don't. Not in Darton County, for heaven's sake. Still, he'd scheduled some training sessions, called de . . ." Mrs. Allen's eyes rolled toward the ceiling as she tried to remember. "Designing? No, that's not it."

"Desensitization?" Jake suggested.

"Yes!" Mrs. Allen said, and her enthusiasm made Sam smile. "The sheriff has hired an out-of-state expert on desensitizing police horses, and he's doing some workshops with this volunteer unit. Folks will bring their own horses and get them bomb-proofed." Mrs. Allen hesitated for a second. "Although, I doubt he means that literally."

Sam laughed. Of course Sheriff Ballard meant they'd train the horses not to shy at unusual things that might send the average horse into a frenzy. This was beginning to sound really fun.

"And what will we do?" Sam asked, but more than helping out, she wished she could ride Ace in the workshop. This time last year, she wouldn't have thought anything could make her cow pony act skittish, but a single trip to the outskirts of the city had shown her she was wrong.

"Well, the first class was supposed to take place at the fairgrounds tomorrow and someone forgot to write it down, or double-booked it, or something like that, and there's already a computer convention scheduled there, with lots of little booths and demonstrations in the arena, which is where the desensitization would have taken place. Not only that, the Police Explorers, a youth group that was supposed to create all the loud distractions—"

"Oh, now I get the part about the clown on the unicycle!" Sam interrupted, nodding. That was just the sort of thing a police horse would have to tolerate during parade duty.

It was beginning to make sense to her now.

"So, the fire truck will run its lights and sirens so that if the horses are around emergency vehicles . . ." Sam mused aloud, and her mind went spinning on.

The big tarp would accustom them to walking over strange footing. The baby stroller would teach them to be careful by strange rolling objects. And if a horse would stand still for having an umbrella opened in its face, or a pistol fired nearby, he'd be tolerant of almost anything.

"Do you know how much I'd love to take Ace through training like that?" Sam sighed.

Such things sure didn't come naturally, no matter how good the horse was. Sam knew that from experience. When she'd ridden Ace into town for the rodeo, he'd spooked at a water truck, noisy children, and other things that police horses could encounter daily.

"Do it," Jake urged. "You know he'll want more volunteers for the posse."

Mrs. Allen cleared her throat and looked a bit strained.

"The thing is, when the sheriff mentioned the amount he'd budgeted for the fairgrounds and offered it to me, I said yes, of course we could stage the desensitization class here, but I'll need some young people to help out."

Sam didn't know how to feel. Even if she didn't get to use Ace, this was an exciting opportunity. She could learn a lot, help Mrs. Allen, and keep an eye on the injured mare. Her teeth sawed at her bottom lip as she imagined how nerve-wracking the strange sounds and scents would be for the mustang.

But she'd be right there, and everyone else would be too busy to discover the hidden horse. And if, by some bizarre chance, someone did go into the barn and see her, wouldn't they think the palomino was just one of Mrs. Allen's rescued mustangs? With luck, even Mrs. Allen would forget about the mare.

Sam sighed and smiled. Everything would work out for Mrs. Allen and the mare, and Ace was just fine the way he was.

"How many kids did he say you'd need to help harass the horses?" Jake asked.

Sam hoped it wouldn't matter that she'd missed about half of what Mrs. Allen had just said. She also hoped Gram would let her put off cleaning the oven, and Brynna would agree to let her organize her bedroom closet some other day, because she'd be helping to train horses for the sheriff's posse, and helping Mrs. Allen make enough money to keep the wild horse sanctuary afloat. How could they possibly say no?

"He didn't say," Mrs. Allen told him. "Just some."

"How many volunteer riders are coming?" Jake persisted.

Mrs. Allen sucked in a breath through pursed lips. "I'm not sure. He mentioned his own horse, Jinx. Your Jinx, Sam," Mrs. Allen added. "Hard to believe Clara at the diner got him for one dollar and a piece of cake! He is the nicest horse. And fast? Well I should say so."

Jake clasped his hands together and let them hang in front of him, forcing himself to be patient.

"And let's see," Mrs. Allen said, finally, "the sheriff told me Katie Sterling and Mr. Martinez are on the posse, so they'll bring Tinkerbell and Teddy Bear, but I don't know who all else. I guess I should have asked."

Jake brushed aside Mrs. Allen's concern. "You'll need more than two," he said, then he looked at Sam. "How 'bout you get Jen and I'll call Darrell, and in the meantime, you phone Sheriff Ballard and see if you can ride Ace during the training."

"Jake, that's really nice, but what about you and

Witch? Or Jen and Silly?" Sam couldn't help thinking her friends would have fun riding in the class, too.

"Because of all that tracking I do," Jake said, shrugging, "Witch is pretty much okay. And Jen's horse is parade trained."

"Great," Sam said, amazed that Jake had jumped into the planning so wholeheartedly.

"Jake, I'm surprised you're not on the posse," Mrs. Allen said.

Jake looked down. Sam couldn't read his expression.

"He calls me for tracking, sometimes," Jake said, and Sam could almost read his mind. Although Jake loved tracking and was considered a local expert, he was working hard to earn college scholarships. Jake was always good at putting what was most important, first.

"Well, then, that explains it," Mrs. Allen said. "I guess I should get started on this truly bizarre shopping list. Oh! But what about your horse?"

Sam knew Mrs. Allen wasn't talking about Ace or the Phantom, but something about the question stirred up a vague worry.

"The palomino?" Sam asked, stalling.

"Yes, dear," Mrs. Allen said.

"I'll just stay with her for a while before I ride home. Then tomorrow, when I come back for the desensitization thing, I'll check on her."

"And this is supposed to stay hush-hush?" Mrs. Allen asked.

"Well, yeah, if that's okay," Sam said.

"For a few days," Mrs. Allen said pointedly, "but it means I'll definitely skip that mixer your Gram wants me to go to—"

"Oh, no, you can still do that," Sam said.

"No, ma'am," Mrs. Allen said. "No matter how hard I try, somehow it'd get out that I'm hiding this horse. One lesson I've learned over the years, Sam, is nothing travels faster than secrets at a church social."

Since Mrs. Allen's shopping list required a drive into Darton, she took a quick shower. While they waited, Sam and Jake stood at the living room window that overlooked the pasture of unadoptable wild horses.

Sam spotted a black mare with a bright bay colt, Licorice and Windfall, then a yellow dun named Fourteen. He had been named that because Mrs. Allen had joked that she had to round out her adopted herd so she wouldn't have an unlucky thirteen wild horses.

"I don't see Faith," Sam told Jake, just as Mrs. Allen returned dressed in a clean skirt and blouse.

"She's at a difficult age—not grown up and not a baby, so she spends a lot of time off on her own," Mrs. Allen said, then added, "I never did give you two lunch. The least I can do is drop you off at home."

"I have Ace," Sam rushed to explain, and Jake flashed her a strained look.

Jake was afoot. Three Ponies was at least five miles away. Also, the temperature kept climbing. Those facts would have made the choice to ride in a vehicle instead of walk a snap decision for most people.

But when the driver was Mrs. Allen, it wasn't an easy offer to accept.

Mrs. Allen's driving had improved briefly after her grandson Gabe had been injured in a car accident, but lately she'd reverted to her old habits. Her tangerine-colored truck careened around the county as if launched in a giant pinball machine.

"Speaking of Ace," Mrs. Allen said, "I called Sheriff Ballard from my bedroom phone and he said that since Dallas is coming anyway—"

"Dallas is going to be on the volunteer posse?" Sam asked, surprised.

"So he says, and I figured Ace could ride along in the trailer with Dallas' horse. He said we'd only need three or four people, and so I asked if I could help and with Jake's friend, your Jen and this out-of-state expert, there's no problem."

"Mrs. Allen, you are just the best!" Sam said, giving the woman's forearm a squeeze.

"Well now, I don't know about that," she said, looking flustered. Then she pointed her index finger at Sam. "Just see that you get here in time to unload all this strange gear."

"I will," Sam said, then crossed her heart. "I promise."

Sam hummed with happiness while Jake weighed the odds of getting home in one piece if he rode in the tangerine-colored truck. Mrs. Allen added tennis balls, floating pool noodles, and maracas to her list.

She'd just stuffed her list into her big black purse when Imp and Angel gave a volley of alarmed barks, then dove under the kitchen table and shivered in silence.

"Now, what do you suppose?" Mrs. Allen said. "They only act like that, I'm ashamed to say, when Dr. Scott comes over, and I surely haven't called him for anything."

Sam's heart slammed against her ribs.

Dr. Scott, the vet. The BLM vet.

A wave of paranoia closed over her. She didn't look at Jake or Mrs. Allen because she was afraid she'd accuse one of them—no, both of them—of calling the vet. After all, Jake had been alone in the house cleaning up after the quail, and Mrs. Allen had been in the house for some time, supposedly making lunch, before she and Jake came in. But Mrs. Allen hadn't made lunch. Maybe she'd called the vet instead.

Wait a minute, Sam told herself. These people were her friends.

Jake had just encouraged her to do something she wanted, even though it meant more work for him.

And Mrs. Allen had arranged for her to do it!

Besides, neither Jake nor Mrs. Allen were shy about speaking their minds or taking action. If they believed Sam was making a terrible mistake, they'd stop her.

"Maybe he was just in the neighborhood?" Sam asked. She glanced at Jake, but he'd helped himself to a big glass of water and now he was stretching out his legs as if warming up for another run.

"Sam," Mrs. Allen said, "that poor young veterinarian is so overworked, he doesn't have time for courtesy calls. At your place, maybe, where Grace will feed him—but here? All I've got to offer is blisters and bites. Oh, hush up, Angel," Mrs. Allen added as a growl emerged from under the table. "Well, we might as well go out and see what he wants. I heard they had a case of West Nile virus over in Blackheel City. True, it's a hundred miles away, but what's distance to a mosquito?"

Sighing fatalistically, Mrs. Allen stood up.

Sam held her breath as the old woman turned and looked into her eyes. "Won't change your mind about having him look at that mare, I suppose?"

"No . . ." Sam knew as the word passed her lips that she could be wrong, but she said it anyway and followed Mrs. Allen outside.

"Guess I'll jog home," Jake said.

"Jake, why don't you stay and—" Sam started.

"'Cause I'm no good at this," Jake said, and Sam

closed her eyes. She didn't have to ask what Jake meant, because she was no different. Neither of them were good at lying.

At first, when Dr. Scott climbed out of his truck, Sam thought he was wearing odd-patterned jeans because of their light-dark patchiness. But the young vet walked stiffly and when he got closer, Sam noticed his jeans were coated in dry mud, some of which had flaked off, and his blue eyes looked red-rimmed and rabbity behind his glasses.

"It appears to me you've had a tough day already, Glen," Mrs. Allen teased, but Dr. Scott wasn't in a joking mood.

"Irrigation system went haywire over in the pasture near Clara's coffee shop. I noticed it last night on my way home because a blue roan colt had got himself stuck and half drowned. He was weak as a new-hatched chick. Each time I tried to let go of him and get back to my truck to radio for help, he'd fall flat down and his nostrils would fill up with mud. I knew he'd drown if I left him. So when the Slocum girl drove past at about two A.M. and her headlights hit us, I flagged her down."

Sam couldn't imagine high-fashion Rachel picking her way across a boggy field to help the veterinarian and a colt. She guessed she should stop always thinking the worst of Rachel.

"She didn't come too close," Dr. Scott went on,

"just pulled to the side of the road and listened to me shout, but she promised—absolutely swore—she'd send someone."

Held there by the vet's story, even though he'd stretched his Achilles tendons in preparation for running home, Jake crossed his arms and grunted as if he knew what was coming next.

"And she didn't?" Sam asked.

"Sure she did," the vet snarled, "just an hour ago, after the colt had already revived and I'd slogged back to my truck to hear a message from yesterday that I"—Dr. Scott's voice grew louder with each word—"in my capacity as an inspector for the Humane Society—was supposed to pay a visit to Blind Faith Mustang Sanctuary on an abuse complaint!"

Jake had tried to slip away unnoticed, but they all turned at the sound of his running shoes hitting the sandy soil as he jogged toward home. He gave a vague wave. Sam could tell he was glad to escape what was coming next.

"An abuse complaint." Mrs. Allen pronounced the syllables as if she could hardly stand them on her tongue. "Well, you needn't have bothered."

"Trudy, I didn't have a choice," Dr. Scott said, flatly. "Even if I wanted to draw my own conclusions without driving out here, I couldn't. A rural vet just starting out is glad for extra contracts like I have with BLM and the Humane Society. I take the extra training, do the extra work, and bank the salaries. That means I can take time to do a few things for free — like care for . . ." The vet snapped his fingers twice, as if the animal's name would magically come to him. "What did your grandson name our favorite mustang?"

"Firefly," Mrs. Allen said, and her affection for the bay colt with the white patch over his eye showed in her smile.

"Right," he said. Dr. Scott looked satisfied and relaxed, then his jaw dropped and his eyes closed in a yawn.

Dr. Scott had lavished weeks of care on the burned and traumatized colt and Firefly had responded to the kindness by bonding with Mrs. Allen's grandson and helping him pass through the bitterness that followed his terrible injury.

But Dr. Scott's enjoyment of the memory lasted only a few seconds.

"So, I've got this complaint of abuse and neglect, and I need to take a quick walk around now. All your horses are in that pen and the pasture, right?" Dr. Scott asked.

Mrs. Allen gave a wooden nod. Sam wondered if Mrs. Allen was insulted, or covering for the hidden horse which wasn't, technically, hers.

"Ace is in with Judge, and —"

The vet made a curt gesture to cut off her explanation.

"I saw him. I noticed most of the wild horses are

close in, on this end of the pasture. That's good." He gave a loud sigh. "Look, I don't mean to be abrupt, but I'd like to get home, clean up, and grab a nap before the next crisis explodes." Dr. Scott yawned again, then a corner of his mouth quirked up. "Truthfully, I don't think this will take long. I don't expect the complaint to pan out."

"Go right ahead," Mrs. Allen said, but the vet was already striding toward the pen where her three saddle horses dozed in the shade.

After a few minutes, Mrs. Allen asked Sam, "Do you want to go back inside? It's cooler there."

She had to keep her eyes on that barn. She had to be ready to explain—she wasn't sure how—why she'd hidden a wild horse if Dr. Scott happened to find it.

"I can't," Sam said.

"Neither can I," Mrs. Allen replied, and the strain on her face told Sam the old woman had more at stake here than she did.

This time last year, Mrs. Allen's ranch had been a clutter of sagging fences, flapping shingles, and wandering horses. Depression had made her so rude and reclusive, word had spread through the ranching community that the artist-rancher had gone from being eccentric to downright peculiar.

"All we need now is for that stallion of yours to come sniffing around," Mrs. Allen whispered.

"What?" Sam gasped.

"I don't expect he will, not during daylight, but many nights when I look out the window, he's down at the pasture gate, wandering back and forth as if he's lost something."

"He did," Sam said, thinking of Firefly. Then she shivered, imagining the stallion moving pale through the moonlight like a restless ghost.

"If you're thinking of Firefly, we both know he would have kicked that youngster out of the band before long. It's what herd stallions do with the young males."

"But then why is he hanging around?" Sam asked.

"Samantha, why on earth would you ask me? I'm not the one who can read that stallion's mind."

If only that were true, Sam thought.

They remained in silence for so long, Sam's mind veered toward home. She really should phone and explain what was going on. She hadn't looked at the clock when they'd been indoors, but Mrs. Allen had said it was nearly noon when they'd finished doctoring the palomino. That must have been at least an hour ago. Someone would be wondering where she was.

"Do you think that mare is Firefly's mother?" Mrs. Allen asked.

"I've been thinking about that," Sam admitted. "I keep going over the times I saw him with the Phantom's herd, but I never saw him paired up.

Mainly, he was just fooling around with the other colts."

Gloom settled over Sam. As they waited, sweating, Sam longed to be the horse psychic that people thought she was.

If the Phantom returned to Deerpath Ranch looking for one of his colts, what would he do for a lead mare?

He'd left the palomino when he knew she'd slow down the rest of the herd, but what if he came back without the others?

Hooves thudded and a sharp neigh cut across the hot afternoon. Sam and Mrs. Allen turned to see Dr. Scott being pursued by Roman, the liver-chestnut gelding who'd appointed himself leader of the adopted herd.

Dr. Scott vaulted over the pasture fence and walked toward them. When he came near enough that his voice could be heard, he called out, "Trudy, we'd better have a talk."

Chapter Seven ❧

"You know, there's an odd glare on those cotton-wood leaves that's making me a little dizzy," Mrs. Allen whispered to Sam as the vet approached.

Sam steadied the old woman's arm, then retrieved the maroon baseball cap from Mrs. Allen's back pocket. She shook out the crumpled cap until it was pretty much its original shape, then handed it to her.

While Mrs. Allen hooked the cap over the back of her head, then tugged it down to shade her eyes, Sam looked up at the trees. She searched for sunbeams of unusual brightness. She didn't see any. Maybe overwork had made Mrs. Allen light-headed.

"You wouldn't have to work so hard if we could

get some kids to volunteer help with the horses," Sam said. "They'd love it, you'd—"

"Need liability insurance," Mrs. Allen muttered.

"That doesn't matter," Sam said, though she didn't know what liability insurance was.

"It does if someone got hurt and her parents sued me. I'd lose everything."

Sam couldn't believe anyone would sue Mrs. Allen. She was spending her nights, days, and money taking care of wild horses. If you were going to sue someone, wouldn't you go after someone who deserved it?

"Well, no one can do all this work alone," Sam said.

"Probably won't matter, once Glen gets done with me." Mrs. Allen hurried the end of her sentence as the vet reached them.

Looking hot and frustrated, Dr. Scott wiped his wrist over his forehead.

"I've done nothing to deserve the looks you two are giving me," the young vet said. "You're shrinking away from me like I'm—I don't know what. A hooded executioner holding an axe?"

"No . . ." Sam drew the word out as if he were being silly.

"Of course not," Mrs. Allen added.

"Here's what my inspection report will say," Dr. Scott began. "Your horses have enough food and water. I saw no sunken backs, protruding hip bones, or ribs indicating they're starving or malnourished, and no potbellies indicating worms."

Sam smiled, but she was so afraid the vet would start toward the barn, her lips kind of jerked.

Dr. Scott took a breath and held up his hand to stall off interruptions. "Most of their coats look okay, not dull with hunks of hair coming out, indicating mineral deficiencies."

Mrs. Allen gave a quick nod as if she'd never had a single doubt.

"However," the vet raised his voice and eyebrows, "they're wandering around a soft pasture, not galloping over lava beds, so their feet could use some work. I'm guessing half of 'em need their teeth floated, too, but this was just a quick visual inspection. I haven't done a hands-on exam for any of them since just before you adopted them from Willow Springs."

"But the bottom line," Mrs. Allen said, "is that you're not going to recommend the Humane Society close me down."

"No, but I will suggest that any time you take in a horse, you get a photo of it on day one, and a letter from the vet on scene testifying to the condition of the animal," Dr. Scott said. "If I hadn't seen those horses before you adopted them, I might have some questions."

"I get it," Sam said. "If Mrs. Allen takes in a horse in bad condition—"

"Someone could say she's to blame. In fact, I bet that's how the complaint came about. Someone who's used to seeing blanketed, stabled horses thought this bunch had been neglected.

"And one more recommendation," Dr. Scott continued. "It would make my job, and the farrier's, a lot easier if you'd try to handle those horses once in a while. Brush 'em and pick up their feet or do something to convince them it's okay to be touched."

Mrs. Allen nodded adamantly, but Sam heard the defeated tsk of her tongue. When Dr. Scott put it that way, it made perfect sense, but where would the extra time come from? And was Mrs. Allen really in shape to hand-gentle wild horses?

"Maybe, after tomorrow's hoopla . . ." Mrs. Allen's voice trailed off.

"The police horse desensitization?" Dr. Scott asked.

Sam flinched. How could he know?

"Why, yes," Mrs. Allen said. Then she shook her head. "I will never get over what a small town this is. I just found out about it this morning and I'm—how would you put it?—hostessing it."

As Dr. Scott listened, Sam noticed his hands moved to rub the small of his back. Spending the night in a mudhole with a struggling yearling must have left him with some sore muscles.

"Heck Ballard let me know the location had been changed, since I said I'd show up, just in case anything unexpected happens," Dr. Scott said. "Another four hours donated."

He said it gruffly, to keep them from thinking he was easy to take advantage of, but Sam already knew the truth. Dr. Scott's life revolved around animals and the people who cared about them.

"It sounds to me like you already do enough volunteer work," Mrs. Allen said.

"This is worth doing. I encouraged Heck Ballard to get the funding for this training, especially for volunteers and their mounts."

Sam figured she could keep the vet distracted from the barn by babbling about how she planned to ride in the training exercise, too, but then a faraway expression crept over Dr. Scott's face.

"I was in Chicago once for a vet conference and a couple of us went down to watch a parade. Some fool planner hadn't given a thought to marching the mounted police unit in front of a mountain man reenactment group."

Sam could picture men costumed in fringed buckskins, moccasins, and fur caps swaggering down the street. She couldn't figure out why it would be foolish to put them next to a group on horseback.

"Everything was just fine until the mountain men started shooting off their black powder rifles."

Sam imagined the thunder and smell coming from behind. . . .

"The horses had been trained to tolerate the sound of handguns, but this was a series of huge, echoing *ka-booms*. Two horses broke ranks. The crowd split and one of the horses got himself cornered at a bus stop, but the other one ran right into a power pole."

Dr. Scott looked distant for a minute, then he finished, "He had to be put down. Right there, while his rider—a big tough-guy police sergeant—stood by crying like a baby."

Dr. Scott scowled at the memory, then yawned once more.

"So that's why you're volunteering your Sunday to help out," Mrs. Allen said. "I'm sure Heck appreciates it."

"What's four more hours?" Dr. Scott shrugged. "Overnight I'll think about what kind of setup we'll use to tend to your wild horses. I'll talk to you tomorrow."

As Sam watched Dr. Scott walk away, she wasn't thinking about the story he'd told or the desensitization of police horses. She felt rescued—partly because he hadn't discovered the mare and partly because Dr. Scott would be here again tomorrow. Just in case.

If the mare's condition worsened overnight, Dr. Scott would be here to help.

Mrs. Allen's tangerine-colored truck sped down the dirt road before dust from the vet's vehicle had even settled.

For a few seconds, Sam savored the feeling of being alone with so many horses. She counted the mustangs, saddle horses, Ace, and the Phantom's lead mare on her fingers. She was surrounded by nineteen horses.

Her gaze swept appreciatively over the ranch. She knew which horse she wanted to spend a little time alone with: the honey-colored mare.

Sam didn't sneak into the barn. Scuffing her boots as she went, she gave the mare plenty of warning that she was coming. Before Sam had even crossed the barn's threshold, the mare's head whipped up from her investigation and her ivory mane swirled around her face. Tail switching from side to side, the mare watched Sam enter.

"Hey, pretty girl," Sam crooned to the horse, and the mare's ears flicked forward to listen.

Even though it was too hot for hugging, Sam had a strong desire to wrap her arms around the mare's neck.

As if the horse read her mind, though, she backed quickly into a corner. She barely favored her bandaged leg, but she paid attention to Sam. Then, as if she suddenly felt trapped, the mare bolted forward, eyes rolling. For the first time since she'd entered the stall, the mare stared around wildly.

She had to be remembering her herd, Sam thought as the mare neighed loudly and longingly, then gave two short, wavering whinnies.

For the first time, Sam compared the mare to Dark Sunshine and sighed. Though she'd calmed down after Tempest's birth, Sunny had never really adjusted to captivity. She always stared toward the Calico Mountains as if her heart still galloped with the wild ones, and Sam didn't want this mare to pine away, too.

"Even if I get in trouble, I'll take you back to him," Sam vowed, and the mare seemed to understand.

When Sam got home, she'd been missed. But not in a good way.

No one threw their arms around her and rejoiced that she'd come safely home.

"It's about time you got here."

Gram's cranky greeting hit Sam as she opened the kitchen door and breathed the chemical fumes of oven cleaner.

"You cleaned the oven," Sam began.

"Someone had to do it," Gram complained.

"I'm here now," Sam protested.

Gram knelt in front of the oven, wearing a pair of elbow-length rubber gloves as she scrubbed.

"I planned on doing it," Sam added. "Do you want me to finish up?"

Gram shook her head and kept working, but somehow Sam thought she read a reprimand in Gram's stiff back. For some reason, it seemed like the opposite of Mrs. Allen's compliments.

If I had a few more helpers like you, Mrs. Allen had said. Or something like that. When the words had settled in, they'd not only made Sam happy she did something well, she wanted to do more for Mrs. Allen.

Musing for a few seconds as she watched Gram angle her arm to reach far into the oven, Sam decided she worked better for praise than guilt.

It really was something she should tell Gram, but what if she didn't take it the right way?

Gram stood up from the job and began peeling off her gloves.

"There's a note there from a girl at school. She wants you to call back."

Sam picked up the note from the kitchen table and smiled.

Ally McClintock, the note said, *wants to do something fun.* Under that Gram had written Ally's phone number.

Allison McClintock was the type teachers called "well-rounded" and popular girls like Rachel Slocum called "geek." Ally wore long, gauzy skirts and her brownish-blond hair made a flyaway halo around her delicate face. She was on the school newspaper with Sam and she was a talented musician who assisted her father, the choir director at the Methodist church, by directing the children's choir. Although socializing made her shy, Ally snapped up chances to perform with her guitar.

Sam didn't blame her. Ally's voice seemed too rich and strong to be coming from the throat of a high school student. Sam had heard Ally play at talent shows, school assemblies, and even the opening of a music store at Crane Crossing Mall, and each time she'd hoped someone would step forward and tell Ally she was going to be a star.

Ally's creativity made Sam feel about as clever as a caveman and Ally was definitely not the sort to stand around whining, "I don't know, what do you want to do?"

Whatever Ally had in mind would be fun.

Gram laid her yellow gloves on the kitchen counter, then gave Sam a considering look. "There's plenty of other housework to do."

Sam didn't like the sound of that. She pushed Ally's airy appeal aside. She'd call her later. Now, she had to fend off whatever super-chore Gram had in mind.

Gram didn't care that Sam liked horsework, not housework. She'd been hoping to spend time with Tempest and Dark Sunshine, or on the phone with Jen, scheming how to do what was best for the Phantom's lead mare.

"I know there is," Sam admitted. "Let me think." If she didn't come up with a chore and jump on it right now, Gram would say something like "Pick up everything downstairs," and that kind of job could last all day.

"Would you like me to dust all the furniture?" Sam suggested.

"No, but . . ." Gram looked surprised. "Thanks, honey."

Sam knew better than to take Gram's approval and run. Laziness would catch up with her by the end of the day and she might not be allowed to go back to Mrs. Allen's tomorrow.

She ended up helping with laundry. As she pulled wet clothes from the washing machine and plopped them in a wicker basket, she told Gram about Mrs. Allen's weariness, the Humane Society complaint, the police horse desensitization planned for tomorrow, and the part she, Jen, Jake, and Darrell would play in it.

"Trudy needs some help," Gram said as Sam lifted the basket by both handles. "It's nice of you kids to pitch in."

"Well, I think Jen will do it. If she can't, I might not be able to ride Ace. . . ." Sam's voice trailed off and she looked toward the phone, but Gram tilted her head to one side as if Sam were trying to get out of work. "But I'll call her later."

Sam had almost angled the basket out the door, when she said to Gram, "Did you know Dallas was going to be on the volunteer posse?"

"I'm not surprised," Gram said. "He sounded downright jealous when I told him I'd been going into town to help out with the therapy horse program."

"Hmmm," Sam said, and then she continued on outside.

Hanging laundry was probably the best chore that didn't involve horses. It definitely smelled better than oven cleaner.

Blaze, the ranch Border collie, had followed her to the clothesline, and now corridors of wet, flapping sheets kept them both cool.

"You're no dummy, are you, boy?" Sam asked the panting dog, but then her thoughts changed direction and Sam found she could do the chore while she thought about the palomino mare.

Clipping a wooden clothespin to one corner of a sheet, then smoothing it along the clothesline, Sam wished she was still at Deerpath Ranch.

When Belle and Faith had been in that stall, they hadn't been left alone for a minute. Now Jake was gone, Mrs. Allen was in town, and Sam was home, too. The injured lead mare was all alone in her captivity.

What if the mare looked at the wooden walls surrounding her and began pawing at boards? What if her struggles widened the cut they'd bandaged so carefully? Could she get a sliver in her chest if she tried to jump out of the stall? But she hadn't looked fearful.

Sam took a T-shirt from the laundry basket, fastened it in place, and wondered how the wild horse had come to know stalls. Picturing the mare's alert ears and watchful eyes, Sam decided the horse not only hadn't acted confined and crazy, she hadn't even looked nervous. If Sam didn't know better, she'd think the mare looked relieved and almost at home.

Sam paused as she bent toward the laundry basket again.

Clues pointed toward the mare's domestication, but ever since Queen, the Phantom's first lead mare, had been taken in by the BLM, this honey-colored horse had helped lead the Phantom's herd. Sam knew that the mare was where she belonged.

Sam was finishing the dinner dishes, staring out the window over the sink, and half wondering why Dallas was standing on the porch outside the bunkhouse kind of expectantly, when it popped into her mind that no one had asked what had happened after she rode away from River Bend that morning.

They hadn't questioned her about the Phantom or asked what she thought had him stirred up.

Sam guessed that was a good thing, since she couldn't have told the truth about the palamino mare, but it was sort of ironic that Dad had refused to let her budge and Brynna had kept her straining like a dog on a leash until the sun came up, and neither of them had wondered what happened next.

Now Dad was dozing in front of the television, Gram was reading a seed catalogue, and Brynna was spreading out even more maps on the kitchen table.

They'd all been interested in her plans for tomorrow. Dad had actually talked with Sheriff Ballard the other day about Lieutenant Preston, the man who'd conduct the training, and Dad thought the work would do Ace good. Brynna had told about a search party she'd ridden on once and the volunteers she'd nicknamed "thrusters"—people who pushed themselves to the front when a photographer appeared to show heroes who'd found a group of lost Boy Scouts.

When Sam had phoned Jen, she'd had to be vague about the mare's condition, but she'd managed to hint that Jen's advice had worked. And Jake turned out to be right about Jen and Silly.

"She's already bomb-proof enough," Jen had said. "But Ace—and you have to swear you won't take this wrong, or I'll shut up now—"

"I know," Sam had said. "He needs some work on confronting unusual stuff."

"Oh, yeah," Jen had said, making Sam laugh.

That was another example of what a good friend Jen was, Sam thought. She'd offered a teeny crumb of criticism about Ace, but not in a mean way, and Sam found she could take it.

Now, with everyone else preoccupied, she could call Jen back and give her more details about tomorrow. She needed to call Ally, too. It was probably too late for whatever fun the other girl had had in mind and Ally would be busy tomorrow, because it was Sunday. Still . . .

Sam was moving to retrieve the note with Ally's phone number on it when she heard tires hit the bridge that led into the ranch yard. A screech of brakes told her the driver had slowed suddenly. Then, sliding through the gray-purple dusk, a car pulled into the yard.

Looking from the kitchen window, Sam wondered if this was what Dallas had been waiting for.

She'd never seen the car before. It rolled jerkily into the yard, throbbing with the bass beat of music playing inside. Mostly emerald green with a white top, it might be one of those classic cars you saw in movies about the fifties. Or sixties.

The car stopped. The music ended. A heavy door opened and closed.

She didn't know the car, but she recognized the guy climbing out of it as Jake's friend Darrell. Dark, slicked-back hair and baggy pants told Sam it couldn't be anyone else.

She'd first heard Darrell's name the day Jake had disabled Gram's car by pulling some wires out from under the hood, making it into an immovable barricade on the road to Willow Springs Wild Horse Center, so that Linc Slocum couldn't drive past.

When Sam had gaped in amazement, Jake had told her his friend Darrell had taught him how to do it. He'd added that Sam was not allowed to meet Darrell because he was kind of a rebel, but of course Sam met him at school.

He wasn't really a bad guy. But what was he doing here? And what did he have in that gunny-sack?

Chapter Eight ॐ

Sam wiped her wet hands on her jeans and slipped out the front door. The door closed behind her. She saw Darrell tighten his grip on the sack as it rocked and swayed.

Now that she was closer, she was pretty sure the sack held something alive. Even so, despite the shifting and swaying gunnysack, Darrell walked as he did down the halls of Darton High. Weight back on his heels with his baggy pants billowing and his eyelids lowered to half-mast. He looked totally cool.

Once he opened his mouth, he'd start talking like a hard guy, as if he were risky to be around.

But he wasn't. Last year when she'd been searching small rodeos for the Phantom, she'd seen how patiently Darrell took care of his unruly little cousin at a carnival.

Darrell had slipped her evidence to write an exposé for the school newspaper, too, and the principal had ended up nabbing Kris Cameron, one of the most popular guys in school, for forging passes to get his friends out of class. Not only that, Darrell had helped her make a hay drop for the wild horses during the snowiest part of winter.

"Hey Forster, you know how to keep a secret."

It was a statement, not a question. Sam sucked in a cautious breath.

Should she turn and run? Moments like this had a nasty way of becoming turning points. And she only had about a fifty-fifty record of turning in the right direction.

The bag was definitely making a sound and she wasn't the only one who'd noticed. Two Rhode Island Red hens that had already scurried into their coop for the night peeked outside and gave cautious clucks.

Darrell shifted the sack to his other hand, then, looking dissatisfied, lifted it up and cradled it in his arms.

"Ow!" Darrell flinched as if whatever was in the bag had hurt him. Did it have teeth? Claws? A stinger?

"Hey man, don't peck your rescuer, know what I mean?" Darrell dangled the bag at eye level as if whatever lurked inside could read his glare.

You know how to keep a secret, he'd said confidently. Before she agreed with him, though, she needed more information.

"Is the secret in the bag?" Sam asked.

"Shh," Darrell said, then looked over both shoulders and back to her. "Yeah, you nailed it. The secret's in the bag and I'm here to make a little deal." Darrell set the bag gently on the ground and rubbed his hands together in anticipation. "Ely tells me you need help raising a ruckus tomorrow."

Darrell's habit of using everyone's last names could have made his sentence confusing. After all, there were six Ely brothers. But Sam had no doubt Darrell was talking about Jake.

"We're helping desensitize the volunteer posse horses tomorrow," Sam admitted.

"'S what I mean," Darrell said. He folded his arms with a sort of streetwise dignity. "You assist me and Fluffy. I'll assist you."

Sam tried to listen to the voice in her brain that begged her to be sensible. She really tried not to be curious, but she couldn't help asking, "Fluffy?"

Darrell pointed at the shifting sack. "My man Fluffy needs a place to live."

Sam knew that as soon as whatever was in the bag came out, she was sunk. She was so soft-hearted with animals that, just a day ago, she'd rescued a daddy longlegs spider by scooping it into a jar and delicately dumping it outside.

Darrell must have known what a pushover she was, because he moved quickly to release the creature from the bag.

Even in the dusky light, the rooster's feathers shone with a cinnamon and black gloss. His fountain of tail feathers glinted iridescent green and his red eyes glared at everything around him. He wasn't very big, but what he lacked in size, he made up for in fierceness. The rooster braced his thin legs apart, hooked his toenails into the dirt, and opened his beak in a challenging *cock-a-doodle-do*.

"His name is not Fluffy," Sam said.

"Sure it is," Darrell said. "And before you ask me where he came from—I can't tell you."

"Why? Because then you'd have to . . ." Sam began sarcastically.

"No, really," Darrell said seriously. "It wouldn't be safe."

The rooster's crow had brought River Bend's chickens crowding out for a look at this newcomer. Sam had no idea how Rusty, Gram's rooster, would react.

"Darrell," Sam began, shaking her head regretfully.

"You can't say no without hearing his side of things," Darrell insisted as if he and the rooster had talked things over before they arrived a River Bend. "Just listen while I tell you three things. Okay?"

"Go," Sam snapped.

"Here's the first thing. I know you've heard of

people putting gaffs or spurs on—" Darrell broke off, and Sam wasn't surprised. She must have looked confused, because she had no idea what he was talking about. "They're like little tiny knives they attach to two roosters' legs," Darrell explained, "before they throw them at each other so they'll fight. Then people bet on which one will be the winner."

Sam had been scratched and pecked by hens unwilling to surrender eggs Gram had ordered her to gather. Those pecks and scratches hurt. She didn't like imagining what damage roosters would do to each other if they were fighting for their lives—and armed with spurs.

"I sort of remember hearing about something like that," Sam said. "But who'd do that around here?"

"I don't know any names, but a few faces looked familiar. I'm not going to tell you where I found Fluffy, but there's a little corner of Darton County with about thirty short A-frame shelters with roosters chained to 'em and every Saturday around midnight, guys bet on which rooster will peck the other's eyes out."

It had to be dangerous for Darrell to go skulking around such a bloody gathering in the dark. No wonder he had a bad reputation.

Sam tried not to be a wimp, but what was Darrell thinking? Whether he peeked furtively from the bushes, or stood shoulder-to-shoulder with the gamblers, it was no place for a teenager.

Actually, Sam thought with a sigh, she knew

exactly what he'd been thinking. He'd rescued a creature that couldn't help itself. It was weird that she and Darrell had that impulse in common.

"Poor roosters. That's awful," Sam said.

"That's nothing," Darrell corrected. "They usually fight to the death, or if they're hurt too badly in the battle—"

"I don't want to know," Sam insisted. "It's a terrible story, but if he's a trained killer, he can't stay here with Gram's chickens."

"Here's the second thing," Darrell said. "I heard one of the guys joking that Fluffy didn't stand a chance 'cause he's a lover, not a fighter."

"Darrell," Sam protested. There was so much wrong with this idea. Betting was illegal. Chicken fighting must be, too. Not to mention chicken-napping. But then she said, "It's Saturday night. He would've been fighting in a couple of hours."

"Yeah," Darrell answered. "That's why I had to break him out."

"But"—Sam dropped her voice to a whisper— "you took him from guys who have to be horrible and violent if they're making money off killing animals for 'fun.'" Sam glanced at the rooster as he investigated the yard. "I don't think they're going to be real forgiving when they figure out what you did."

"They won't," Darrell said confidently. Then, as if rethinking the possibility, he added, "And what are they going to find if they do?" Darrell held his hands up in mock innocence. "I won't have the bird, if you help me out. I don't have anywhere to keep Fluffy."

"Will you quit calling him that?" Sam asked in frustration. "I'm not dumb. I know you're just trying to make me sympathetic, and I already am, but—hey! Why aren't you taking him to Jake?" Sam asked.

"That's the first place they'd look," Darrell said. "At my buddy's house."

Sam didn't remind Darrell he'd just said the bad guys wouldn't catch him. Instead, she glanced toward Darrell's car as if answers lay there.

"You figure he could pose like a hood ornament?" Darrell joked.

"No."

Sam tried to think of a solution, but the only thing that popped into her mind was how easily and generously Mrs. Allen had accepted the honey-colored mare. With fewer questions than Sam had just asked Darrell, Mrs. Allen had agreed to keep the horse and keep her a secret.

Was chicken-fighting illegal? Sam didn't know, but taking in a wild horse was. It was a federal crime, but Mrs. Allen had trusted Sam not to do something "wrong" without a reason.

"Okay, I'll do it."

"Excellent."

"I don't know how," she said, glancing toward the house. She hadn't turned on the porch light when she darted out, so if Gram and Dad or

Brynna were looking this way, they probably couldn't see what was going on. But what was she going to do with a rooster? Especially one that might—no matter what Darrell had overheard—have been trained to fight.

"You'll think of something," Darrell said. His hand jammed into his cavernous pocket and his car keys jingled. Then he squatted for a second and addressed the rooster. "Stay cool."

Sam smiled. This kid was weird, but he had a good heart.

Darrell pushed back to his feet and strode toward his car. He hadn't gone far when he turned back.

"Oh yeah, Forster," Darrell called as if he'd just remembered. "Third thing."

"Yeah?" she asked.

"Even if you'd said no to Fluffy, I would have helped with the noise-making tomorrow."

Sam groaned, but she wasn't really sorry for helping the doomed chicken.

"I have this killer piece of plastic pipe," Darrell went on, "and when I blow into it, the sound's just like a didgeridoo."

"A what?"

"You know those Australian bush horns? Don't you think that'd be perfect to test a horse's nerves?"

"Or a human's," Sam said pointedly.

Darrell was chuckling when the front porch light flashed on. He froze.

"Samantha, who's out there?" Gram called. "One of your friends?"

Darrell looked at Sam as if her answer held him in more suspense than it did Gram.

"Yeah," Sam admitted. Then, as Darrell broke into a grin and jutted his thumb upward in approval, she added, "but he's just leaving."

"All right, dear," Gram said, but before she closed the screen door, she asked, "Sam? Did I hear the rooster crowing? Whatever do you suppose has gotten into him?"

"Yeah, Sam?" Darrell whispered.

She set her jaw and tried to give him the same kind of threatening gaze he used on other people, but Darrell just chuckled and walked toward his car.

He'd almost reached it when he looked over his shoulder.

"Thanks, Forster," he said. "You're all right."

Sam got up early the next morning. Excitement over the palomino mare and Ace's introduction to desensitization had been buzzing in Sam's head all night. She couldn't have slept much longer.

It only took a few minutes to groom Ace and load him in the trailer next to Amigo, and Darrell and Jen arrived before Dallas was ready to go.

As they rode in the backseat of Darrell's car, Sam noticed Jen's fidgeting. She crossed her legs, jiggled her foot, uncrossed her legs, and polished the toe of one boot on the back of the other leg of her jeans.

Jen wanted to hear more about the honey-colored mare, but she was being patient, pretending fascination with each word Darrell said.

First, Darrell talked about the trip he and Jake had made to the junkyard the night before, looking for cool things to use as distractions in the class. Then, Sam and Darrell talked about the new chicken pen she and Gram had improvised, about Fluffy settling in so quickly that he was already taking a dust bath when Darrell arrived that morning, and about Gram's unexpected excitement over starting a second flock.

Only once had Jen's eyes slid sideways to meet Sam's, and still, Jen hadn't uttered a word about the injured mare. But Sam could read her best friend's mind, so she wasn't surprised when Jen whispered, "I'm dying to see her," as they arrived at Deerpath Ranch.

If Darrell heard, he didn't care.

"Cool! Ely brought the fire truck," Darrell said as he unloaded a big plastic bag full of clattering aluminum cans from the trunk of his car. Hauling it with him, he moved off noisily toward Jake and a table set up with coffee and doughnuts.

At last the girls could talk in private.

But when Sam spotted Mrs. Allen opening the wrought-iron gate that led to the garden path up to her house, she forgot what she'd been about to tell Jen.

Sam waved in greeting, but she was surprised that Mrs. Allen, who usually wore swirly skirts and cartwheel-sized hats around company, had dressed in a gray shirt and jeans so old they were white everywhere but the cobwebbing over Mrs. Allen's knees.

She's ready for work, Sam thought. *Ready to take my place, so I can ride Ace in the training.*

Should she feel guilty that Mrs. Allen was going to do a job the sheriff had originally planned for kids?

When Mrs. Allen returned her wave with a sly grin, Sam decided the answer was no. Not only wasn't Mrs. Allen gloomy about the work that lay ahead, as clearly as if she'd spoken, Mrs. Allen was reminding Sam of the hidden horse and her part in concealing her.

Sam felt a conspiratorial thrill.

She knew she could trust Mrs. Allen to keep all the visitors from noticing as she slipped away with Jen.

"The posse's just getting here," Sam muttered, as she noticed the horse trailer from Sterling Stables and a plain brown one she didn't recognize. "We can sneak into the barn and see her, if we're really careful."

"And really lucky," Jen said. She nodded toward Sheriff Ballard. Using a clipboard, he seemed to be checking in the volunteer members of his posse. "Aren't you supposed to be on that list?"

"I don't know," Sam said.

She felt a little queasy. Sheriff Ballard was her friend and he trusted her, but it had only been two months since he'd warned her to quit thinking with her heart instead of her head. He'd told her flat out that people who did the wrong things for what they thought were the right reasons got into serious trouble.

And she was doing it again.

"We'll hurry," Sam said, but just as she looked away from Sheriff Ballard, her eyes took in a man lining up pieces of lumber that he'd dragged into an arrangement like railroad tracks. Even though he wasn't in uniform, Sam would bet he was the policeman teaching the class. His manner was crisp as he directed Jake and Darrell in how to help.

"—distract and not terrify them . . ." he was saying.

Mrs. Allen approached the lawman almost shyly. Sam could tell she was offering to help, but the man continued to aim most of his requests to Jake.

Sam felt a twinge of resentment, but it didn't last.

Fine, she thought. Let Jake be the boss of everything. Mrs. Allen probably didn't care, and Sam had more important things to do. Besides, she wasn't eager to face two police officers when she had a questionable horse hidden just across the yard.

Jen matched Sam's steps as they cut across the ranch yard. Sam was relieved that Jen walked normally. There was none of the arms-circled-around-herself care and stiffness that had hampered her friend's movements just days ago. Jen's recovery from being gored by a bull was almost complete.

Sam noticed the barn door was closed and nodded with satisfaction. Mrs. Allen would make a pretty good role model.

Sam shoved the barn door open about a foot, and Jen slipped in ahead of her.

A quick thud of hooves on straw drew Sam's eyes to the palomino mare. The movement in the box stall was like a swirl of sun.

"She's amazing," Jen said as they walked farther into the dim barn. "Oh man, if we ever get our palomino breeding program back up—"

"Jen, she's wild," Sam reprimanded her.

Jen considered the palomino for what felt like a full minute. "If you say so," Jen said finally.

Why couldn't Jen see that everything about the mare—her ragged mane, rough coat, and the snarls in her tail—looked wild? She just happened to have a sweet temperament.

Jen used her index finger to push her glasses up her nose, then bent to study the front leg that the mare held just above her straw bedding.

"That swelling's really minor," Jen said.

"It's gone down a lot," Sam said.

"I won't try to touch her, but I bet there's not much heat there. It doesn't look infected," Jen observed.

"I hope not," Sam said on a sigh. "I want to turn

her loose as soon as I can."

"Sam!"

Both girls gasped, but in an instant, they recognized Jake's voice, coming muffled through the barn door.

Quickly and quietly, Sam and Jen raced for the door. They sure didn't want him to open it. If the mare saw all those unfamiliar horses, she'd be certain to call to them.

Trying hard to keep her expression blank, Sam eased the door open an inch. "Yes?"

"Get out here or you're gonna be missed," Jake snapped. "They're almost ready to start."

"Okay," Sam said.

Though she'd noticed Jen putting her hands on her hips at Jake's bossy tone, Sam didn't feel like fighting. Maybe later. Now, she wouldn't do a thing to attract attention to herself, because she was a terrible actress and a worse liar.

Jake didn't give her much room to emerge from the barn. She realized he'd stayed close on purpose when they bumped shoulders and he whispered, "How is she?"

Jake's broad shoulders had blocked the view through the open barn door, Sam realized, as she said, "Looks good."

Jake nodded, and walked silently beside Sam and Jen.

He pretended not to hear Jen say, "How maddening is that? Just when I'm set to tell him he's a domineering jerk, he acts like he cares."

Sam didn't have time to answer. As they entered the ranch yard, she realized Jake was right. Things were almost underway and she still hadn't saddled Ace.

"C'mon," Jake said, leading them through the horses and trailers.

"Okay," Sam said, then she blinked, recognizing Ace tied to a River Bend horse trailer. "Did Dallas saddle up Ace and Amigo?"

"Guess so," Jake said.

As Sam scanned the ranch yard, she wondered if she'd ever get her fill of watching horses. She loved hearing their nickers and stamping, watching them back quickly from trailers or sidestep away from a raised saddle. Everything they did was wonderful to her.

"There's Jinx!"

Sam pointed out the gleaming grulla-bronze gelding tied to a Darton County Police Department horse trailer. The mustang was fast and beautiful. As Sheriff Ballard's horse, he'd left behind his days as a failed cow pony, bucking horse, and bad-luck charm. Now, he was mastering the skills of a police horse and he'd lead the volunteer posse.

Ace lunged to the end of his tie rope and kicked at the trailer when he saw Sam was distracted. The kick echoed.

"Ace!" Sam said. The horse didn't act the least bit chagrined as Sam climbed into the saddle and picked up her reins before unsnapping the tie rope.

Then, Sam saw another horse she knew and loved. "And Katie Sterling brought Tinkerbell!"

The mustang looked like a mahogany-brown Percheron. No one had expected a wild horse with draft blood to become the best jumper in the area. Schooling at Sterling Stables was helping him make a name for himself in the show ring, too.

Sam urged Ace closer, then shortened her reins.

Even though the two horses appeared to get along now, it hadn't always been like this. In the week Tinkerbell had spent at River Bend Ranch, Ace had shown his jealousy with flattened ears, kicks, and bites.

Now, Sam leaned from her saddle to pet Tinkerbell's neck. He nuzzled Sam in recognition. If anyone ever had to come looking for her, she hoped they'd ride Tinkerbell. For level-headed endurance and strength, she couldn't imagine a better horse.

"Teddy Bear's turning out fine," Jake said as they passed a curly coated young horse ridden by Mr. Martinez, the Darton banker who'd hired Jake and Dad to school Teddy Bear.

"Don't be so humble," Jen said as she strolled up. "Mr. Martinez told my Dad that you transformed that horse from a dangerous prankster to the perfect saddle horse."

Jake shrugged off the compliment. "He's one of those Eureka County curlies. They're good horses."

Jen didn't waste any more words insisting that Jake was a superb rider and trainer. Instead, she turned toward Sam.

"Those Eureka County horses really are pretty interesting," Jen told Sam. "Mr. Martinez says they're descended from horses brought to Nevada by some Russian settlers. The wide-set eyes and curly coat," Jen pointed as she talked, "are typical, but another thing that's really cool is they're hypoallergenic."

"Really?" Sam asked. She remembered a friend in her middle school who'd been so allergic to fur-bearing animals that a single cat hair on someone's clothes could make her sick.

"That's what Mr. Martinez told us. In fact, he wants to keep Teddy Bear closer to home, instead of in Clara's pasture, because his son who's allergic to animals isn't allergic to Teddy Bear."

"You need to meet Lieutenant Preston," Jake interrupted, nodding across the ranch yard.

The man that Jake indicated looked young and lanky. His hair was parted on the side and combed down like a little boy dressed up for Sunday school. His ears kind of stuck out, too, like a little kid still growing into his body. Though the man's neatly combed hair was turning white, it had been black. It was the kind of hair Gram called salt and pepper.

As Sam watched Lieutenant Preston, her worries floated away. He didn't look like a detective who'd intuitively gravitate to the barn, fling open the door, and shout "Ah ha!" at the hidden mustang. He didn't look worthy of the admiration in Jake's voice, either. He was just an older man, standing there talking to Mrs. Allen.

Still in her saddle, Sam watched him as she would a wild animal. Something about him had made an impression on Jake, and that wasn't easy to do. Then, Lieutenant Preston looked away from Mrs. Allen, toward Sam and Jen and Jake. Impatience flashed over him and he strode to meet them.

Dressed in shined shoes, khaki pants, and a short-sleeved blue shirt, he had a get-out-of-my-way walk. She would bet he could stride right through a riot and it would part around him. His eyes alone would make people step back. They sure didn't fit with his boyish haircut. Ice blue and cold, those eyes should've been in the face of a gunfighter or a tundra wolf.

Let me out of here, Sam thought. She was sure he'd picked up her uneasiness just as Ace had. Her bay mustang tossed his head even though her reins hung loose to his bit. He sidestepped, glancing at the other horses, searching for the source of Sam's worry. Then he stopped and his ears swiveled to point not at Darrell, who'd come to stand beside them, but at Lieutenant Preston.

As he drew closer, Sam thought the edge of his

trimmed mustache looked sharp. She caught a scent that reminded her of Brynna's uniforms when they'd just come from the dry cleaners. And he was watching her.

Of course he was.

The police could tell when someone was hiding something.

For a minute, Sam tried to convince herself he was only looking at her because she was mounted, but that wasn't it. His eyes skimmed over Darrell, Jake, and Jen. Even though Darrell had a bad reputation and tough-guy swagger to match, even though Jake had the muscles and youngest brother chip-on-his-shoulder attitude, and Jen regarded everyone with the superior air of a genius, the lieutenant watched Sam.

"Samantha, this is Lieutenant Preston," Mrs. Allen said proudly. Sam hadn't even noticed she'd been trailing behind him. "Although he prefers not to be called lieutenant because he's retired."

Mrs. Allen's smile said she thought the man's modesty was magnificent.

"Hello, Mr. —" Sam began.

"Just Preston will do," Lieutenant Preston said. He reached up and she reached down. His hand clasped hers so she couldn't get away and his wolfish eyes watched hers so closely, he was probably counting her blinks. "Good to meet you."

Liar, Sam thought.

Out loud, she said, "Thanks."

As he released her hand, Sam wondered why she'd been born to attempt things that would lead to turmoil.

He shook Jen's hand and said it was nice to meet her, too, but he glanced back at Sam. Had Sheriff Ballard said something about her, or did Preston know by looking at her that she was a troublemaker?

Sam strained to listen beyond her circle of friends, past the horses and riders, to the closed-up barn. Did the retired policeman hear something she didn't? Like the hidden mare whinnying in despair?

But Sam heard nothing. At least, not yet.

Chapter Nine ❧

Members of the volunteer posse warmed up their horses, walking or jogging them around the property, much to the interest of Mrs. Allen's saddle horses. The pintos, Calico and Ginger, pressed their chests against the fence, nodding their heads. Judge, a big bay, paced along the fence line, stopping only to paw and snort at the trespassers.

The saddle horses weren't the only ones to notice the commotion. Sam stared across the ranch yard, past Mrs. Allen's house and garden to the pastured mustangs. Playing it safe, they veered close to the fences, snatched glimpses of the newcomers, then darted away—but not too far.

Her gaze wandered past the boundaries of Mrs.

Allen's ranch, toward the hot springs where she'd seen the Phantom three times. What if the stallion had been lingering there, plotting to round up his lead mare, then all this activity drove him away?

Settle down, Sam told herself, but she knew that wouldn't happen. She recognized this anxious, paranoid feeling. It clamped around her like a sarcophagus any time she tried to lie. She knew it was wrong and her brain wouldn't let her forget it.

When Sheriff Ballard and Preston motioned Jake, Jen, and Mrs. Allen over to them, Sam followed. She wasn't sure exactly where she fit in here, but she went anyway.

"You"—Preston's clipped voice claimed Sam's attention—"aren't really part of our four-person riot. I'll let you know if I need you."

He didn't sound rude, just efficient. She'd been dismissed to go hang out with the other riders. But curiosity kept her around, eavesdropping on what she would have been doing if she hadn't wanted to be part of the class.

"Start slow and easy, then build up to true chaos," Preston explained to her friends. "Jake got here first, so I've told him what I'd like to see you do. See him for assignments."

Jake set his jaw.

Proud but uncomfortable, Sam thought, as Jake fixed his eyes on a spot a yard ahead of his boots and the others nodded and mumbled agreement.

When Preston, all businesslike and brisk despite the growing August heat, turned to Sheriff Ballard, Sam noticed how different they were on the outside.

With a droopy mustache, shaggy hair he'd likely cut himself, and alert eyes, Heck Ballard looked like an Old West sheriff, but Sam knew he was obsessed with technology. He loved anything that could be programmed, and she wondered what kind of computer advancement he'd sacrificed to pay for this horsemanship workshop.

But there were some things computers couldn't do, Sam thought, like search the high desert for a downed aircraft or lost child. Sheriff Ballard knew those jobs could be done best from the back of a dependable horse.

As if he'd read her mind—a dangerous thing today—Sheriff Ballard clapped his hand on Ace's shoulder and told Sam, "Glad I've got you on horseback. Wish I had a couple more just like you."

Warmth washed over Sam at the sheriff's appreciation.

"Thanks," she mumbled, but Preston had focused on Sheriff Ballard's words as if they weren't a compliment, but a complaint.

"This group might not make up a big search party, but six is the ideal number for the class," Preston said as he scanned the group on horseback. "What have we got, three women and three men?"

"Four men, if you count me and Jinx, and you'd

better, since we aim to be your star pupils," Sheriff Ballard joked. He glanced down at his clipboard again. Dragging his index finger past the names, he said, "All three women are experienced equestrians."

Sam blushed again. She felt as proud as if she'd earned a blue ribbon.

"Dallas and I can hold our own—" He paused at Jen's half-smothered laugh. "Mr. Martinez rides when he can. That goes for Dr. Yung, too. What those two lack in saddle time, they make up for with brains.

"As for horses," the sheriff went on, "we've got good ones. Six geldings and a mare. Four bays, one sorrel, one black, and my grulla. Mostly Quarter Horse crosses and mustangs. All pretty much bomb-proof."

Sam smiled. The first time she'd heard that expression, she hadn't really understood. Now she knew it was an exaggeration for a horse so dependable it wouldn't act up if a bomb exploded behind him.

"Bomb-proof? We'll see about that," Preston replied as if Sheriff Ballard had thrown down a dare.

Again, Sam noticed that Preston didn't sound rude, just skeptical.

He probably had a right to doubt Sheriff Ballard's claim.

After all, he was from the city and saw the horses and riders before him as ranch born and bred. Even

Ace, born on the range, where he'd handled every natural challenge, from flash floods to being leaped over by one of his own kind, had encountered city sights and sounds that unnerved him.

Right now, for instance, Ace's ears were pointed toward Jake and Darrell as they hung a string of plastic ribbons between two trees.

To Sam, they looked kind of like those things that hung down in a drive-through car wash, but Ace had never seen one. He watched them stir in the faint, hot breeze, intent on figuring them out.

His curiosity was a good sign, Sam thought, but she wondered how her gelding would react if she rode him through the long, tickling strands.

As Sheriff Ballard mounted Jinx, Preston called to the other riders.

"Gather around. That's it. Just bring your horses into a half circle around me."

Sam watched as six other horses moved close. None nipped or kicked, although the black mare shot Teddy Bear an ear-flattened glare when his rider's stirrup struck her rider's.

Preston studied each horse and rider. He didn't look a bit intimidated by his position afoot.

"I'm Preston," he began, "formerly with the Fairfield Police Department near Los Angeles, California. . . ."

Sam focused on the horses and barely kept herself from smooching to Tinkerbell, while the instructor droned through his introduction. Then he got to the interesting part.

". . . on the street, then graduated to mounted patrol and stayed on there until January of this year. Then I took early retirement to pursue a personal interest—namely, the theft of my police horse, Officer Cha Cha Marengo."

Everyone gasped. Sam looked down at Jen just as her friend looked up. They both shook their heads. Who would be stupid enough to steal a police horse?

"The clues I'm following have taken me to Washington, D.C., Rhode Island, Oregon, Arizona, and now, Darton, Nevada. Along the way I've been in touch with Sheriff Ballard, since it seems you've had a little horse thieving around these parts, too. None of that has much to do with you folks, except that the sheriff and I got to talking about this posse and he offered me a chance to teach you folks a bit about what I do best—train riders to teach their horses to be trustworthy."

Officer Cha Cha Marengo. The name strummed like the notes of a Spanish guitar through Sam's mind.

But when the group rustled with excitement, Sam only smiled automatically, because she was thinking about horse thieves. Preston had to be talking about Karl Mannix, the man who'd stolen Hotspot and her foal Shy Boots, but Sam couldn't believe there was a connection.

Karl Mannix was a wimp. He seemed like the kind of thief who watched for an opportunity to make quick money, then jumped on it. Sam didn't know where the Fairfield Police Department kept its horses, but she couldn't believe Mannix would be gutsy enough to break in and steal one.

Preston cleared his throat, pulling Sam's attention back, before he went on.

"I wish I had Honey—you don't think I called her Cha Cha Marengo on the beat, do ya?—here to demonstrate for you. I never called on that horse to do anything she wouldn't try, including dashing into a steel culvert—you know, one of those big ribbed water pipes?—only six feet tall and next to nothing in diameter." He shook his head with a fond expression. "The felon hiding in there claimed he nearly went deaf from the hammering of her hooves coming after him, closer and closer. He swore he started to run, then he looked back over his shoulder and Honey's eyes were glowing red. He also said she was snorting fire.

"Now, I don't know that we can teach your mounts to do that, but today we'll be desensitizing your horses to strange stuff. After that, with some shared trust, there's no telling where you'll go together."

Sam reached through Ace's coarse black mane to rub his warm neck. As if on cue, every rider gave his or her horse a pat, rewarding it for some achievement in its future, but Sam knew Ace had already given her more than any horse should be asked to give.

"Now that you all know who I am and why I'm here," Preston said, "I'd like you folks to do the same, and don't forget to say why you've volunteered for the posse. You can introduce your horse, too, if he's too shy to speak up."

Faint laughter was still subsiding as Katie Sterling began.

"I'm Katie Sterling and this is Tinkerbell," she said, fingers toying with the unbraided lock of mane at the base of the horse's gleaming neck. "As for why I'm here, well, my family owns Sterling Stables, and we raise Morgan performance horses and dabble in just about anything to do with equines. This community has been really good to us and, I don't know," she said, shrugging, "it's just a way of giving back, a little, I guess."

Sam felt like applauding when Katie finished.

Mr. Martinez must have felt the same way. Although he was a bank president, his reason for being there was almost the same as Katie's. Teddy Bear underlined his rider's comments by sticking his long, pink tongue out.

"This is Nightingale," said the familiar-looking man on a black mare with two hind socks. "She's half Arab and half Thoroughbred. I rent her from Sterling Stables and you may remember her as having the second fastest time in the claiming race in October."

"Oh, yeah!" Sam said quietly, and others nodded as well, remembering the race in which the sheriff had won Jinx.

"As for me," Nightingale's rider continued, "I'm Peter Yung—"

"Doctor Peter Yung," Sheriff Ballard added, and Sam remembered seeing the doctor in the first aid station at the rodeo during the summer.

"—I enjoy riding and I thought my skills might be of use to the sheriff's department sometime when an ambulance isn't at hand."

For that, Dr. Yung got a small round of applause.

Then, it was Dallas' turn.

"Well, shoot, there's nothin' fancy about me or why I'm here," Dallas said. "I'm Dallas Green, foreman of Wyatt Forster's River Bend Ranch. Since he got those two young cowhands ridin' full time, Wyatt's just not working me and Amigo hard enough. So, here we are."

Sam felt her cheeks heat and redden as faces turned to her next.

"My name is Samantha Forster—"

"Speak up, darlin', we can't hear you!" Darrell called.

Everyone except Sam burst into laughter, but Sam was appalled.

Not that Darrell seemed to care how much he'd embarrassed her. He was high-fiving Jake with one hand and holding a megaphone in the other.

A megaphone? Sam had no idea where he'd gotten it, but she felt a little better as she imagined breaking it over his head.

"I'm Samantha Forster," she started over again, more loudly. "My horse Ace is a mustang and he's perfect for ranch work, but sometimes man-made things kind of freak him out."

It wasn't exactly what she meant to say, but when Sam heard a murmur of agreement, as if other ranch horses were the same, she decided she'd said enough. Besides, she wanted to save her energy for dismembering Darrell.

The last to speak was a rider in chaps and a pearl-snapped shirt. About Brynna's age, the woman leaned her forearm on her saddle horn and introduced herself as Barbara Ridge and her horse as Laramie. "As for his breeding, all I know's he's quick and tough. As for why I'm here, it's kinda personal—"

"You don't have to—" Preston's concerned tone startled Sam.

"But I want to," Barbara Ridge cut him off. "You see, I have a son who's—well, Freddy has Down syndrome and his judgment isn't always the best. Not so long ago he was lost overnight. He's fine," she responded to the swell of concerned voices, "but there was no mounted posse to go out and find him." The woman cleared her throat and her chin lifted. "To tell you the truth, I'll do whatever it takes to spare another mother the torture of a night like the one I had, waiting for Freddy to come home."

Preston let a moment of silence pass before rubbing his hands together.

"Perfect," he said. "That's what we're all here for. By lunchtime, your horses should be learning that unfamiliar sights, sounds, and smells won't usually hurt them. Smells are the trickiest, and since none of our chaos volunteers"—Preston gestured toward Jen, Jake, Darrell, and Mrs. Allen—"have brought llamas or a ferret on a leash, two things that unsettled my first equine partner, Tex, we'll save the more exotic things for a second workshop.

"However," his voice cracked over the squeaking of saddle leather and shifting hooves, "before we start doing crazy stuff, I'll tell you a secret."

Gooseflesh crept down Sam's nape and over her arms. She wasn't up for any more secrets.

In a low voice, Preston said, "The best way to desensitize a horse is to give it complete trust in you. Today, you won't know what's coming at you from one minute to the next any more than you would in a real-life search-and-rescue situation.

"Stay calm for your horse," he ordered. "If you panic, so will he. Even though you're volunteers and won't be focused on law enforcement—you know, having bad guys trying to climb your saddle and take your gun—you might be riding in flood or fire. If you get 'freaked out,' as Miss Forster said, by a flaming branch falling across your path, or a minivan floating past on the La Charla River, your horse will do the same. He might not still be under your saddle by the time you get your wits about you, and he sure won't be instantly responsive if he hears you panting and whimpering."

"Stay cool," Darrell said, just as he had to the rooster the night before.

"That's about the size of it," Preston said, and though he'd used a joking tone for his instructions, the volunteers were sobered by his real-life examples. For a minute, the only sound was that of Teddy rolling his bit.

After that, the desensitization process began. The horses took turns walking, trotting, and loping over crackling plastic tarps.

Ace did fine at a walk, leaving each hoof in place for a few seconds before lifting the next.

Teddy Bear reacted by hopping straight up in the air as if he'd stepped on something alive, so he had to repeat the exercise until he didn't try to hurdle the plastic, swerve around it, or balk with his head low-ered and feelings hurt.

Tinkerbell didn't seem to notice the tarp beneath his bell-shaped hooves, but when Jake turned on the flashing lights and siren of the fire engine, the giant horse trembled.

Did he recall the earthquake, the fallen barn he'd pulled off Ace, and the volunteer fire department truck rushing to gas mains that had ruptured and burned? Tinkerbell had been a hero then, but maybe he didn't remember it that way.

Sam wanted to hug the frightened gelding, but she quickly saw that Katie Sterling had a better approach.

"No big deal, Tink," Katie told him in a cheerful voice. "That's just an itty, bitty truck. You could stomp it into a pancake. This time, just walk on by."

He didn't that time, or the next, but eventually he walked past the fire engine paired with Ace at his side and after that, he did it alone, even when Jake flashed the lights and whooped the siren at the same time.

Darrell and Jen bounced tennis balls around the horses and, when Preston insisted, gently lobbed the balls against the horses' shoulders. As the first ball struck his shoulder, Ace halted. He gave an insulted grumble, then ignored the rest.

Only the ranch gelding Laramie objected strongly, snapping at the balls with square yellow teeth.

Preston gestured for Sam to dismount and asked Mrs. Allen to lead Ace to water while Sam carried an air mattress over her head and popped it back and forth to Preston in front of, then behind, each horse.

Why did he pick me as his partner? she wondered. Darrell was careening around whining NASCAR sounds while pushing a baby stroller. Jake opened and closed an umbrella under each horse's nose and each one except Tinkerbell half reared away from it. Jen rode a bicycle, weaving among them.

Sam sighed as Nightingale lifted her prancing hooves and stared askance at the yellow air mattress. So maybe Preston hadn't picked one of the others because they were busy. But why had he asked Mrs. Allen to take charge of Ace, when he could have asked her to play Pass the Air Mattress?

He wants to keep me under surveillance, Sam thought hopelessly.

She was relieved when he called for a break.

With no horse to water and no appetite for the sodas and store-bought cookies Mrs. Allen had arranged on a folding table over an hour ago, Sam sneaked away to check on the Phantom's lead mare.

Sam's steps quickened as she neared the barn, but no one was close by as she slipped inside and it was a good thing.

The palomino wasn't happy. She didn't seem to be in pain; in fact, she stamped a rear hoof, redistributing her weight to her injured leg as she did.

"You're limping less than you were just this morning," Sam said, then clucked her tongue at the horse.

But the mare was restless and resentful. She flashed bared teeth at this lone human, and Sam didn't blame her.

"I know, girl," Sam said, but she found herself talking to the rippling ivory tail the mare turned toward her. "You're not used to being cooped up. You want to be out running with your herd." Sam sucked in a breath, telling herself she wasn't lying to the horse. "It won't be long, I promise."

When Sam slipped back out, Jen ambushed her with a despairing look. Then she grabbed Sam's elbow and hissed into her ear, "Do you want to get caught?"

"Of course not," Sam snapped. "I just—"

"Just want to see something so creepy you won't be able to sleep tonight?" Jen asked.

Sam dug her bootheels in, refusing to be towed along.

"No, not really."

"Yes, you do," Jen insisted. She gave Sam's arm a yank, then winced at the pain in her own healing rib.

"No fair," Sam said, walking grudgingly beside her friend. "I didn't do that. You hurt yourself."

"Yeah, yeah," Jen muttered. "Just come with me. You won't be sorry."

At first, Sam had no clue what Jen wanted her to see.

"What?" Sam demanded.

"It's right in front of your face," Jen said, but Sam saw nothing.

Nothing except Mrs. Allen standing about ten feet away, talking to Preston.

"Is it going well?" Mrs. Allen asked, touching her open-necked purple blouse.

"Things went real easy, but doing this on the street will be trickier."

Then, as Preston began explaining how he'd gotten to know Heck Ballard while trailing a horse thief with the unlikely name of Christopher Mudge, Sam's mind screeched to a halt.

Purple blouse? Mrs. Allen wasn't wearing a purple blouse. She was, actually, but she hadn't been two hours ago. And now, instead of demolished jeans, Mrs. Allen wore one of her long, black skirts. Her earlobes shone with silver concho earrings, too.

Why in the world had she changed clothes? And put on magenta lipstick?

"So, you took early retirement to travel around the United States searching for your lost palomino," Mrs. Allen said.

"My lost partner," Preston corrected.

"That's noble of you, Lieutenant, but all that traveling must be hard on your family . . . ?"

Why did Mrs. Allen's voice quirk up at the end like that? She hadn't really asked him a question.

But apparently he thought she had, because he gave a grim laugh and said, "Both my kids are in college and I've been divorced for just over a year. Nobody misses me at home."

Mrs. Allen looked down at her boot toes, then back up, kind of sideways.

"I find that impossible to believe," she replied.

"Oh my!" Sam gasped.

"Oh, your poor dry throat? Let's get you a soda," Jen said, pulling at Sam's arm again.

Sam stared over her shoulder while she stumbled after Jen.

Jen was right. It was creepy, disturbing, even, to hear Mrs. Allen flirt with Preston. Yes, flirt. Add their ages together and they had to be 150 years old, right? But if they weren't flirting, why were they joking over a missing button on his shirt and a camper full of convenience foods and instant coffee, and why in the world would a policeman, the kind of rugged guy who absolutely defined competence, say, "I've learned to be pretty darned independent"?

"You're speechless," Jen said with a satisfied nod.

"And a little sick," Sam said.

"I told you it was worth seeing."

"I guess," Sam said, but then, as she watched the posse reassemble for the next exercise, in which they'd be dragging things, she forgot where she'd last seen Ace. She shouldn't have let Preston make her hand him over to Mrs. Allen.

Mrs. Allen had other things on her mind now, like Preston.

Sam shivered at that thought.

A little tendril of fear unfurled in her mind. She didn't like what she was thinking.

So, don't think about it, she told herself.

"What's wrong?" Jake asked.

Sam blinked. She'd barely talked to Jake at all

this morning, and all of a sudden he was next to her.

"Nothing," Sam said.

"You just turned pale—"

"No, I—"

"—and you never do that."

Sam tried to swallow, but it was impossible. Something as big as her fist obstructed her throat.

Jen and Jake, who were practically sworn enemies, looked at each other as if they should join forces to watch over Sam. When she rushed toward the snack table, Jen and Jake were right behind her.

She could trust Mrs. Allen.

Don't think about it. Sam popped the top on a generic orange soda. She drank gulp after gulp, even though it was warm and syrupy from sitting in the sun.

When Darrell sidled into their tight-knit group, she stared at him.

"Don't blame me," Jen told Jake as Sam stopped swallowing. "All I did was show her the old people making eyes at each other."

"Making eyes," Jake repeated slowly. Then he waved a hand in front of Sam's face. "You sure you're okay?"

"I'm fine," Sam said through chattering teeth. "Go make bundles of sticks and rags like the lieutenant told you to."

Sam decided she must be doing a good job of not thinking about . . . that . . . when her mind registered the fact that Jake not only obeyed her, he tolerated her snarling with no more than a shrug.

If you fall flat on your face from heatstroke, his expression said, *it's your own fault.*

But Sam caught him glancing at her again once he'd joined Darrell.

Fine, they could look all they wanted, she thought. But when Darrell took up his megaphone again and said, "Samantha, stay hydrated, darlin'," Sam had had enough.

In fact, she'd had more than enough after Darrell's embarrassing shout of, "Speak up, darlin'."

As she approached Darrell and Jake, Sam snagged Ace's reins from where Mrs. Allen had tied him. Then, she kept walking, relentless as a robot.

Darrell bounced around, pretending to shadowbox, obviously delighted that she was coming at him with eyes full of payback.

She was within two feet of Darrell when she closed the fingers on her right hand into a fist and swung for his mouth.

He jerked aside, but her fist grazed his jawbone.

Sam gasped. She dropped Ace's reins. She whimpered and curled her left hand around her right as if she were holding a delicate newborn mouse.

"Oh, man," Darrell yelped, but not in pain. "Ely, why haven't you taught her how to throw a punch?"

"I didn't think—" Jake began, looking bewildered.

Darrell held Sam's wrist and looked kindly into her eyes. No matter how she tried to tug loose, he wouldn't let her go. "Never, never, fold your thumb inside your fist when you hit someone." He spoke slowly and softly, as if each word held astounding importance. "You can get hurt that way."

"No kidding," she said between her teeth.

Both guys stood so close, maybe no one else had seen her do a better job of embarrassing herself than Darrell had. Maybe no one else could even guess she was about to cry.

Wrong.

"You all right?" Preston asked briskly.

Where had he come from?

"I'm fine," Sam managed.

"We need to get back to work," Preston said. "Shooting blanks comes next."

She saw him notice Ace, ground-tied despite the bustle around him, and then the man with the salt-and-pepper hair moved off, checking a revolver that looked completely real to Sam, no matter what kind of ammunition was inside it.

Sam swept her left hand at her reins and managed to get back into Ace's saddle. Everything around her was blurry, but it wasn't pain in her hand that made tears start into her eyes.

"Sam, are you positive you're okay?" Jen asked, peering owlishly at Sam.

Sam nodded.

She'd be totally fine if she could keep things from adding up to disaster.

Just don't think about it, she ordered herself again.

Don't think about lost horses. There must be thousands of lost horses in the United States.

Don't think about Preston tracking his stolen horse to this barren Nevada county.

Don't think about the fact that the horse he's searching for is a palomino mare and she'd found one.

All that meant nothing. Nothing at all.

Chapter Ten &

Once the idea popped into Sam's head, it wouldn't leave.

What if the Phantom's honey-colored mare was the police horse Cha Cha Marengo? Sam's gloom deepened as she remembered that Preston had mentioned that he didn't call his "partner" by her registered name. Instead, he'd called her Honey.

"In the course of your duties, it's likely you'll have to drag something—an obstruction off the road, a stranded person from a creek, and so on," Preston was saying now. "So we'll play a pulling game until lunchtime, then we'll go back to desensitization."

"Laramie already knows how to work a rope," said the middle-aged cowgirl. "So maybe he and I should practice something else."

Sam had been thinking the same thing. A good cow horse like Ace knew that after his rider roped a calf, he backed up, keeping the rope taut until the rider jumped from the saddle, worked her way down the rope, and put the calf on his side for branding or doctoring.

Preston nodded. "Those horses that have worked cattle might have a head start on the others, but this is a little different. The horse may have to back away from his burden, or turn and pull it behind him. That can be a little scarier, but it's no time to let your mount think for himself like a cow horse is apt to do. You want him to keep dragging whatever's at the end of your rope until you tell him to stop."

They were about to begin the dragging exercise, when Dr. Scott arrived. Sam had almost forgotten he was coming. Renewed worry surged through her. What would Dr. Scott do while they were dragging stuff? He couldn't go tend Mrs. Allen's horses alone, so he'd just be killing time. What if he wandered toward the barn and heard the palomino nickering to the other horses?

Sam knew she couldn't stop him from doing that, so she just watched as the young vet climbed out of his truck and decided she was not cut out to be a crook.

"Hey, Glen!"

"Good to see you, Doc!"

Everyone greeted the vet warmly. Despite the fact that he was always bustling and busy, he was well liked. He must do as good a job with all the animals in the county as he did with River Bend's, Sam thought.

Once he'd told Sam she was a natural with horses. When she'd sidestepped the chance to work with a young, burned mustang, he'd made her feel guilty. He'd said she was selfish not to share her talent.

Sam sighed, and hoped he'd feel the same about the injured mare in the barn.

With his blond hair shining and his black glasses squared away on the bridge of his nose, Dr. Scott looked well rested for a change. He gave a quick wave, then unloaded a big cardboard box from his truck.

"I brought your picnic," he called out, and when he heard a smattering of applause, he added, "Sheriff Ballard ordered me to pick 'em up from Clara's coffee shop in Alkali. You just go on with what you're doing and I'll put them where they'll stay cool. And don't worry if the cake is missing from yours," joked the vet who had a reputation for always being hungry, "I'm sure it's just a mistake!"

Laughter followed him and Sam sat relaxed in her saddle, lined up and waiting her turn at the bundle dragging. With Tinkerbell in front of him and Jinx behind, Ace stood loose and calm.

It was a perfect day for Ace, Sam thought. He liked working and nothing had scared him yet. He knew both of the other geldings and they had nothing to prove to one another.

They took turns backing and dragging.

From what Sam could tell, Darrell and Jake had made the bundles out of feed sacks stuffed with all kinds of things. Some were puffy with rags, others lumpy with rocks. A few horses had to pull real objects.

Tinkerbell had to back up, pulling along a small tack trunk. Though he flicked his ears and demanded a sniffing inspection of the trunk before he'd pull it, the draft horse succeeded.

He was lucky, Sam thought later, because the tack trunk wasn't half as weird as what Jake and Darrell had set up for Ace.

When she moved to the head of the line, Sam saw Jen hold up her hands and wave them.

What did Jen mean by that? Shaking her head, Jen seemed to deny she had anything to do with what lay on the ground for Sam to drag.

The mannequin had seen better days. Its head was on backward. One arm twisted at an abnormal angle that reminded Sam of pyramid paintings. Its pallid body bore lots of dents from time spent in the junkyard.

It still looked vaguely human, though, and Sam was surprised when Ace didn't demand a sniff test.

Instead, the little bay shifted from hoof to hoof, eager to see why Sam had unsnapped her rope from its holder.

Ace trembled when Sam's loop settled over one of the mannequin's legs on the first try.

Amazing, Sam thought as she wheeled Ace, then clucked him forward. The mustang flashed one puzzled glance over his shoulder, then gave a snort and dragged the mannequin with ease.

"Yay, Ace!" Jen cheered.

"Too easy," Darrell shouted, and the other volunteers must have agreed, because Jake got applause when he darted forward and looped the handle of a plastic bag filled with aluminum cans around the mannequin's wrist.

Ace paused to watch, but when Sam stirred her legs slightly, the little gelding dragged on.

Preston held up a hand for her to halt, then said, "Let's try some fireworks."

Ace's neck arched, positioning his eyes to study Preston as he struck a flare. The thing looked like a stick of dynamite, Sam thought, but when it hissed into glaring pink flame, Ace only retreated one step, then kept watching. When Preston tossed the flare and it rolled to a stop in front of Ace, the horse lowered his head and breathed in the sulphurous scent. He seemed interested in the unfamiliar object, but when Sam asked him to pull the mannequin past it, he didn't hesitate.

Sam leaned forward to plant a kiss on her horse's mane.

"You are such a good boy," she told him, and Ace gave an "aw-shucks" swish of his tail.

But they weren't finished.

"I'd like to try him with one more real-life situation," Preston said, and when Sam hesitated, he added, "It won't hurt your horse, I promise."

"Okay," Sam said.

She tried to keep her uncertainty from showing in how she held the reins while the gray-haired man donned leather gloves and a protective vest, then lay down on the ground. He grabbed her rope, widened her loop, then slipped it over his torso.

Sam could tell that Ace was as confused as she was.

"Do you want me to do that?" Darrell volunteered.

Sheriff Ballard and Preston laughed at Darrell's polite concern.

"You just tryin' to be helpful, or are you afraid that old man will hurt himself?" Sheriff Ballard called.

Darrell held up both hands as if there was no safe way to answer. Then, as Preston pulled the rope snug around his own chest, Darrell retreated.

I don't know about this, Sam thought. She tried to ignore her rogue thought that suggested that if Ace happened to gallop off, dragging Preston behind, there wasn't much chance he'd sneak around and find the palomino mare.

"Ready?" Preston's head lifted from the dirt as if he were doing a sit-up.

"Yeah," Sam said.

Preston pointed, "Don't let him slack off until we reach the water trough, okay?"

The water trough was about twenty yards away.

"Okay," Sam agreed. "I'll take it slow."

"At a trot," Preston instructed. "And don't worry if I'm yelling and carrying on," Preston warned, "that's part of the training. Just keep going."

At a trot? Wouldn't friction skin the shirt right off the man? And after the shirt, maybe a layer of flesh?

Why, Sam wondered, couldn't Ace pull Darrell or Jake or someone else? *Anyone* else.

Sam looked over to see Jen nervously twirling the ends of her braids. She met Sam's questioning look with a shrug.

"Giddyup!" Preston yelled, as if Sam had stalled long enough.

She turned Ace so that he faced away from the retired policeman's feet, leaned forward in the saddle, and urged him into a trot. Sensing that this was different, that something alive squirmed at the end of his rope, Ace quickened his walk.

But Preston had said a trot, so Sam tapped Ace's sides with her heels and he finally picked up his hooves and moved faster.

If Preston thought his yodeling yell would make Ace spook, he was wrong. The mustang's jog took them across the ranch yard until Sam lifted her rein hand for him to stop.

Ace's forelegs were precisely even with the trough.

Sam looked over her shoulder. For a minute Preston didn't move. Was he waiting for her to go on?

"Did you mean Ace was supposed to trot as far as the trough, or did you want us to pull you even with—"

"You're good," Preston grunted. "Stop." He rolled onto his right side, used both arms to push upright, then stood. "Didn't think he'd do it, first try." Grimacing, he pulled the rope off over his head, then nodded in appreciation. "That little bay can pull some."

"Thanks," Sam said, but she wasn't surprised when Preston called all the riders together.

"We're going to break a little early for lunch, then take turns riding a gauntlet," Preston said. He stood stiffly straight. "I'll explain the gauntlet at"—he lifted his arm as if it were unjointed wood and peered at his watch—"twelve thirty. In the meantime, rest your horses, grab yourself some lunch, and be thinking of ways to bomb-proof your horse at home."

Just as Preston started to move off, Mr. Martinez asked, "Can you give us an example of how to do that?"

Preston gave a pained smile, then explained, "The opportunities are all around. If you've got a river, make your horse an expert at water crossings. If you have a bagpipe or accordion you play badly, serenade your horse until he doesn't hightail it out of earshot. Maybe you just bought a new tent for camping. Practice setting it up where the horse can learn that all that flapping won't hurt him."

"He did that all in one breath," Sheriff Ballard commented.

Preston flashed him a frown, then said, "If there's nothing else, eat up."

Sam wondered if she was the only one who noticed that, instead of lining up for a brown bag, Preston limped to the camper he'd parked near the entrance to Mrs. Allen's ranch.

"Guess we don't get a turn dragging stuff," Sheriff Ballard said, dismounting as he talked to Jinx. Hooking a stirrup over his saddle horn, the sheriff loosened the cinch so that it swung below the grulla's sweaty belly.

Sam did the same. She slipped Ace's bit, too, then glanced over her shoulder in time to see Preston heaving himself into his camper.

"I didn't mean to hurt him," she told the sheriff.

"Don't think you did. Not much," the sheriff said. "Besides, he asked for it."

Great, Sam thought.

Then, as if he knew she was planning on sneaking

away to check on the palomino mare, Sheriff Ballard walked beside her to pick up lunch.

Mrs. Allen had spread out blankets on the grass, and everyone sat close together, trying to fit in the patches of shade.

Jen and Sam staked their claim on half of a blanket, then rolled up their sleeves and opened their collars. Still hot, Sam would have tugged off her boots and socks and wiggled her toes in the grass, but she was afraid she'd want to stay barefoot all day and that just wouldn't work for riding.

"Check this out," Jen mumbled.

Sam looked up. Darrell swaggered over wearing Jake's black Stetson. Then, though there was only a foot of blanket between the girls and Dr. Yung, he flung himself down full length. The hat shot off his head but Darrell snagged it, rolled flat on his back, plucked a blade of grass, and stuck it between his teeth.

Squinting sunward, he asked, "Do I look like a cowpoke?"

Jen's and Sam's eyes met. Trying not to laugh, they opened their lunch sacks without comment.

"Hey!" Darrell insisted, "I said, do I—"

"No, but you smell like a cow," Jen said quietly. She unwrapped her sandwich and peered under a corner of bread. "Is that close enough?"

As Darrell snorted his appreciation for Jen's wit, Dr. Yung watched openly. Head tilted to one side and brows raised, he seemed fascinated with the alien culture of teenagers.

Darrell kept his eyes closed as he fanned himself with Jake's hat.

"Sam," he said, "tell Jennifer that I can always tell when a woman's hiding her true feelings with sarcasm."

"If it happens all the time, it might not be sarcasm," Jen pointed out.

Darrell gave an exaggerated sigh, then commented to anyone listening, "The sassiest ones are the most smitten."

"Smitten?" Jen asked. She pushed her glasses up her nose and rearranged her braids to lie flat over each shoulder. Then, when she couldn't come up with anything better, repeated, "Smitten?"

Sam couldn't choke back her laughter any longer. Maybe Jen had finally met her sarcastic match.

Darrell opened his eyes, made a toy gun of his hand, and shot it into the air in celebration.

"Told ya," he said, then pulled the Stetson down so that only his smug smile showed.

Sam was still giggling when Jen muttered, "I don't know what you think is so funny."

Gesturing toward her lips, Sam pretended she couldn't talk with her mouth full.

It was a good thing Jen didn't notice that Sam's sandwich, apple, chips, and cake sat untouched before her. Then Jake came to retrieve his hat,

Preston returned, and there was really too much going on to answer her friend.

As her laughter subsided, Sam's face tightened once more with worry. Concern for the palomino mare settled over her again, hiding her appetite.

She watched Preston gulp down his sandwich as if he were making up for lost time.

Had he washed a scrape and applied some antiseptic while he was in his camper? Had he bandaged an Ace-induced abrasion? While she'd been laughing at Jen and Darrell, had he slipped into the barn, discovered the injured mustang, then called a federal marshal to come arrest her?

Sam took such a deep breath, and exhaled so loudly, that Jen frowned at her.

"What?" Jen asked.

"You know," Sam responded, and Jen's understanding nod said she did.

This nerve-racking day was going on way too long.

"Lieutenant Preston, can you—" Katie Sterling started to say.

"Just Preston," he corrected her.

Katie nodded, but kept talking. "—tell us any more about the horse theft ring you're trying to break up? As I mentioned, we have a commercial stable, so . . ."

"*Trying* is sort of the key word. Honey was stolen two years ago and—well, I've got to back up a bit for this all to make sense." He looked around a bit awkwardly. "Sure you want to hear the whole story?"

"Of course," Mrs. Allen said. Then, Barbara Ridge's "You bet," overlapped Jake's "Sure."

"Okay," Preston said, satisfied. "The Fairfield Police Department had an agreement to use the university's agriculture department corrals. Campus police patrolled a little extra for us in exchange for some in-service training a couple times a year. That only matters because whoever took Honey got past the campus police."

"Did they get all the police horses?" Jen asked.

"No, they almost got Spanky. He was a big bay and there was a trick to loading him. We found him wandering near the freeway. The others were spooked, but still locked up. Honey's stall was open and she was gone. She was always an easy loader," he said wistfully.

"What did she look like?" Mrs. Allen interrupted.

The man clearly didn't mind being sidetracked from his story.

"She was a beauty," he said. "A Quarter Horse built for speed and endurance. She'd be about ten, now, in her prime. She was rare among police horses — being both a mare and a palomino — so she had to work harder to be taken seriously. But she did it."

From nearby, Nightingale whinnied to the captive mustangs. A raspy neigh, probably Roman's, answered, before Preston went on.

"If they'd gotten all six police horses, we probably could've hung in there a little longer, spent more time and money on our investigation, but we had nothin' except the ransom note until—"

"They sent a ransom note to a police department?" Darrell yelped.

"Kinda ironic, isn't it?" Preston asked. "I mean, we're not gonna pay it, and it puts a piece of evidence in our hands." He drew a deep breath. "Not that it helped until we got two breaks."

Sam saw the volunteers lean forward as if they were listening to a ghost story around a campfire.

"A Fell driving pony was stolen from a Washington, D.C., horse trailer. A ransom note was sent on this one, too, but the owner just happened to be a congressman's wife. The heat was pretty intense to solve that case. That's why we heard about it out in California, and we thought, huh, another horse stolen, another ransom note sent. This could be our guy.

"The case got such publicity, a few other victims finally stepped up. We heard about an American Saddlebred stallion stolen in Providence, Rhode Island, and two Arabian mares from Scottsdale, Arizona."

"Did the owners pay?" Mrs. Allen asked.

"All except the senator's wife," Preston said, nodding. "But the animals weren't returned."

Disappointed sighs came from all around. Sam

knew one of them was hers.

"And the horses, were they ever found?" Dr. Yung asked gingerly.

"Actually," Preston said, "some were."

"Really?" Jen said solemnly. "I would have thought—"

"The Fell pony was found on the beach at Chincoteague Island, as if someone was trying to get him out to Assateague among the wild ponies, and the two Arab mares surfaced together at a breeders sale in London, Ohio, after they were found together in an urban park."

"Does that mean"—Mr. Martinez seemed to pick through his own ideas—"that the thief wants the money, won't risk returning the horses, and yet is too softhearted to destroy them?" He shook his head, as if his theory was absurd.

"That's what we're trying to figure out," Sheriff Ballard said. "It's a mystery."

It was a mystery, but something about the story was familiar to Sam. Did the thefts remind her of Hotspot's disappearance? Not the ransom note, because there'd been no demand for money when Linc Slocum's Appaloosa disappeared. Not the softhearted thief. Although Sam thought it had been Karl Mannix, and Shy Boots had been given to a petting zoo instead of being destroyed, some other clue was jiggling around in her brain, waiting to be recognized.

Sam looked up to see Jake watching her. Had he

thought of something? His solemn brown eyes told her nothing.

"Our second break," Preston went on, "came when we picked up an ex-jockey known as Bug Boy."

"In his better days, he could get right up on a Thoroughbred's neck and stick there like a flea," Sheriff Ballard added, explaining the nickname.

"We only had him for outstanding traffic tickets, but there were sixteen of them, and he tried to dodge a thousand-dollar fine by telling us about a former partner in crime named Mucho Mudge."

"Where do they come up with these names?" Mrs. Allen muttered.

Preston laughed outright at Mrs. Allen's puzzlement.

Sheriff Ballard smiled and said, "I get a kick out of aliases. Sometimes they're linked to the criminal's real name, but not often enough. This guy we're after has gone by Christopher Mudge, Kit Mudge, and Mucho Mudge and probably a few other names, since we haven't caught him yet."

"So Bug Boy told you Mucho was stealing the horses?" Katie Sterling prodded.

"Horses and other animals."

Preston went on to explain that Mudge was part of an ongoing investigation nationwide.

The thefts had started on the East Coast. Pedigreed dogs and cats—not trophy winners, but beloved pets who were somewhat successful in show rings—began disappearing. By not snatching from big breeders, the thieves managed to operate for years without a single report to the police.

"It was blackmail," Preston said. "People were promised their pets would get food, water, and vet care if they paid up. Since they didn't want anything to happen to their beloved animals . . ."

"The thieves weren't too greedy, either," Sheriff Ballard added. "They kept the ransoms in the five- to twenty-five-thousand-dollar range—"

"But the animals were never seen again," Preston finished.

"Until the horses," Jen insisted.

"Right," Sheriff Ballard agreed.

"When Mudge hooked up with Bug Boy, he thought he'd struck it rich. Being a jockey, Bug Boy could steal a horse and ride it away quicker than Mudge could stick a Chihuahua in a briefcase."

While his audience laughed, Preston opened a new soft drink can.

"So now that you know who you're after, the case is almost solved?" asked Mr. Martinez.

"It should be, but all this information is a year old, and though we have Bug Boy's information linking him to all this, Mudge doesn't have a record, at least not under any of the names we know. And Bug Boy only communicated with him over the phone.

"Without a physical description, and a department with the manpower to devote to the case,"

Preston went on, "we were kind of spinning our wheels."

"So when Preston won the lottery, he struck out on his own." Sheriff Ballard pointed his thumb toward Preston.

"You won the lottery?" Barbara Ridge said and gasped, flattening her hand against her chest.

"A little one," Preston said. His face turned crimson.

"Sorry 'bout that," Sheriff Ballard muttered, but Preston was already talking over him.

"Cracking this case would've been easy if we'd nabbed Bug Boy earlier. All the agencies thought the horses were being killed, but it turned out that as soon as the ransom had been paid, the horses were just taken a few hundred miles from the kidnap scene and released in some open area. To quote Bug Boy, 'None of us had the stomach for killin' horses, even if they were prissy good-for-nothing's.'"

The line should have been funny, but Preston's voice was grim. As they waited to find out why, no one laughed.

"According to Bug Boy, a new rider, an ex-con they called Cowboy, elbowed his way into the operation. He announced he was the new mastermind and he was changing three things. First off, he'd replace Bug Boy. Second, all stolen horses were dead horses, whether the ransom was paid or not. Last thing was that any one with questions could come see him."

Preston paused.

Then, though his glance swept over all of them, it stopped on Sam.

"I don't mind telling you I've dealt with some pretty rough characters during my career," Preston said. "And Bug Boy is no innocent, but his eyes were round and darn scared when he told me 'Ain't nobody wanted to ask Cowboy a thing.'"

Chapter Eleven ∽

Why was he staring at her while he was talking about horse thieves?

Sam's hands turned cold. Her arms felt like they'd frozen and then she shivered, even though the temperature must have reached ninety degrees.

She must have been giving off invisible icicles, because when Preston finished giving directions for the gauntlet and everyone else stood up to get ready, Jen reached over, grabbed Sam's hand, and squeezed it with concern.

"Don't panic," Jen said quietly. "He looked at you because—"

"I wasn't imagining it, then?" Sam said, wishing Preston's stare had been produced by her paranoia.

"Definitely not," Jen said. "But I'm convinced it's because Sheriff Ballard told him about Hotspot's disappearance and your role in it."

"Wonderful," Sam sighed. "Just because I tried to help your boyfriend —"

"Don't go there," Jen snapped, but she took Sam's hands and pulled her to her feet with a sympathetic smile. "Go pick up those marachas and jitterbug 'til you've terrified every horse here."

"Jitterbug?" Sam asked, but Jen gave her a shove between the shoulder blades, and she went.

Each horse ran the gauntlet alone, while the other riders lined up facing each other. Preston had explained that the point was for each horse to ignore the noise and visual distraction and listen to his rider, so those in the gauntlet used kazoos, plastic bags filled with aluminum cans, pom-poms, and other things to create chaotic rows for the horses to pass between.

Preston had gone to his truck cab and retrieved a bunch of helium-filled balloons he'd bought in Darton. When he gave them to Mrs. Allen and instructed her to stroll near the horses, she looked as pleased as if he'd handed her a bouquet of roses.

Though Sam started out feeling silly waving a pink pool noodle in one hand and a maraca in the other, it was fun. By the time her turn came, Ace had been watching for nearly an hour. He survived his trip through the gauntlet easily. When Preston dismissed the volunteer riders, Sam had managed not to think about the Phantom's lead mare for at least fifteen minutes.

Dallas had left with Ace and Amigo. Sam, Jen, Darrell, and Jake were piling all the desensitization gear into boxes and the adults were talking nearby when Sam saw Mrs. Allen do something strange.

She released the balloons one by one and when they'd all floated away, colors dimmed to black dots in the sky, she looked sadly at Sam. Then she turned to Preston.

"I've got to show you something," she said. "It's in the barn."

Sam felt as if red ants covered every inch of her body. Jen dropped the plastic pipe she'd been picking up and Jake slowly put his thumbs in his pockets. Only Darrell didn't halt his movements and stare.

No! Sam wanted to leap the clutter between her and Mrs. Allen and clap her hand over the old lady's mouth. But she trusted Mrs. Allen. She couldn't be about to do what Sam's paranoid mind was thinking.

Black skirts swishing back from her boots, Mrs. Allen led the way toward the barn. Preston, Dr. Scott, and Sheriff Ballard looked at each other, shrugged, and fell in behind her.

Finally, Sam grabbed Jen's forearm and demanded, "Is this because she likes him?"

That got Darrell's attention. Suddenly he noticed the tension around him.

"Is what because — ?" Darrell began.

"He gave her the balloons," Sam continued, "so she's . . ."

Dizzy and confused, it took Sam a few seconds to realize Jake was talking to her.

"You've got to go," he was saying, nodding toward the barn. "Tell your side of things."

"He's right," Jen said.

Maybe because Sam had never heard Jen agree with Jake in her life, she ran.

Preston, Sheriff Ballard, and Dr. Scott were already inside the barn by the time Sam reached it. Panting from exertion, Sam looked back for her friends, then at Mrs. Allen.

With crossed arms and a mournful expression, Mrs. Allen waited at the door.

"How could you?" Sam demanded as soon as she had enough breath. The words hurt as if they'd been ripped from roots sunk deep inside her chest.

"How could I not, Sam?" Mrs. Allen asked.

"By keeping your word to me!"

Mrs. Allen winced, but she wore the look of an adult who's done what's best for a child as she said, "He's searched two years for her. She belongs to him. I'm sorry to disappoint you."

"Disappoint? You didn't disappoint me." Sam's voice spiraled in a high-pitched sound that was almost out of control. She stopped. She swallowed. Then, she said, "How about betray? You betrayed me and the wild horses, and I don't know how you could do it."

Sam was still shaking her head as she squeezed into the barn. Dr. Scott and Sheriff Ballard looked at her with blame on their faces, but Preston didn't even glance at her. For him, there was nothing but the horse.

"Honey," he said on a sigh.

He moved closer, pressing against the box stall while the mare studied him.

Her golden ears tipped so far forward, she seemed to point at him. She looked away, gazing at Sam as if she couldn't believe her eyes, but a heartbeat later, the palomino was staring at him again.

Moving like a man in a dream, Preston slid back the bolt on the stall door.

The mare didn't retreat even a half step, but Preston changed his mind. He took a deep breath, slid the bolt closed again and turned on Sam.

She knew exactly what he was doing. She'd seen the reaction in Dad, Jake, Dallas, and every cowboy she knew. He might be a cop, not a cowboy, but he wasn't about to show his feelings in front of them all. He'd keep his love and relief for later.

Right now, Preston dumped two years' worth of frustration on her.

"That's my horse. Her registered name is Cha Cha Marengo. At the time she was stolen she was serving as a police horse for Fairfield County."

He said it like she hadn't heard his story. He sounded like a robot, as if he'd rehearsed this moment so often, he couldn't deviate from the script.

"I don't think it's her," Sam began. "This horse has been running with a wild herd for a long time. Since before Christmas, for sure."

"Two years," he said, and his eyes accused her.

"Wait. You don't think . . ." Sam sucked in more air. Still, she couldn't seem to go on. Sure, she'd hidden the horse overnight, but that was all. "Even if it is her, and I don't think it is—I didn't steal her."

Preston's eyes said he'd heard it all before. Criminals didn't confess on the spot. They tried denial first.

Sam studied him. "That's not what you're thinking, is it?"

"Uh-huh," he said.

Sam couldn't look away. Like a mouse hypnotized by a cobra, she knew she shouldn't let him gaze at her this way, but his pale blue eyes were mesmerizing. They didn't quite agree with her, but they didn't disagree, either. They implored her to keep talking.

"I rescued her," Sam insisted. She had evidence. She could prove what she was saying. "Take a look at that front right leg," she said, pointing. "Under the bandages."

Preston started to look, but that would have meant lowering his magnetic stare.

"That could have happened in transit," Preston

suggested, but he didn't say outright that she was lying. Then, in case she wasn't smart enough to know what he meant by *in transit*, he added, "When you were moving her from wherever to this ranch."

"No! Go ahead and look her over." Sam's arms flew out in a be-my-guest motion, and she finally broke away from his stare. "Or have Dr. Scott look her over."

Sam turned to the vet. He looked so disappointed.

When she tried to explain what Jake had said about the mare's injuries, she couldn't.

She cleared her throat, but nothing physical kept her silent. For most of her life, Jake had protected her. Now it was her turn to protect Jake.

If things kept going downhill, if everyone believed Preston instead of her, she didn't want Jake involved. Being arrested as an accessory to grand theft probably wouldn't help his chances of getting into college.

"Dr. Scott," Sam said formally, "the palomino has a bruise on her chest from a fight with another mare. I saw that happen last week."

"And the cut? When did that happen?" Through his glasses, Dr. Scott's eyes accused her of knowing about the wound when he'd been there yesterday.

When she didn't answer, the vet moved to the stall door.

"I'll have a look at her," he said.

"Check under her top lip for a tattoo identifying

her as a police horse. It'll be there," Preston said.

The vet nodded.

He believes me, Sam thought as he opened the door cautiously, and braced for the territorial charge of a wild horse. He sighed when it didn't come, when the mare just watched him with curiosity and lifted her front hoof a bit higher.

Sheriff Ballard moved to stand beside Preston.

Straw rustled behind Sam and she didn't have to look to feel Jake and Jen supporting her. Darrell was probably standing back there, too. Like an invisible net, her friends' support held her up.

"Preston, do you know what could have happened to her if I'd left her out there without her herd?" Sam asked, but she didn't let him answer. "Start with coyotes, I guess that would be the most likely, but this time last year there was a cougar and her year-old kitten out there. What do you think they'd do to a horse who couldn't run away?"

"What about bears?" he asked sarcastically.

It took Sam a few second to understand, and then her mind chorused, "Lions and tigers and bears, oh my!" from *The Wizard of Oz.* Preston thought she was making excuses, and not very good ones.

"I saw the cougars last year at Aspen Creek," Jen said.

"Aspen Creek is where I found her yesterday morning," Sam said, realizing she'd just admitted she'd had the horse for twenty-four hours without reporting it.

Not that it mattered, Sam thought. Mrs. Allen would have told them if she hadn't.

"Trees up there are still marked," Jake offered. "And there's a coyote den upstream from where the mare was, with signs they're feeding pups." He paused, but when Preston remained unconvinced, Jake added, "Take a look for yourself. There are tracks so clear your granny could read 'em without her glasses."

Preston stiffened at Jake's sarcasm. You could tell the retired cop was used to dealing with guys who used humor to cover their emotions or to fight without throwing a punch. For a minute, he squinted at Jake, sizing him up.

"Are all you kids in on this?" he asked.

"There's no 'this' to be in on!" Sam kept her voice just short of a shout. "I've seen her running with a wild herd since last year. She was the lead mare. That's how she got in the fight. I don't know how she got cut, but I didn't see it until yesterday morning. I brought her here because it was the closest place to get help." Sam stopped to draw a breath. All the fight seemed to have drained out of her. "And if you don't believe the truth, I can't force you."

"It's not my job to say whether you're telling the truth," Preston said in an offhand tone. "I'm just a private horse owner, not a judge. But I'm pressing charges, and the sheriff can take you away. Don't think you'll need handcuffs, do you?"

He joked in a dark way, but Sam could tell he

really wanted her out of there. He wanted all of them gone so that he could be alone with his horse.

"She's right about the coyotes and cougars," Sheriff Ballard commented.

Preston didn't seem to hear the sheriff. "Might as well tell me how you came into possession of her. Was it from Mudge directly, or one of his accomplices?" he asked. "Maybe the judge will go a little easier on you if you cooperate. Although," his voice grew louder, "I wouldn't count on it. There are more girls in juvenile detention facilities every day."

Sam knew he was trying to scare her. It worked, but she tried not to react.

Preston sucked in a breath and shook his head. "But most females don't get sent up. Those who do have generally committed violent offenses. It'd be a shame if a judge looked at all the stolen horses you've been associated with and tried to put you back on the straight and narrow path by locking you up."

This time, Preston didn't sound like he was joking.

Sam whirled toward Sheriff Ballard.

"You know the story behind Hotspot!"

"That'd be the Appaloosa, but wasn't there an ownership question on a buckskin, too?"

Dark Sunshine. Sam remembered the hidden bill of sale proving the mustang mare belonged to Curtis Flickinger, the man who'd starved and whipped her and threatened to steal the Phantom.

"And now Honey?" Preston pretended to mull things over. "Quite a coincidence, you always being in the middle of this stuff."

"She didn't do anything wrong." Jake's voice was no more than a whisper. "Showed some bad judgment, but she's fourteen years old."

"Jake." Mrs. Allen warned Jake to turn down the antagonism in his voice.

"Yeah?" Preston said. He looked willing to listen to Jake, but any hero worship Jake had felt toward the retired officer was long gone.

Jake's lazy tomcat look hid a desire to fight. Sam wasn't the only one who recognized it. Darrell grabbed Jake's arm.

"C'mon, buddy," Darrell coaxed.

"There's no need to bully her," Jake told Preston.

Sam didn't feel bullied, exactly, and she was about to say so when Jen's sensible voice sliced across Jake's threatening one.

"You can't browbeat and harass someone into a confession," she said, shrugging. "We'll testify that's exactly what he did and it won't hold up in court."

"Everyone's an expert on the criminal justice system as it appears on TV," Preston joked. Then he looked around. Suddenly he seemed to realize where he was and who he was talking to. "But I can tell you guys aren't hardened criminals."

If that was supposed to be an apology, it didn't work.

Jen couldn't have lifted her chin much higher. She was insulted on Sam's behalf. And Jake just stared at Preston as if he was waiting for an excuse to fight.

Dr. Scott stood up from examining the mare. He wiped his hands on the front of his jeans, then spread them as if pointing out the palomino's quiet temperament.

She couldn't possibly be a wild horse, the vet's gesture said, and that's when the sheriff turned to Sam.

"Why did you do it?" Sheriff Ballard asked.

Why did I? Sam thought, but she didn't know. It was like trying to remember a dream. When you first woke, it was so clear and vivid that your muscles still shook from some marathon-across-the-moon you'd run, or the green horse you'd ridden. Then, as real life crowded in to fill up your mind, you couldn't remember the story of your dream. In fact you might forget you even had one.

Why did I do it? She wondered again, and suddenly she remembered. In memory, she saw the palomino galloping across the range, veering around rocks and jumping sagebrush. Her creamy mane billowed and her golden legs matched the Phantom's silver ones in a wild and beautiful race.

"I had a reason," Sam said.

Then, Dr. Scott asked, "Couldn't you have asked me for help?"

His injured tone underlined the question, and for a second Sam felt guilty. But then she looked at Mrs. Allen. She'd trusted her, too.

Sam shrugged.

"Samantha, I'd like you to go out and sit in my car," Sheriff Ballard said.

"Are you arresting her?" Jen demanded.

"Of course not. You all can go with her." The sheriff's gesture took in Jen, Jake, and Darrell.

"Ballard?" Preston asked sharply.

"I've known this girl's family since before she was born," Sheriff Ballard said, "and I've come to know Sam pretty well lately." The glance he shot her added, *A little too well.* "One thing I've learned is that Samantha Forster might not always be right, but she's always kind. If she brought your horse in from the range, the mare needed help. And there's no way on God's green earth she was involved in a horse theft ring!"

"When you look at the timing and circumstances . . ." Preston began, but his voice tapered off and Sam could tell he didn't even believe himself anymore.

"Preston, I know you're used to makin' snap decisions—right, wrong or good, bad—that's part of the job. But give this a few seconds to play out. Take a minute to think. You won't be sorry."

Gently, Jen gripped Sam's arm and nodded toward the barn door. Sam knew her friend was right. If Preston wanted to back down, he wouldn't do it in front of an audience.

They were almost through the barn door when Preston's few words told Sam he knew she hadn't stolen Honey from a corral in California. He knew she'd been roaming the range and that Sam had wanted her to stay free.

"She didn't belong out there, you know."

Sam faced him. "If you could have seen her . . ."

Preston turned his back on Sam and looked at his horse. He mumbled a few more words. Sam wasn't positive, but she thought Preston said, "I wish I had."

Chapter Twelve ❧

When Sam arrived home, she saw Fluffy the rooster and his River Bend counterpart play-fighting. From opposite sides of the fence Gram had erected, the roosters made flying feints at each other, then retired to take noisy, squawking dust baths with their hens.

Those were the last pleasant sounds Sam heard for hours.

Once Sam got inside the white ranch house, Dad told her he was disappointed in her.

Gram said Sam had let her down.

Brynna claimed she was sad and stunned, and wondered if Sam had considered that her actions could get Brynna fired.

Sam decided she'd rather have spent the night in one of the chicken coops.

She didn't like Sunday evenings, anyway. With the weekend over and homework to do, she always felt melancholy, but this was the worst Sunday night she could remember.

Preston had agreed not to press charges if Dad came to get her, so it was a good thing that Dallas had already taken Ace home with Amigo.

When Dad arrived, it was clear that Mrs. Allen had already told him something.

Face hard and unmoving as dark wood, Dad had banished her to the cab of his truck while he talked with Preston and Heck Ballard.

From there, she couldn't hear anything. It was like watching television with the sound off, except that it was the drama of her life playing out, and she had a lot of interest in what was happening.

When she saw Dad shake hands with both men, Sam figured he was coming back to the truck to yell at her. Before he did, though, he took both of Mrs. Allen's hands in his and leaned forward to speak in what might be regret that Sam was his daughter.

At last he stalked back to the truck, yanked open the driver's door and, without a glance at Sam, climbed in.

"Dad? What did they tell you?" she had asked.

He'd started the truck as if he was inside it all alone.

"How was I supposed to know the mare wasn't wild?"

Dad eased the gear shift into reverse and backed around to leave Deerpath Ranch. Once they were headed out the gate, he still didn't respond.

"I would've told Brynna, but I knew she'd have to bring her in, and she's the Phantom's lead mare," Sam explained.

The truck bounced over ruts and onto the smooth highway and still Dad said nothing.

"I trusted Mrs. Allen, and she didn't tell me I was doing anything wrong. Then, out of the blue, she just told Lieutenant Preston the palomino was his. If he hadn't shown up, no one would be mad at me and the horse would be out where she belongs."

Her ears hurt. In the tight confinement of the truck cab, her own voice ricocheted off the windows and windshield and bounced back at her.

"You know I didn't steal her, don't you?"

Dad had given a curt nod, but that was all. He hadn't told her what he would have done for the mare if he'd been in her place. He hadn't agreed that Preston should be grateful to her for finding his long-lost police horse. He hadn't even answered when she asked if she'd be punished.

Dad had just stared out the truck's windshield until they pulled across the bridge over the La Charla River and drove into River Bend's ranch yard.

He stopped the truck and put on the emergency

brake. Without looking at her he said, "I am down-right embarrassed by you, girl. That's all I'm gonna say."

Sam had run from the car to the front porch, aware of Dallas, Ross, and Pepper watching from the bunk house and of Ace neighing from the ten-acre pasture.

Eyes clouded with tears, she'd tripped going into the kitchen, but when she tried to run upstairs and close her bedroom door against everyone's disapproval, Gram had called her back to tell her what a mistake she'd made. Then Brynna had joined in, and the worst part was that Brynna had tears in her eyes when she talked about losing her job.

Now, tears ran into Sam's ears as she lay crying on her bed.

Honey was fine. Dr. Scott had said so. He'd admitted that Jake had done a good job of tending her cut. He said there was nothing a vet would've done that Jake hadn't. So if Mrs. Allen hadn't broken her promise to keep the mare's presence a secret, none of this would have happened. Sam wouldn't be in trouble. No one would have forgotten every single good thing she'd done in her life and focused on the bad.

Best of all, the honey-colored mare would be poised to return to freedom. In days, the Phantom's lead mare would have been back where she belonged.

But Mrs. Allen hadn't kept her promise. Sam

stared up at her bedroom ceiling, but her mind didn't conjure images of horses cavorting among clouds. She saw no fantasies at all, only swoops and whorls of old plaster.

She would never tell anyone's secrets. Sam sniffed, reached for a tissue from the box on her nightstand, and accidentally knocked her alarm clock to the floor. When she rolled over to get it, she bumped Cougar and he yowled.

"I'm sorry. Come here, baby," Sam said, trying to draw the cat's soft body close for comfort. But the cat didn't want a hug. He squirmed and growled, and when she tried to coax him to stay, he gave her knuckles a quick bite that drew blood.

Sam sucked at her knuckles and listened to the sounds of voices and footsteps waft up from downstairs. She stopped crying and strained to hear what they were saying. They were probably talking about her and how they'd punish her. Why didn't they just come up, tell her, and get it over with?

The torture of waiting was part of the punishment, Sam decided, but suddenly her mind was filled with Jake's face. And Jen's. Then Darrell's.

Her friends were the best. Sam remembered them lining up beside her and almost started crying again. Tomorrow at school, everyone was getting hugs whether they wanted them or not.

Sam turned on her left side and stared toward her bedroom window. Dusk wasn't far off, so why hadn't someone come up to explain what was going on? She didn't want to leave her room to shower because she was afraid someone would call her down to dinner. Or bring it up to her, if she was confined to her room. They had to feed her, didn't they? She'd refuse whatever they offered, of course, but wasn't it kind of medieval to starve her for punishment?

Finally, Sam couldn't stand her dirty hair and sticky skin anymore. She showered, did her homework, searched her backpack for food, ate the gross packet of peanuts Brynna had given her from her last plane trip, and crawled into bed.

More than anything, thought Sam, she wanted to call Jen. But then she revised her wish. More than that, she wanted to walk down to the river and find the Phantom there waiting for her. She wanted him to kneel in the shallows and invite her to climb upon his back, and then they'd gallop away to his hidden valley where nothing bad ever happened.

Sam yawned. Her eyes closed. Just as she fell asleep, the mattress dipped. Cougar crept across her quilt, curled up in the crook behind her knees, and settled down for the night.

Dad drove her to the bus stop Monday morning.

As soon as Sam climbed into the truck and closed the door, she noticed Dad hadn't brought her a cup of cocoa to sip on the way. In fact, he hadn't even brought himself a cup of coffee.

Trying to head off a lecture, Sam asked, "Can we just not talk about this?"

"I reckon that's what I'd like, too," Dad said. Then, before her shoulders could sag in relief, he went on. "But this isn't something we can skip over. You thought you knew what was best for that horse, but the horse wasn't the only thing to consider. The horse is never the only thing to consider. This time, you mighta thought of Preston and Heck Ballard. And Trudy Allen."

Sam shifted in her seat. Dad didn't know how Mrs. Allen had let her down.

"Really think about Trudy a minute, will you? And her rescue ranch, and her already under investigation for animal cruelty before you dumped a wrecked horse on her. And what about Jake?"

"Jake can take care of himself," Sam said, smiling.

"Oh yeah, I heard he wanted to have it out with Preston, a retired cop. Heck had himself a chuckle over that, but I don't happen to think it's a bit cute. What if they'd really gotten into it and Jake had been arrested for assault?"

Sam looked down at her folded hands and wished the miles would pass faster beneath the truck's tires.

Finally Dad pulled over to the side of the road. Sam looked up. They'd arrived at the bus stop. She could see Jen in a hot-pink blouse and jeans. Standing on tiptoe, trying to see Sam, Jen looked like a flamingo.

When Sam grabbed for the door, Dad's hand touched her arm, but it was his cold eyes that stopped her.

"Louise always thought she knew what was best, too, and it got her killed."

Sam sucked in a breath. Dad almost never talked about Mom. This wasn't fair.

"You think that's harsh? It is, but it's true. You do not always know what's right."

Sam stared at her hands lying limp on her knees as she waited. Her fingers were pale, as if all her energy had drained out and they'd wilted.

"To give you time to think this over, you won't be riding this week. Not at all, so don't ask. You go to school and you come home. Anyone wants to see you, they can come over, but no secret talks will go on. You'll sit at the kitchen table. Same goes for telephone calls. Someone will be listening to everything you say."

"Don't I deserve some privacy?" Sam asked.

"You can have all you want when you're alone. Other than that, no. You pretty much gave it up when you kept the mare a secret."

"But you didn't ask! I came home after riding out early in the morning and you didn't even ask!"

"Samantha, you know staying quiet amounted to a lie. I just won't have it. One other thing. I hear you were pretty rough on Trudy Allen. You're phoning her with an apology."

"Oh, no, I'm not."

"Samantha —"

"She lied to me, Dad. She promised to keep a secret and she told!"

"How old are you Samantha, fourteen or four? Some secrets just can't be kept."

"But she promised."

Dad sounded worn out when he said, "She promised before she knew Preston's police horse had been stolen and you had it! Cat's sake, girl, use the brain you were born with. Now, here comes the bus. Go to school and learn something useful."

Sam felt like a sleepwalker as she climbed out of the truck. She closed the door and leaned against it for a minute, her mind spinning.

When the bus driver tapped his horn to hurry her along, Sam saw Jen had already disappeared inside the bus. She sprinted to join her friend.

"So, how'd that go?" Jen asked once Sam was settled next to her.

"How'd what go?" Sam asked, wishing she'd develop a tougher skin. Just because she hadn't burst into tears when Dad was yelling at her didn't mean she hadn't felt like doing it.

"Well, the truck was kind of jouncing around and you and your dad were leaning toward each other and unless you had the radio turned up really loud, I kind of heard —"

Sam gave Jen a friendly shove to make her hush.

"It was terrible," Sam said.

"Let me distract you with my mom's struggles trying to get Golden Rose ready for this weekend's parade," Jen said. "I'm not sure she'll disgrace the Kenworthy palominos forever, but . . . Want to come live with us?" Jen asked when Sam kept staring out the bus window, watching the range slip past.

Sam pretended to consider Jen's offer.

"Your dad doesn't like me," she said finally.

"Sure he does," Jen said. "He just thinks you're sassy, have the Forster stubborn streak, and that you're a bad influence on his darling daughter."

"Ha!" Sam said and Jen laughed.

"Little does he know," Jen said in a sly tone. When she went even further to amuse Sam with an evil laugh and waggling eyebrows, Sam remembered that she owed her best friend a hug.

The school day passed quickly. Sam was a little baffled that she hadn't seen Jake or Darrell all day, but the order and structure of classes and bells had Sam feeling almost normal by the time she reached Journalism class.

"Ally!" she said as soon as she saw the girl who'd called on Saturday.

Allison looked even more delicate than usual. Besides the violet veins that showed in her hands and temples, dark shadows covered the tender skin under her eyes. She stood just inside the classroom door, holding her school books in front of her like a shield. Sam wondered why she hadn't taken a seat yet.

When Allison didn't say anything, Sam touched her arm. It always surprised her that the other girl was actually taller than she was.

"I'm so sorry I didn't call you back," Sam said, talking over her shoulder as she moved toward her desk. "I had the worst weekend!"

"Yeah?" Ally said weakly, but she didn't follow along. "Me too."

Sam didn't really think about what Ally had said. She was too eager to take some film into the darkroom.

As photo editor, Sam had a choice of using digital or traditional photography in the school newspaper, and though digital was easiest, she loved traditional black-and-white photography. Even more than that, she adored the darkroom.

She liked the solitude and the process of swishing the photo paper around in chemicals and watching things develop. In the quiet little lab, she controlled the amount of darkness and light, and enlarged what she thought was important.

After Mr. Blair had taken roll, Sam slipped inside the darkroom and sighed at the peace and quiet. It was a haven, especially today.

Sam realized she'd been humming when Ally appeared beside her in the darkness and she fell silent. Sam waited for Ally to convey a message from

Mr. Blair, but Ally just stood there.

"What's up?" Sam asked, finally.

"When you didn't call Saturday, I thought I might get a chance to talk to you at church yesterday."

Rather than pour out the details of the desensitization class, Sam said, "I had this horse thing to do. Sorry."

Since she was concentrating on her work, it was several minutes before Sam turned to look Ally full in her face. Of course the red photo lights cast an eerie glow, but Ally's expression was strained and anxious.

"You said you had a terrible weekend, too," Sam began. She didn't get a chance to finish.

"He took my money," Ally whispered. "I was saving to buy a mandolin. I've always wanted one. That's why I started making money of my own — because there never seems to be any extra . . ."

Sam's mind raced, trying to make sense of the torrent of words pouring from Ally's mouth, but she didn't want to interrupt her.

". . . started babysitting and playing my guitar at parties where they actually paid me to entertain. Of course I wanted to help out with family finances, and I know a church choir director doesn't make much money and it's not easy being a single parent, but I wanted something of my own, too, the mandolin . . ."

So Ally was talking about her father. Mr. McClintock was a tall, thin man. Secretly, Sam had always thought he looked like a mortician, but he was a talented musician who devoted his life to the church choir, even though she'd heard people say it was a case of "pearls before swine," because he was so good, few in the congregation appreciated him.

". . . but then he stopped asking permission. He just took my money!" Outrage had made Ally's voice rise to a normal tone and Sam watched the darkroom door, too. "It made me mad that he was sneaking, so I kept moving it—first in my guitar case, then in the can the tennis balls came in for my P.E. class last year. That worked for a long time," Ally said proudly. "Remember last year in English, we read 'The Pur-loined Letter'? And in it, that secret letter everyone was looking for was framed on the wall or something like that? Well, I tried it and it worked! I hid my money in plain sight. For months that can rolled around on my bedroom floor, but then I made the mistake of putting a handful of quarters in it and I guess he must have bumped it with his foot, and . . ."

Sam tried not to let her shock and disillusionment show on her face.

The church choir director was stealing from his own daughter. Couldn't he just ask for a raise?

"Ally," Sam said, "that's not right."

"I know, and—" Ally glanced wide-eyed toward the darkroom door when someone bumped a desk outside, but no one came in. "That's not the worst of it." Ally took a deep breath. "I shouldn't tell you, but I have to tell someone."

Dread made Sam shiver, but she told Ally, "Go ahead."

"You promise you won't tell?" Ally stared at her with beseeching eyes.

"Believe me, you couldn't have picked a better person or a better day to ask that," Sam insisted.

"Okay, if you promise."

"Absolutely," Sam said.

"Saturday, when I called you, he'd been acting weird, and then he said there was a special choir practice and I knew that wasn't true, and when he came home late . . ." Ally glanced at the darkroom door again and lowered her voice to a whisper. "He smelled like cigarette smoke and no one's allowed to smoke inside the church! I was scared and I asked him where he'd really been, and he . . ." Ally pushed up the sleeves of her blouse. Even in the red darkroom light, Sam could see twin bruises on Ally's forearms. "Shook me. Really hard."

"Oh, Ally," Sam said.

"He apologized Sunday morning before church," Ally said, "but—"

"That's not enough. No way. Something's wrong. Ally, you've got to talk to someone," Sam insisted.

As she watched, Ally's face was transformed from scared to watchful.

"I'm talking to *you*," she said.

"Sure," Sam told her, "but I mean, someone who can help. The minister, Mr. Blair, or maybe your counselor. Wait, do you know Mrs. Ely?"

Sam paused.

Ally held a hand over her mouth as if she regretted opening it in the first place. *You've got to do better than this,* Sam told herself, then softened her tone and tried to sound more convincing. "Mrs. Ely is really nice, and so smart. Or, like I said, maybe Mr. Blair?"

"No." Ally's voice was strangely level.

"If you want," Sam said, quickly, "I'll ask Mr. Blair what we should do."

"You can't talk about this to anyone," Ally hissed, glancing at the door a third time.

Was Zeke playing drums in the other room? Was Rjay hitting his fist against the classroom wall for order? He did that sometimes, but Sam was pretty sure what she heard was the sound of her own blood pounding through her veins, fast and hard and panicked.

"Ally, you've got to get him some help. Maybe your dad's sick, or . . ."

Drugs, Sam thought. Doesn't it sound like drugs? Stealing money, acting weird . . .

Without warning, Ally buried her face in her hands.

"What have I done?" she whispered.

Sam had never heard anyone say that in real life. Ally was so overwhelmed, her hands shook and her teeth chattered as if she were cold.

"It's okay," Sam said, patting Ally's shoulder.

"I shouldn't have told," Ally said. She shook her

head repeatedly. The lab light turned her hair crimson as fire. "It isn't that bad. It was just hard to keep inside, but I should have. I thought I could trust you."

"You can," Sam said dully. She hated traitors. She couldn't become one. "I won't tell. We'll think of something."

"Really?" Ally said, looking up at Sam. "He could lose his job if you tell, and he's never hurt me before. I bet he won't do it again. I think he's just—"

The bell to end class rang and Ally didn't finish.

"We'll think of something," Sam repeated as Ally left the darkroom. The door slid closed behind her, shutting out the light. "But I don't know what."

After a long, quiet ride home, Sam and Jen climbed the steps down from the school bus.

"Cheer up. They won't be so mad when you get home," Jen said.

"Oh, it's not—" Sam pressed her lips closed. She'd almost told Jen what she was really twisted in knots over. "It's not that bad. I've got lots of reading in English this week."

Jen nodded in understanding. "And I've got loads of physics! Yeah!" She gave an excited thumbs-up and Sam thought, again, that her best friend was definitely one of a kind.

The afternoon weather couldn't have been better and Sam tried to push aside her worries and be glad of that.

It was warm, but a cool breeze scudded clouds around overhead, keeping the *playa* from radiating heat waves up to sizzle through her shoes on her walk home.

Now that Sam was alone, this new secret crowded out other thoughts. She'd tried to block Ally from her mind while she was around Jen. It was hard not to ask for her best friend's help, but she had promised not to tell.

Sam stared skyward, searching for a giant puppeteer in the fat white clouds.

"Is this a little joke?" Sam whispered. "Something to teach me a lesson?"

Sam didn't hear an answer.

"Hello?" Sam called.

Gram had told her that unanswered prayers were really answers. She hadn't quite puzzled that out, yet, and she hadn't really been praying, but anyone who knew what had happened yesterday and then what had happened today, would agree Samantha Anne Forster was being teased by something bigger than herself.

Maybe if Ally hadn't told her this secret on the very same day she'd gotten in Dad's face about Mrs. Allen breaking her word, Sam wouldn't have noticed, but this was just too much of a coincidence. She'd sworn not to be like Mrs. Allen, but Ally had bruises!

Sam knew she'd have to tell, but shouldn't she try to convince Ally it was the right thing to do before she told anyone else?

Or at least before she told another person. Sam smiled. No one could blame her for telling Ace when she got home. And Dad couldn't get mad. She wasn't allowed to ride or leave the ranch, but Dad hadn't said anything about hanging out with her horses.

Thoughts of Tempest stirred in Sam's mind and she wondered why the Phantom had come so near the corral in the middle of Friday night.

Sam stopped walking. Her backpack weighed heavy against her shoulders, but she had to think. She turned the silver horsehair bracelet around and around her wrist, staring toward the Calico Mountain range until her eyes lost focus.

She shook her head.

What if . . .

No, it was too big a "what if."

But what if the Phantom had known the honey-colored mare was too injured to rejoin the herd? Could he have come for Dark Sunshine to take her place?

Sam walked a little faster. She loved the Phantom, but he couldn't have Dark Sunshine and Tempest.

She'd call Mrs. Allen and ask if the Phantom was hanging around Deerpath Ranch, waiting for Honey's recovery. And what about Preston? He loved Honey. He'd probably keep her at Mrs. Allen's while she recovered. That meant he'd be hanging around, and Sam didn't want Preston to see the stallion.

Sam's eyes wandered toward the Calico Mountains again.

Why could she still see the moon, smudged silver white against the blue sky? Chills raised gooseflesh on her arms. She rubbed them, looking around for bobbing rabbit brush or pinion pine swaying in the wind, but there was no wind. No cloud had slid over the sun, either.

The Phantom's distant call floated across the range.

Sam stared hard at the Calico Mountains, but she didn't see him. She wheeled around, back in the direction of the bus stop. Nothing moved there or on the alkali flats. And the trail toward Lost Canyon lay empty.

She'd turned in a complete circle by the time she spotted the Phantom right where she'd looked in the first place, far ahead on a rocky ridge.

Only his coat's silver glimmer told her it was him. Only the familiar sound told her how he'd look if she stood close enough to see.

Head high and level, forelock blowing back and mouth open, the stallion summoned her as if she were a wandering herd member. White movement against the red-gray rocks might mean he'd dipped his head, stopping for a breath.

Then he neighed again, and the cry entreated her to gather together with the others.

Was she right? Is that what the great stallion was

saying? Sam strained to understand, but then the truth came to her: if she was right, he wasn't calling her.

He could be summoning Honey or Dark Sunshine, even Tempest, but the Phantom knew she couldn't run to him like a wild filly.

Sam's eyes were still straining to make out his form. She was still staring at the same red-gray rocks when the mustang vanished.

She drew in a breath. When the stallion did that—just appeared and disappeared as if he were no flesh-and-blood horse, but a ghost—she knew how he'd earned his name.

Sam was almost home when she recognized the connection between Hotspot and the horse theft ring. Maybe all she'd needed was the Phantom's appearance to jiggle her thoughts into order.

The connection was blackmail.

There hadn't been a ransom note, but the word that had been ringing in her mind since yesterday was *blackmail*.

The day Sam had driven out toward Cowkiller Caldera with Ryan to hide Hotspot and her foal Shy Boots, they'd glimpsed Karl Mannix. Ryan had said he didn't think the man his father had hired was really a cowboy, but he was supposed to be a cattle expert who raised black Angus cattle.

Then Ryan had said he'd overhead Jen's dad and Mrs. Coley, the Slocums' housekeeper, saying that the relationship between Karl Mannix and Linc Slocum had less to do with black Angus and more to do with black*mail*.

Sam began sprinting toward home. She had to phone Mrs. Allen anyway and apologize. She might as well ask if the old lady would have Preston call when he came to visit Honey, and give her a description on the man he'd called Chris Mudge.

She'd always assumed Karl Mannix spelled his name with a *K*, but she'd never seen it written down. What if he spelled his first name with a *C*?

Carl Mannix and Chris Mudge had the same initials. Both had been around stolen horses, and those horses had been freed in nearby open space. Maybe that wasn't a coincidence, either.

What if Linc Slocum had received a ransom note, but hadn't told anyone?

Sam ran even faster. She didn't care if her backpack hammered her spine, because she'd just remembered the man called Cowboy. If Mannix had been around here, Cowboy might have been, too.

He was probably no more a cowboy than the ex-jockey was a bug boy, but what if he was? What if Cowboy looked and acted like a real cowboy? It would be easy for him to fit into life in Darton County, where he'd spot horses whose owners might pay fat ransoms.

Although Linc Slocum was the only horse owner Sam would classify as rich, Katie Sterling's farm looked pretty prosperous. Glossy Morgans grazed in its emerald pastures and Tinkerbell was already gaining a reputation as a show jumper.

Sam pictured Blue Wings. Dad's beautiful new mustang moved with the grace and style of a champion Paso Fino, and River Bend Ranch was large and well cared for. Dad wouldn't pay a ransom for a horse any more than Preston would, but it wouldn't be solely because it was wrong.

An outsider wouldn't guess they were one more flood or drought or fire away from losing everything.

Sam gritted her teeth in resignation.

She didn't like Preston and he didn't like her, but if they worked together with Sheriff Ballard, they might unravel the secrets of the horse theft ring before it was too late.

Chapter Thirteen ❧

*A*fter a hurried apology to Mrs. Allen, Sam asked if Preston was still hanging around Deerpath Ranch.

"He is," Mrs. Allen replied. "But he and Heck Ballard are on their way over to talk to you."

"She's still mad at me," Sam had said when she'd hung up the phone.

Gram hadn't been surprised. "Samantha, that was not the most heartfelt request for forgiveness I've ever heard."

Gram wasn't as angry as she'd been the night before. She just continued rolling out pie dough, then sprinkled it with flour from the tips of her fingers.

"Well, I'm not really sorry," Sam said, holding her reddish-brown hair up off her neck. "Preston-whoever-he-is has his horse back, but now the Phantom doesn't have a lead mare."

Gram stared at Sam aghast. "You've regressed."

"What does that mean?" Sam asked.

"In this case," Gram said as she settled the bottom pie crust into a pan, "it means you're not acting your age. Instead of growing up, you're acting like a child."

Dad had said the same thing that morning, asking if she was fourteen or four. Either Dad and Gram had discussed this, or she really was acting immature.

Sam watched Gram mound sugared blackberries into the pie crust, and tried to explain.

"Here's the thing. Preston—and don't you think it's kind of weird that he only goes by one name?—anyway, Preston has lived without his palomino for two years. He's used to being without her," Sam said, "and the Phantom isn't. Before long, he'll be moving his herd for winter, and he needs her."

Gram held her breath as she moved the top pie crust onto the fruit. After she'd crimped the edge with her fingers, she looked up at Sam, blew a wayward lock of gray hair out of her eyes, and asked, "How long were you in San Francisco?"

Sam blinked. It was kind of a random question and she didn't know why Gram was asking until she said, "Two years."

"And this horse you call the Phantom, the one you can't live without, the one you make so much trouble over—"

"Okay," Sam said. "I know, I was away from him for two years."

"Would it be fine with you if someone kept him from you on purpose? Maybe forever?"

Sam froze. It was an awful thought.

"No, Gram," Sam said. "You win."

Gram smiled. "Oh, good. I'll just put this in the oven so we have fresh pie when your visitors arrive."

The men didn't come in for pie. Gram was a little offended, but Sam knew it was her fault. They weren't mad at her, but they wanted to make the point that Sam was not part of the investigation. They'd ask her some questions and listen to her ideas, but that was all.

Sam hadn't really expected to go out with them, searching for clues, but she had hoped that if they hung around long enough, she'd figure out a way, over pie and coffee, to ask questions that would help Ally.

But they didn't come inside and she couldn't just blurt out Ally's secret the way Mrs. Allen had hers.

Standing in the ranch yard, the three of them watched the horses in the ten-acre pasture while Sam explained the similarities she'd found between Mannix and Mudge. At first, she thought both Preston and Sheriff Ballard appreciated her ideas.

"Crooks usually stay with what they're good at," Preston said. "If he successfully stole horses in other states, Chris Mudge could be trying his hand at it here in Nevada as Carl Mannix."

"Using the same initials for each alias is a pretty common memory device," Sheriff Ballard said.

"But we're no farther along than we were after talking to Sawyer, Fairchild, and Baldy Harris," Preston said, frustrated.

Admiration at the man's thoroughness—after all, he'd talked to an old mustanger, a livestock sales expert, and a disgusting buyer of horses for meat— flashed through Sam's mind before Preston snapped his fingers.

"Do you have a photo of him?" Preston asked Sam.

"No," Sam said. "Someone at Gold Dust Ranch might, but I doubt it."

"So we're pretty much back where we started," Preston said.

His remark told Sam that the men had already come to the same conclusion she had. They were just hoping she'd have more evidence.

"We've got casts of his truck tires, and several of us, including Sam, have seen him. If he's around we'll recognize him," the sheriff said.

"For sure," Sam said. "I've never met anyone else who looked like a praying mantis."

A flicker of interest showed in Preston's eyes.

"Do you want me to describe him for you?" Sam asked.

Preston shrugged and pulled a notebook from his pocket. "Couldn't hurt."

Sam closed her eyes, "looking" at the man in her mind's eye as she described him. "He's got a big parrot-beak nose, thick glasses, and watery blue eyes. Like I said, he's built kind of geeky, like a praying mantis."

Preston frowned at the repetition. Maybe he wasn't familiar with insects, Sam thought, but she continued. "When he worked for Linc, he wore outdoor clothes that fit but didn't look right on him. You know, like he wasn't really the outdoorsy type. After I looked at his soft little hands, I really didn't think he was. Oh, and he always had a cold, or else hay fever."

Preston looked up from his notebook with grim satisfaction.

"You mean allergies?" he asked.

"Yeah," Sam answered.

For the first time, his mouth almost formed a smile.

Preston snapped his notebook closed and his expression turned into a grin so wide, Sam would have thought his team had won.

"What is it?" Sheriff Ballard asked.

"Just something Bug Boy recalled from his phone conversations with Mudge. He said Mudge was always sniffing and sneezing. Bug Boy couldn't figure out why a man who blew his nose so much around fur-bearing animals would choose to make a living with horses and hay."

This was so cool, Sam thought. If she wasn't having too much fun to wander off for even a few minutes, she'd call Jake to tell him how great things were going. Despite yesterday.

But then the men got ready to go.

"Thanks for your help." Preston shook Sam's hand so quickly that his hand seemed to just slide by.

"What will we do next?" Sam asked.

"We"—Preston gestured to include Sam—"won't do anything."

"I know," Sam said softly. Why did he have to make such a big deal of it?

"But we"—Preston pointed back and forth between himself and Sheriff Ballard—"will take a drive over to Gold Dust Ranch to interview . . ." He glanced at his notebook again. "Ryan Slocum and Helen Coley."

Sam felt a pulse of satisfaction. Even if they'd already come up with the idea, so had she.

"What about Linc?" Sam asked.

Sheriff Ballard looked at Preston. Was this something they hadn't quite firmed up yet? Or were they trying to keep her in the dark about some scheme involving Linc? Sam didn't blame them, really, but she couldn't help being curious.

"I'll have to get back to you on that, Sam," Sheriff Ballard said.

"But I, uh . . ." Sam began. Was she letting a chance to help Ally get away?

But she'd promised not to tell, and if there was one thing she despised, it was someone who went back on her word. So, she kept quiet, but she promised herself that she'd harass Ally until she gave in and allowed someone to help her.

Later that night, Sam had a second chance to tell.

She usually slept well on school nights, but tonight she was listening for the Phantom to return. And worrying about Ally. When Sam had called the McClintock house after dinner, Ally had said in an airy voice that she was fine, but Sam knew the girl's words didn't mean anything.

Frustrated by the way she kept half waking again and again, Sam finally got up and went downstairs.

She heard a clink. Someone was in the kitchen, and she'd bet that someone was eating blackberry pie.

Sam lifted the hem of her nightgown as she descended the stairs, and Cougar followed one step behind. When she pushed open the swinging door between the living room and kitchen, she saw Brynna sitting sideways on one chair with her feet up on another. Her stepmother's red hair streamed loose around her shoulders and her nightgown was pulled up short by her pregnancy, but she was working.

On the kitchen table, a small triangle of pie and a glass of milk sat amid the clutter of maps and markers.

"I felt restless and had leg cramps," Brynna confessed as Sam came in.

"Are you still working with those maps?" Sam asked. It was a dumb question, she thought, since Brynna was surrounded by them.

"These wild horse problems won't stop," Brynna mused as she stared at the biggest map. "Domestic horses keep showing up mixed in with wild herds."

Brynna said it as if it happened all the time, but Sam didn't think it did.

"First there was Hotspot, then Lass, and now Honey—"

"Wait," Sam said, "not Lass."

Sam had seen the chocolate-brown Rocky Mountain mare with the Phantom, but Lass sure hadn't joined his herd. In fact, she'd snubbed him worse than any mare Sam had ever seen with the Phantom.

"I agree," Brynna said, "I just hope the BLM doesn't—" Brynna broke off, and for a woman who hadn't blinked at wearing a gun to corner horse rustlers last September, she looked awfully nervous.

"Doesn't what?" Sam asked.

"Pick up a pattern of wild horse problems and ask me to do something about it," Brynna finished.

Then, Brynna leaned forward and reentered her world of maps.

She'd missed her chance, Sam thought. She'd been about to ask Brynna some vague but important questions about helping Ally.

Should she give up and go to bed, Sam wondered, or have some pie? She watched Brynna sigh and rearrange the maps, then hold her index finger in place on one map and stretch to check something on another.

One of the nice things about her stepmother was that she hadn't murmured a single word about why Sam was awake so late.

"I think I'll have a piece of pie," Sam said. Brynna just nodded.

Sam had sliced a piece a little bigger than Brynna's and was carrying it back to the table when muffled steps sounded on the stairs. Seconds later, Gram peeked into the kitchen. She wore a red corduroy robe and smelled of baby powder. Her eyebrows arched in surprise.

"I guess that pie was better than I thought," she said, but she settled into her chair between Brynna's and Sam's without cutting a slice for herself.

Sam concentrated. How could she ask something about Ally without telling her secret?

Gram's arrival tore Brynna away from her maps. She grabbed her pie and took a bite.

"I didn't mean to disturb your work," Gram said, but Brynna waved her hand.

"Don't be silly," Brynna said. "I've been meaning to ask you something, anyway. How old is Trudy?"

"Too old," Sam blurted, but she could have bitten

her tongue a second later.

"As a matter of fact, we're the same age," Gram said flatly.

"I didn't mean too old for anything," Sam said. "Just . . ."

On her very first day back on River Bend Ranch, Dad had told her she'd just missed a good chance to keep her mouth shut. Sam remedied the mistake and pressed her lips together.

"Too old for a boyfriend?" Gram asked.

"That's what I was getting at, too!" Brynna giggled.

"Trudy and I are both sixty-two," Gram said, and though Sam tried to keep a straight face, she must have reacted, because Gram added, "Lands, Samantha. That's not ancient, you know." But she smirked a little when she said, "Even if that Preston is only a lad of fifty-five."

"Yuck," Sam moaned.

"Preston and Trudy," Brynna announced. "Tell me that doesn't sound like a soap opera."

"Oh, hush," Gram said. "They're both single, both devoted to horses—"

"And he just won the lottery," Sam said. "That should help."

For a second, it was so quiet Sam heard the grandfather clock's pendulum swing in the living room.

"What?" she said. "I was just thinking about

keeping Blind Faith Sanctuary open. That's all."

Gram tsked her tongue. "If money is your prime objective, I guess we don't have to worry about you falling for any local boys. Ranchers' sons don't drive Ferraris and wear designer clothes—except for one."

"And he likes her best friend," Brynna teased.

Insulted by their not-so-subtle hints, Sam gave a huff.

"Money is so far down my list of things I'd look for in a boyfriend," Sam said.

"Go on," Brynna said. She scooted closer to the table and rubbed her hands together as if she could hardly wait to hear Sam's list.

Actually, she didn't have one. And she wouldn't share it if she did.

"I don't think so," Sam said. Pushing back from the table, she carried her empty plate to the sink and rinsed it off. "I'm going to bed."

Gossiping with Jen was one thing, but gossiping with her grandma and stepmother was just plain weird.

"Nighty-night," Brynna called.

"Sweet dreams," Gram said.

They were still laughing as Sam trotted upstairs to bed. Just the same, as she was falling asleep, an ugly thought intruded. The pattern Brynna hadn't wanted to put into words came to Sam. Three domestic horses, all mares, had been found running with the Phantom's herd. What if the BLM questioned

Brynna's judgment in leaving the Phantom out on the range where he seemed to be stealing mare after mare? Once Sam fell asleep, she still tossed and turned and wondered.

The next day at school, Sam panicked. Ally wasn't in English.

"I hope Ally's okay," Sam said to Jen at lunchtime.

"It's a beautiful Indian summer day," Jen said, gesturing at the trees edging the lunch area. "She's probably sunbathing and reading a book."

"I bet you're right," Sam said, but when Ally wasn't in Journalism, either, Sam asked Mr. Blair for a pass to the pay phone by the quad.

Rachel Slocum, dressed in a crocheted top, short black skirt, and sandals with heels so high she tottered, stood up from her desk, eyes intent on Sam.

"Use the phone on the wall, Forster," Mr. Blair told her.

"Please," Sam begged. "I can't call from here. I have to check on Ally, and it's personal."

"Everything is," Mr. Blair grumbled. "Go, but make it quick."

As Sam headed for the classroom door, Rachel sidled up to her and whispered, "If you had anything to do with the sheriff coming to my house last night . . ." Her voice trailed off, scary as the tip of a snake's tail disappearing around a corner.

Sam recoiled, but Mr. Blair saved her from answering.

"Forster! Go or don't. Slocum, put a sock in it."

"Well, I never!" Rachel retorted. She tossed her hair back at his rudeness, then flounced to a computer terminal in the rear of the room.

Sam kept walking. As if she didn't have enough to worry about, Rachel, and maybe the entire Slocum family, was angry with her. She gave a heavy sigh. At least she had the right change for the phone, and Ally answered on the first ring.

It turned out Jen had been right. Ally was fine. Sort of.

"I didn't come to school because I was afraid you were going to try to push me into telling someone," Ally snapped.

"Don't be afraid of me," Sam said. "But you've still got to tell."

"No, I don't. Everything's fine."

"If you had any idea what I've been thinking all day because you weren't here—"

"Sam, you hardly know me," Ally said.

"Well, then . . ."

Sam stared at a group of sparrows on the quad. They were squabbling over a piece of bread crust no bigger than a dime when a starling darted down and grabbed it.

"I guess that wasn't a very nice thing to say," Ally amended, finally.

"It doesn't matter," Sam said. "You've got to tell someone."

"I won't do it," Ally insisted.

"Okay, then I will," Sam said.

"Go ahead. I'll say you made it up!"

"But you have bruises!"

"I'll stay home until they're gone, or I'll tell them some story. Something really good. You know how creative I am. . . ." Then all of the anger faded from Ally's voice and she sounded like a little girl. "Do you think my dad's some kind of an addict, Sam?"

Sam sighed. There were lots of warning signs — money disappearing, erratic behavior, lying, but Sam remembered Dad telling her she might not always know what was right.

Sam shielded the mouthpiece of the phone even though she couldn't see anyone nearby or far away. Then, instead of answering Ally's question herself, she asked, "What do you think?"

"I think he might be," Ally said in a tiny voice. "So, what will I do? Where will I live if I turn him in?"

"I don't know," Sam said, "but we'll figure something out."

After school, Sam was walking toward the lines of school buses, scanning dozens of loud groups of other students for Jen, when Darrell and Jake headed her way.

Darrell wore baggy pants and a shiny red bowling

shirt. The red shirt reminded her of Fluffy and the other fighting roosters and the fact that Saturday was coming and they hadn't done a thing to stop the bloody contests.

When Darrell sprinted ahead of Jake to catch her, Sam saw her chance.

"It's time!" Darrell yelled.

"Darrell," Sam hissed, "quick, before Jake gets here. . . ."

He looked confused, but happy to go along with her.

"Anything you want, darlin'," he drawled.

"Stop it. Just tell me where the roosters are kept and I'll tell my dad and he and our cowboys will go out and set them loose."

"No." Darrell shook his head uncertainly. "I don't think so."

Sam pressed her advantage before Jake caught up with them. "Okay, don't tell me. Let's do it together. How fun would that be?"

"Bad idea," Darrell said, glancing back over his shoulder. Jake was just a few feet away.

"But what about all the other Fluffies?" Sam pleaded. "We've got to rescue them before Saturday night."

Frowning, Darrell nodded, but then he confused her, by saying to Jake, "I tell ya, it's time. See how down she looks? Oh yeah, Ely, it's most definitely time."

Sam kept walking toward her bus until Darrell spun her around to face him.

"It's time for your on-the-spot punching class in five easy steps."

"Just in time," Sam said, pretending to draw her fist back for a punch. "But I've got to catch the bus."

It was a shame, too, Sam thought, because Jen would love watching a spontaneous punching class.

"All ya need to remember is a simple series of dos and don'ts," Darrell instructed. "As we mentioned before, don't fold your thumb inside your fist. Jake?"

"Do jab in and out, quickly," Jake said in a colorless voice.

"Don't fold your thumb over your knuckles," Darrell cautioned.

"And do be prepared for your hand to hurt like crazy," Jake said.

"Now for the Ely brothers' secret sock," Darrell announced.

"Oh no, what are you doin'?" Jake asked.

"Some secrets are meant to be told, brother," Darrell said.

"I don't care about that," Jake said. "Go ahead and tell anyone you want, but not Sam. Knowing her, she'll try to use it sometime, and when it doesn't work—"

"But it does. It just depends on how the Ely sock is, you know, dealt out!" Darrell crowed.

"Don't trust it," Jake insisted. "How old was I

when I showed it to you? Eleven? Twelve?"

"So it's not a secret anymore?" Darrell asked.

"That stupid hammer fist? No, of course it's no secret," Jake said. "About the only thing it's good for is breaking noses, and only if you're the tall one." Jake paused and pretended to whisper to Darrell. "In case ya haven't noticed, Samantha Anne is never gonna be the tall one."

Sam soaked up the punching information, glad to have it from these guys since she was pretty sure Dad never would have taught it to her. She was memorizing the dos, don'ts, and the hand position of the Ely Brothers' Super Sock when she heard the air brake on Bus 9, her bus.

"Gotta go!" Sam yelled to Jake and Darrell.

She had to run for it. Her bus was rolling forward, on its way. Jen was waving from the window, and Sam just barely made it.

Chapter Fourteen ∞

A black-and-white sheriff's car was idling at the bus stop when Sam and Jen climbed down the bus stairs to start walking home that afternoon.

"What did you do, now?" Jen asked.

"Me?" Sam's heart thumped with worry. She hadn't heard anything in three days about the honey-colored mare.

"Wow. Could things get any weirder?" Jen asked as big tires skidded on dirt, bringing Linc Slocum's champagne-colored Jeep up beside the police car, almost as if he'd been following him.

Linc climbed out of his Jeep. He didn't slam the door closed. Instead, Linc fidgeted beside the Jeep as if he wasn't sure what to do next. Then, as if he realized he wasn't going to fade into the background in his snakeskin boots, turquoise blazer, and brick-colored shirt tucked into matching pants, Linc clapped a gray cowboy hat on his head and clomped up to the sheriff's car.

Sam wanted to surge forward, right after him, to find out what was going on, but Linc shot her and Jen a look over his shoulder. Sam stopped. That look had been almost concerned, but he must have been thinking about whatever had brought him here, because a second later, his shoulders twitched in a shrug that meant Linc was dismissing them as unimportant.

Whatever he was thinking, Sam realized she and Jen could probably learn more if they hung back instead of crowding close to listen in.

"I got this letter," Linc boomed as he flapped a piece of paper at the sheriff's car window.

"Hold on."

Sheriff Ballard gestured Linc back so that he could open the driver's door without bowling the man over.

"You got to look at this," Linc said.

"I'm after doing just that, Linc. Relax."

"I'm just trying to do right by my kids," Linc said.

Jen drew back, reacting to Linc's words with disbelief. Although Linc treated Rachel like a princess, he and Ryan weren't getting along. And Linc "doing right" was hard to believe, unless he saw a profit in it.

Sheriff Ballard turned his back to the girls and tilted his head in a confidential way. Sam couldn't hear what he was saying, but Linc's voice rumbled a puzzling response.

"I admit I'm the one who reported Trudy Allen for her treatment of those poor horses. It's a crime the way she keeps them locked up like that."

Stunned by Linc's hypocrisy, Sam gasped. Linc Slocum had tried every tactic—legal and illegal—to catch the Phantom. He'd had Flick, a criminal with the roping skill of a rodeo champ, rope the stallion from the back of a truck, then leave him tied to a barrel full of concrete. The Phantom still had scars on his neck from fighting the rope and weight, but he'd escaped.

How could Linc condemn Mrs. Allen as cruel for penning mustangs in a wide, green pasture?

"Down, girl," Jen whispered.

Sam heard her own loud breaths and forced herself to stay quiet, since Linc was still talking.

". . . ought to be shut down and her property sold at auction . . ."

Of course, Sam thought. There was his motive for reporting Mrs. Allen to the Humane Society. He'd been after her land for years, and he'd thought of another strategy to try to get it.

"That cruel old woman should have the same treatment she gives those ponies, don't you think, Samantha?" Linc pivoted toward her.

The look on his face was crafty. He knew she'd been listening and he hoped she'd be on his side.

Sam played dumb. "Huh?" she said.

One side of Linc's mouth lifted in a sneer.

"Kids," he snorted, but then Sheriff Ballard took over.

"Linc, I'd like to stick to the business at hand—if there is any." He touched Linc's elbow, guiding him away a few steps.

"Oh, there surely is, Sheriff."

"Girls," Sheriff Ballard said, "if you could sit over there on the boulder for a couple minutes and give us a little privacy?"

"Okay," Sam and Jen said together. They hurried to do as the Sheriff asked, but kept listening.

"I appreciate it," he said, but just then Linc's voice soared louder than before.

"You've gotta do something!" he insisted. "The law's meant to protect me just like anyone else."

The sheriff grimaced and made a settling gesture with one hand.

"Now who's this from?" he asked as he took the letter with the other.

"Danged if I know. The coward didn't sign it!"

Muttering, Sheriff Ballard bent his head to read.

"This is too creepy," Sam whispered as she and Jen sat side by side on the cold boulder. "He's not acting right."

"He never acts right, but he seems scared," Jen

said. "Don't you think?"

Sheriff Ballard turned the letter over, examined it front and back, then rubbed his thumb over the paper. Holding the letter at eye level, he considered the stationery and print rather than rereading it. At last he let out a sigh.

"It's anonymous," Linc said.

"I can see that." Sheriff Ballard's voice was low, but Sam caught a few words. Whoever . . . payoff . . . Then the sheriff demanded, "Explain this part."

Linc leaned over to read the passage Sheriff Ballard was pointing at.

"A 'standing ten-thousand-dollar fee.' That part?" Linc asked.

Why were those words familiar? They jolted Sam like an electric shock.

"I can't say I understand, either," Linc admitted. "Standing offers are a part of doing business. I have standing offers on some property in Mississippi. You know, if someone should ever come around to wanting to sell, my offer is right there, waiting. But ten thousand dollars? Who'd make an offer that small? Not me. Besides"—Linc made a show of reading the exact wording in the letter—"this says the standing offer is 'for services rendered.' What's that about, Sheriff? You tell me. I have no idea, whatsoever."

"He's lying," Jen whispered to Sam.

"All that blustering so the sheriff can hardly think," Sam said, agreeing with Jen.

"And watch how he keeps fixating on the letter. He won't meet Sheriff Ballard's eyes."

Sam nodded.

"Okay, Linc, settle down. Let me see if I have this right. Put in simple terms, the letter writer wants to meet you at Apple Mills during the Harvest Home parade this Saturday. . . ."

Jen grabbed Sam's arm and forcefully mouthed something.

"What?" Sam whispered back, but Jen shushed her and leaned so far forward she almost slid off the boulder as she concentrated on Linc and the sheriff.

"That's tomorrow, I—" Linc must have noticed the sheriff's impatience, because he interrupted himself to say, "Yes sir, Sheriff."

"—and this anonymous person wants ten thousand dollars on an old debt that you know nothing about—"

"Yes, sir. I don't owe anyone ten thousand dollars for services rendered. Nobody."

"And another ten thousand on a standing offer."

"That's the way I read it, too, Sheriff."

"So, how can I help you?" Sheriff Ballard asked.

Linc jerked back in amazement.

"Come along and protect me!"

"From what, Linc? No crime's been committed, has it?"

"I'm shocked at you, Heck. In the old days they used to hang—" Linc's jaw snapped shut.

Had he been about to say something incriminating? Sam wondered. Or had he realized he'd gone too far?

Sam glanced at Sheriff Ballard and for just a second he looked as patient as a predator. A flash of memory told Sam she'd seen the same expression on a coyote waiting at a ground squirrel's hole.

The sheriff must have heard something in Linc's blustering that she hadn't, Sam thought, but Sheriff Ballard finally filled the tense silence.

"Except for specifying an unusual meeting place—a parade on the other side of the county—I don't see any threat here. Don't show up in Apple Mills." Sheriff Ballard handed the letter back to Linc. "Far be it from me to give you financial advice, Linc, but if you owe someone money—"

"I don't owe that mangy crook a red cent!" Linc shouted.

"Sounds like you know who you're dealin' with," Sheriff Ballard said. "Maybe if you told me—"

Linc snorted. "I don't owe *any* mangy crook twenty thousand dollars, that's all. Can't you just come along and make sure this unscrupulous person doesn't extort money out of me?"

"What do you really want, Linc. Me involved in your financial affairs? You plan to go along with some kind of payoff, then you want us to follow the money?"

"Who's us?" Linc interrupted.

"Darton County's taxpayers, that's who," the sheriff snapped.

Seeing that he wasn't making any progress, Linc cleared his throat, took off his hat, and stared at it. Then he looked into the sheriff's face for the first time.

"I've caused you trouble in the past, Sheriff, but I'm changin' my ways. For my kids, like I said before. And the truth is, if I'm in physical danger from this polecat—" Linc shook his head. "Only reason I'm going to meet him at the Harvest Home parade is because I don't want him coming to my house and being around my daughter."

Wow, Sam thought. If Linc wasn't being sincere, he'd fooled them all. Suddenly he had Sheriff Ballard's cooperation.

The sheriff gave a quick nod. "I'll be there."

"Thanks, Sheriff; you don't know how much this means to me. Now if we could just make some plans. You know"—Linc gave a short laugh—"synchronize our watches and stuff like that."

"I'll be in touch, Linc. Right now I have business with these ladies. Hard tellin' what kind of trouble they'll be in if they're too late getting home."

Sam flinched. He was right. How could she have forgotten Dad's command to come straight home after school?

"I'll give them a ride," Linc offered.

Jen rushed in with an excuse before Sam realized they needed one.

"Thanks, but we're on an exercise program for P.E.," Jen said solemnly. "We're supposed to walk at least a thousand steps each day."

"We are?" Sam blurted.

Jen gave a long-suffering sigh. She smoothed a few loose strands of hair back from her temples, toward her tight braids, then straightened her glasses on her nose.

"You were standing right next to me in the gym when the teacher told us." Jen patted Sam's shoulder, turned toward the men, and added, "I guess I was paying closer attention. Because of my broken ribs, I can't do much else but walk." Jen pulled up the edge of her blouse to show a little plastic counter clipped to her jeans' pocket. "See, this records each and every step."

Before Jen went on, Linc backed away, nodding.

"I'll be waiting for your call, Sheriff," he said, and then he was gone.

"We're riding in that parade!" Jen came out with the words as if she'd been about to explode, waiting for Linc to leave. "My family, I mean, with the Kenworthy palominos."

"Is that what you said after you sank your fingers into my arm?" Sam asked.

"Are you, now?" Sheriff Ballard asked Jen.

"Sure, my dad's riding Sundance and I'll ride Silly. My mom's been working with Golden Rose, and they want to try her out in this parade, because it's so small, and we'll kind of bracket her between us." Jen's breath caught. Then she blushed. "I could go undercover for you, if you want. I mean, I'd have a good vantage point, being on horseback."

"Good vantage point for what?" Sam asked quietly.

"Watching whatever goes down," Jen said, as if she were on a television crime show.

Sheriff Ballard smiled, but it didn't look as if he'd completely dismissed what Jen said, and Sam was confused.

"Like, you'd be watching Linc to see who's trying to get money from him?" she asked.

Jen took a deep breath and looked at both Sam and the sheriff.

"Okay, at the risk of sounding like I'm fantasizing, here's what I've been thinking, ever since I heard Preston talk about the horse theft ring. . . ." Jen's voice trailed off and she blushed even redder.

"Go ahead," the sheriff told her. His encouragement seemed to be the push that Jen needed.

"What if Linc arranged for Hotspot's theft, with Karl Mannix, but he didn't pay up because Karl made such a mess of it—letting Hotspot escape and leaving Shy Boots in a petting zoo. But maybe Karl was involved with that guy Cowboy and he thought Cowboy might shoot Shy Boots, so he just left the colt the first place he thought of."

Sam gasped, but she remembered Preston saying that Cowboy had decreed any stolen horse a dead horse.

"Or maybe Linc's deal was that Mannix was just supposed to make the foal disappear, but Hotspot was supposed to turn up right away."

"But then the Phantom ruined everything," Sam said, remembering the flurry of hoofprints in the dirt up in Cowkiller Caldera.

"Right," Jen said, pointing at Sam, and then they both looked at Sheriff Ballard.

With crossed arms, the sheriff leaned back against his car. He watched them carefully but he didn't say a word. Finally, though, he nodded.

"Okay, so in this fantasy of mine," Jen said in a self-mocking tone, "Karl has come back for his money. After all, Linc offered him ten thousand dollars for the job—'the services rendered'—but Linc didn't pay up."

"If he didn't pay Karl then, when it happened at the beginning of the summer, why would he pay him now?" Sam asked.

"He's holding something over Linc's head," Jen said. "I'm positive."

"Like what?" Sam asked.

"Blackmail," Jen said ominously.

Sam whirled toward the sheriff so quickly, she had to push her auburn bangs back from her eyes. "When you talked with Ryan and Mrs. Coley yesterday, did they say anything about blackmail?"

"I can't comment on that, Sam," the sheriff said in a level tone.

Sam made a frustrated sound, but Jen just looked more convinced that she was right.

"My dad has always thought it was strange that Linc didn't fight to get Hotspot. Dad offered to go after her, since we all knew she was running with the Phantom's herd, but Linc said no, he wanted to leave it up to the BLM. Remember," Jen said, turning toward Sam, "he really discouraged Ryan from catching her, too."

"That's right," Sam said, turning toward the sheriff. "They had a huge fight about it. I bet he thought you'd discover something that would incriminate him and prove that he knew about the rest of the horse theft ring, the whole Bug Boy operation."

The sheriff pushed away from his car, standing up straight with an indulgent smile. "Thanks for the suggestions."

"So, what do you think?" Jen insisted.

"I think you have some good ideas and it can't hurt for you to keep your eyes open while you're riding in the parade."

As Jen clapped her hands in delight, Sam protested, "What about me? Hey, since I'm Jen's best friend, it would make total sense for me to ride with them."

"Not going to happen, Miss Forster," the sheriff said, smiling. "There's no reason to put you in the middle of this."

"If Jen's riding Silly, Jed's riding Sundance, and Lila's riding Golden Rose, Mantilla will be left behind. There's going to be an extra palomino," Sam pointed out.

"I appreciate your offer," the sheriff said, "but no."

Sam squinted into the distance, then said, "I know. I won't ride. I'll impersonate a typical teenager. No one would recognize me if I dressed up in a short skirt and sunglasses and looked like . . . Rachel!"

"No kidding!"

Jen's outburst only slowed Sam down for a second. She glared at her friend and kept talking. "Really, though, I always wear T-shirts and jeans and if I dressed in some kind of girly outfit, then walked around jabbering on a cell phone, I could stand right next to Karl Mannix and Linc and neither of them would recognize me."

Sam knew she'd made a good case because now Jen was nodding along with her, but Sheriff Ballard wasn't convinced.

"Again, I appreciate your willingness to sacrifice for the good of the community and its horses, but it's my understanding that you're grounded, Sam."

Even the county sheriff knew when she was grounded, Sam thought in grouchy despair.

"When I grow up, I'm not living in a small town," she complained.

"Of course you are," Jen said. "You're living right next door to me."

"Speaking of that, I'm driving you both home. Now."

Sheriff Ballard held open the passenger-side door of the police cruiser.

Sam followed him around to that side of the car. Then she made one last try to be part of the action.

"If riding in the parade was official police business, even my dad couldn't say no," Sam said as she slid in and fastened the middle seat belt.

The sheriff waited for Jen to get in and close the door before he said, "I think we'll have it covered."

Sam sighed. Her argument had just fizzled out and she was lucky Sheriff Ballard hadn't brought up the fact that just a couple of days ago, she'd been under suspicion of horse theft herself.

As Sheriff Ballard drove toward Gold Dust Ranch, Sam wondered what Linc had meant about not wanting the guy around Rachel. She believed Karl Mannix could be involved in stealing animals, but as far as people went, he seemed harmless.

But Linc's concern had reminded her of something she should know. Sometime months ago, hadn't someone told her Rachel had revealed some information about the Phantom? But who? She sighed. Maybe so many weird things were going on, everything seemed significant.

First the Phantom had shown up at River Bend. Then Blind Faith Mustang Sanctuary had been investigated. The Phantom's lead mare had turned out to be Cha Cha Marengo the police horse, now all this stuff about a ten-thousand-dollar standing offer . . .

Oh, and she couldn't forget Fluffy the fighting rooster and Ally's dad! No wonder she was imagining things about Rachel.

"Did you moan?" Jen whispered to Sam.

"Probably," Sam answered. "One small brain can only hold so much stuff."

Jen scooted a little closer and said, "After the parade, I'll call and tell you everything."

Sam sighed. That would help. "From a pay phone, though," she insisted. "Don't wait until you get home or you might forget something."

"Promise," Jen said.

"Pinky swear," Sam said.

Laughing, she and Jen linked little fingers and were about to repeat their vow when something else crossed Sam's mind. She swiveled in her seat to address Sheriff Ballard.

"What if it's not Karl Mannix who wrote the letter?"

"Good point," Jen said. "That's why I said it was sort of a fantasy, except for one thing . . ."

Jen's voice trailed off and she looked meaningfully at Sam, but Sheriff Ballard was answering her question.

"Just because it would tie up a few loose ends doesn't mean it's the solution," Sheriff Ballard agreed as the electronic gates of Gold Dust Ranch swung open to let him drive through. "In police work, you can make lots of wrong turns and go down lots of blind alleys before you find the truth. It's just part of the job."

When the sheriff braked in front of the foreman's house and gave a wave to surprised-looking Lila Kenworthy as she came onto the porch, Jen climbed out.

"It's okay, Mom," Jen laughed.

"Jen, wait," Sam said before her friend started explaining her arrival in a police car. "What's the one thing that makes you think it's not a fantasy?"

Jen squared her shoulders and prepared to answer.

"Let me guess," Sheriff Ballard cut in. He leaned forward in the driver's seat to peer out at Jen. "It was when he said, 'In the old days they used to hang—'"

"'Horse thieves,'" Jen finished for him. She gave a decisive nod.

"Nice working with you, Miss Kenworthy. If high school doesn't work out, maybe we can find a place for you in the sheriff's department," Sheriff Ballard joked.

"Jennifer Marie Kenworthy," Lila said in despair, "what have you been up to?"

As they drove away, Sam and the sheriff were smiling, but as they turned left toward River Bend Ranch, Heck Ballard's grin vanished.

He adjusted a knob on his police car radio, then glanced at her.

"Guess I should explain why I was waiting for

you at the bus stop," he said.

Suddenly, Sam felt as if there weren't enough oxygen molecules in the police car. She took two deep breaths before speaking.

"You didn't just pull over because Linc was following you?"

"No." Sheriff Ballard swallowed so hard that Sam heard him.

"What's wrong?" she asked in a small voice.

"Sam, there's been an emergency at River Bend Ranch and your Gram wanted me to come get you and explain what's happened."

Chapter Fifteen ❧

Frightening images appeared, like framed pictures on the wall, in Sam's memory. She saw dogs attacking Jeepers-Creepers and Dad falling. She saw Brynna's revolver, shiny and cleaned, slipped into a holster she seldom wore and never used. She saw red-haired Pepper laughing as he rode with risky abandon, trying to prove he was a real buckaroo. And Gram . . . but Sheriff Ballard had just said Gram had asked him to help out, hadn't he?

"What happened?" Sam asked.

"No one's dead," Sheriff Ballard said.

"That's good," Sam said, blinking as she grappled with the sheriff's bluntness.

"Your stepmom's pregnant," he began.

"I know," Sam replied. Why would the sheriff say something so obvious?

"I mean, she's still pregnant," he amended.

Brynna had stayed healthy and strong by continuing to work outside with the horses during her pregnancy, but she'd been warned not to climb on the catwalks above the loading chutes at Willow Springs Wild Horse Center. She'd gotten dizzy up there.

"Did Brynna fall?" Sam asked.

"No. She's okay, but she was moving some maps and files around—I guess her staff is painting her office over the weekend—and she started—" Sheriff Ballard broke off. "What they think is that she went into false labor."

"False labor," Sam repeated, but the words made no sense. Weren't you either in labor, having a baby, or not in labor?

"The symptoms are the same, I guess, but it's so early, they're hoping it's not *premature* labor."

Okay. Premature labor made sense, but Sam counted the months on her fingers. The baby wasn't due until December. If Brynna delivered her little sister or brother now, three months early, what would be missing? Which parts of a baby formed in the last three months?

"Don't look at me like that, Sam. I'm no midwife. I can perform an emergency delivery. I've done two of them, but I don't know about premature labor. All I know is, your grandmother said to tell you that plenty of six-month babies survive."

Survive? That wasn't the word Sam wanted to hear applied to their baby. Thrive, maybe, or flourish would be good, but survive was too much like *exist*. It just wasn't good enough for a new member of the Forster family.

Sam looked around for the first time since Sheriff Ballard had left Gold Dust Ranch. They were headed for River Bend, away from Darton.

"Why aren't we driving to the hospital? That's where they took Brynna, isn't it?"

"Yep," the sheriff said. "Your dad and Gram are with her, but they won't let anyone under sixteen in to see her—"

"That's ridiculous!" Sam shouted. "What do they think I'm going to do? Jump rope in the elevator? Ride a skateboard down the halls?"

"Simmer down," the sheriff said. "None of us made the rules."

"Okay," Sam said meekly. She really didn't know what had gotten into her, so she bit her lip to stop any more outbursts.

"Your Gram hadn't talked to a doctor yet when she called, but they'd been told Brynna would need to stay in the hospital for observation for at least twenty-four hours. That bein' the case, they wanted you to go on home and hold down the fort."

Sam nodded, though that old-time expression Gram and Dallas used grated on her nerves.

"Tomorrow, I guess you have some West Nile virus vaccinations coming in from Reno? Wyatt said you need to make sure that whichever ranch hand picks it up has a cooler. That vaccine shouldn't get warm on the way to your place. Does that all make sense to you?"

"Sure," Sam said, though it sounded like busy work to her, something to keep her occupied while she waited in scared boredom at the ranch. "So, they didn't know when they talked to you if it was false labor or premature?"

"They're hoping for a false alarm," the sheriff said, as his cruiser rumbled over the bridge over the La Charla River into the ranch yard.

The white house with green shutters, the cozy bunkhouse, and the big barn looked familiar, but also somehow threatened. When she scanned the ten-acre pasture, Sam saw the red gleam of Brynna's blind mare Penny. The sorrel stood at the gate as if she was waiting for word of her mistress.

Suddenly Sam longed to get out of the car. She wanted to run into the house, up the stairs to her room, and slam the door against the trouble crowding toward her. Still, she tried to be polite.

"Thanks for the ride, and for telling me," Sam said.

Before the car stopped, she grabbed for the backpack she'd slung into the backseat. She opened the car door, swung her feet onto the ground of home, and focused on the front porch.

"Hey, before I go, do you suppose I could see that filly of yours?" the sheriff asked.

His voice worked like a bungee cord, pulling her back.

"Tempest? Sure," Sam said, then noticed all three hands, in from the range though it was only afternoon, standing near the bunkhouse.

She couldn't read their expressions, but just in case they were watching her with pity, Sam squared her shoulders, bent to rumple Blaze's ears, then led the sheriff toward the small pasture where Tempest and Dark Sunshine grazed.

The pasture was empty and her heart lurched.

"They must be inside the barn," Sam said, and of course they were.

Sam heard the rustle of straw and the clump of hooves before she and the sheriff passed into the barn. As she did, though, for the first time in at least a month, Sam glanced back at the board nailed above the doorway. There it was, the little wooden horse Dallas had carved, stained with white shoe polish, then set there as a good luck charm.

Though she knew it was silly, the sight made her feel better.

So did Tempest's greeting.

"You squeal like a little piggy," Sam told the filly.

Even in the dim barn, Tempest's coat flashed obsidian bright. Her tiny mouth showed pink as she whinnied for Sam's attention, then sidled up to the side of the box stall and rolled her eyes at the sheriff.

"Aren't you the feisty one," the sheriff said. "How soon 'til you wean her?"

"Around Thanksgiving," Sam said. "Brynna said before—" Sam broke off when her voice started shaking. Get a grip, she told herself, then went on, "before Christmas, so all Tempest's and Sunny's carrying on doesn't wake the baby."

Dark Sunshine stood back from her own baby, ears pricked forward because she saw Sam and trusted her. She was also braced to attack, because she didn't know the man beside Sam.

"It's okay, girl," Sam told the mare. "No one's here to hurt either of you."

"Your buckskin belonged to another one of Slocum's bad companions, didn't she?" Sheriff Ballard mused.

Weren't there enough nightmares waiting for her to go to sleep tonight? Why did Sheriff Ballard have to bring up Flick, the bullwhip-wielding criminal who'd roped the Phantom for Linc, then threatened her and Jake on a lonely canyon rim?

"Yeah," Sam admitted.

"Probably I should check and see when he gets released from prison," the sheriff said.

"Why?" Sam asked. "It was . . ." Her voice trailed off as she tried to remember when she and Jake had faced Flick in Lost Canyon. "It's only been a year since he was locked up. He couldn't be out yet, could he?"

"Can't see him returning to these parts where people know what he is," the sheriff said. "Doesn't hurt to check."

Sam heard the sheriff sidestep her question. That meant he could be out of jail. And she'd spend tonight alone in the big, creaky ranch house.

Then, almost as if he wanted to give her something different to worry about, Sheriff Ballard said, "We need to talk about you and Preston."

Instead of insisting there was nothing to talk about, Sam said, "Okay."

"I know you care about horses more than just about anything. I also know you're a good girl," he said.

But . . .

Sam could hear the qualifier before he spoke it. In fact, this conversation was sounding really familiar. Not that she was bored with it. Instead, she wondered if Preston had changed his mind. What if he was pressing charges against her after all?

"You care about truth, honor, justice, and big value words like that. I know your mom would be proud of you," he said.

Sam took a deep breath and held it. That wasn't what she'd expected to hear. But Heck Ballard had been her mother's friend. He probably knew what he was talking about.

"Thanks," Sam said.

"All the same, you've got to stay safe until we can channel your enthusiasm into the right project, okay?" he asked.

Sam reminded herself that Heck Ballard had also investigated Mom's death. Like Dad, he blamed Mom's car crash and drowning on her being preoccupied with wild horses and antelope.

"Okay," Sam said. She tried to keep the resentment out of her voice.

"This isn't the same old thing, Sam. Remember, I mentioned Preston."

Sam nodded for him to go on.

"By the sound of things, Preston and Mrs. Allen are putting together something—come to think of it, she said it was your idea," the sheriff said. "Don't know the details, but it's some way to get city folks to come out and help with the sanctuary horses. Does that make sense?"

"Sort of," Sam said. "But Mrs. Allen said she'd have to get, uh, liability insurance and that it was unbelievably expensive."

"I guess winnin' the lottery'll help with that," Sheriff Ballard said, "'cause they're looking into it, pretty seriously."

"That's great!" Sam said, and she meant it, but she had to ask, "Are they, like . . ."

"In love?" the sheriff asked.

At the same time, Sam finished her sentence with ". . . hooking up?"

Sheriff Ballard laughed so loudly, Tempest and Sunny shied back from the side of their stall and trotted into their pasture. Finally his laughter faded into a chuckle.

"Got me, Sam," he said. "I'm just a country sheriff, and a confirmed bachelor, at that."

"But what do you think?" Sam persisted. "Gram and Brynna were talking about them, too, but Mrs. Allen and Preston have only known each other for a few days and, well, aren't they kind of old for love at first sight?"

"I give up," Sheriff Ballard said, holding both hands over his head. "Don't ask me about anything 'cept crooks and horses. Other than that, I'm ignorant as a jackrabbit."

As they walked back to his police car, Sam and Sheriff Ballard were rejoined by Blaze. The Border collie bumped against Sam's leg, staying close.

"I'm going to be at that Harvest Home parade tomorrow, babysitting Slocum, so you stay out of trouble, hear?" Sheriff Ballard said as he opened his black door.

"I will," Sam said.

The sheriff raised one eyebrow skeptically. "Yeah, well, I hope so. Preston's going to be over at Deerpath Ranch. The vet told him his mare's fine for riding, and he's been working with her ever since."

"Okay," Sam said, though she didn't see what that had to do with her behaving herself.

The sheriff stared at her over the roof of his police car. "If something comes up and you take it into your head to go ridin' to the rescue, ask him to go along with you."

"I'm grounded," Sam reminded him.

"Yeah, that's what I heard, but just the same." He studied her for a reaction, so finally Sam nodded. "Like him or not," the sheriff said, "Preston knows his way around horses and trouble, and that seems to be your favorite combination."

Since she was late beginning her chores, Sam left her backpack on the front porch and got busy. She kept listening for the phone to ring. Part of her wanted to go inside and sit there, staring at it, waiting to hear news of Brynna and the baby, but she knew she'd hear it ring through the open kitchen window, and she knew Gram or Dad would give her plenty of time to answer, so she kept working.

It was almost dark when she knocked on the bunkhouse door.

Sam smelled frying onions and heard them sputtering in a cast-iron pan as Dallas opened the door. Instantly, Pepper and Ross crowded around him, too.

"Want to come in?" Dallas invited. "We're not havin' anything fancy, but you're sure welcome."

"And you can pick what you wanna watch on TV," Pepper said. He gestured to a small screen with a scratchy picture. "We don't care what it is."

Ross nodded in agreement, and the cowboys' kindness touched Sam.

"No, I'm just checking to be sure everything's all set up for the vaccinations," she said to Dallas.

Could she have said it worse? Who was she to be checking up on Dallas, who'd been foreman of the ranch forever? He knew more about it than anyone, maybe even more than Dad and Gram.

But Dallas gave no sign that it was a lame thing to say.

"Yeah, we're all ready," Dallas said. "Ross's driving in first thing. Phil promised he'd have it for us by ten o'clock."

"He's keeping it in the bait cooler until we get there," Pepper put in.

Phil's Fill Up was the gas station next to Clara's coffee shop. Because those two buildings made up the entire business district of Alkali, Nevada, Phil stocked chicken feed, groceries, and other necessities — including night crawlers for fishing — in his little convenience store. So he was keeping the individual hypodermics filled with vaccine for West Nile virus in with the bait.

It wasn't much of a joke, but Sam smiled, as Pepper had probably hoped she would.

"I'm not worried about Brynna and the baby," Sam protested when all three cowboys kept watching her.

"No reason to worry, I guess," Dallas said. "Now

you just go over and fix yourself something your grandma wouldn't approve of for dinner, and watch you some television. If you get lonesome, or if you get a call and want to tell us what the folks have to say, just come on back over."

"I will," Sam said. She turned to go.

"No need to if you don't feel like it," Dallas added, "but I'd surely like to know that everything's all right."

Chapter Sixteen ❧

The phone rang just minutes after Sam walked into the house with Blaze romping at her heels. She must have stared at it like it was a rattlesnake, because Blaze lowered his head and growled. His tail swung low and uncertain.

"Hello?"

"Honey, it's Dad."

"Good," she said. Sam wanted to say more, but her throat tightened and all she could do was press the telephone so tightly against her ear.

"It's just false labor," he said. "Everything's okay, but in case it turns into something else, and since we live so far out, they want us to stay awhile."

"How long?" Sam asked.

"That depends. The doctor said she could leave as early as tomorrow afternoon, or late as Sunday morning. Course she's puttin' up quite a fuss."

Dad's voice sounded almost proud.

"Brynna's fine, then? And the baby?" Sam felt embarrassed by her eagerness. For a long while she'd resented Brynna and the baby that she feared would take her place in Dad's heart, but now she ached at the thought that something bad could happen to either of them.

"Fine as frog hair," Dad joked, but then his voice dropped, "and that is a relief."

"For me, too," Sam admitted.

They finished their conversation by talking about chores, vaccinations, and fastening the shutters and barn door because of the high winds kicking up all over Darton County.

"It's just a fall windstorm," Sam muttered to Blaze. "Wind gusts of forty-five miles an hour— which is what Dad said—are no big deal. We might lose some shingles, but not the roof."

Blaze stared up at Sam, brown eyes fixed on her face, ears pricked to catch every word. "You can sleep in my room if you want," she told him, and the dog's tail wagged. "No chasing Cougar across my bed, though, understand?"

As Sam hurried across the ranch yard to tell Dallas, Pepper, and Ross about Brynna and the baby, the wind felt like a warning. It snatched her hair out behind her, then blew it back in her face. A tumbleweed bounded prickly and huge across the ranch yard and Sam wondered why the weather always took a turn for the worse when she was home alone.

"Already fastened everything down," Dallas said after Sam told him the news and mentioned Dad's concern for doors and shutters banging in the night. "Don't you worry."

Excited by the blustery weather, the horses in the ten-acre pasture galloped and snorted, jostling shoulder to shoulder across the dry autumn grass. Spooked by this first storm in his new home, Blue pressed close to Popcorn and Ace, then burst into a run that ended with a worried neigh.

Sunny and Tempest stayed silent. In the falling darkness, Sam couldn't see their outlines, so maybe Dallas had locked them into the barn for the night.

Sam ate canned soup and toast for dinner. She opened the cookie jar, took out two oatmeal cookies, and poured a glass of milk. She felt restless.

After one bite, she knew what was wrong. She was worried about Ally.

Sam stared at her reflection in the kitchen window. Darkness had turned everything beyond it black and dust spat at the glass, but the light overhead showed her safe and warm, even if she was alone.

It was Friday night. Was Ally facing an entire weekend alone with a madman?

Okay, that's overdoing it, Sam told herself. *He's not a madman.* She slapped her palm against the kitchen table. *He's a choir director.*

She was starting to stand up, to get something to sop up the milk that had splashed over the lip of her glass, as the phone rang. If it was Dad again, the news couldn't be good.

"Hello," Sam said. For a minute there was no response, but then she heard Ally speak. The voice that had been rich and sweet as milk chocolate when Ally had sung the national anthem on the first day at school was now raspy from tears.

"Sam, I don't know whether to be happy or—" Ally's sentence stopped in the middle, but she went on. "My dad bought me a mandolin."

"Wow, Ally, that's great!"

So why was she crying? Sam wondered.

"Kind of," Ally said. "The car was just packed with stuff. He made about a dozen trips back and forth, fighting the wind, carrying all kinds of groceries—steaks and fresh raspberries, and pink boxes tied up with string from that French bakery. One was filled with cream puffs sprinkled with powdered sugar and the other had little chocolate éclairs."

"Maybe he's trying to say he's sorry," Sam said, but some instinct told her to be suspicious. Mr. McClintock's sudden generosity was too much.

"I hope you're right, but he got me a new dress, too. It's—I don't know—like a prom dress or something, all glittery green." Ally was quiet for a minute. "It's beautiful, but Sam—I saw the price tag. It costs more than he makes in a—"

Suddenly there was silence.

"Ally?" Sam said.

"I've got to hang up," Ally whispered. "Here he comes."

Sam's scalp tightened in alarm. She waited for Ally to say more.

She heard only a dial tone.

For a few seconds after she hung up, Sam fought to convince herself that Ally was fine.

After all, her dad had apologized by giving her loads of gifts, hadn't he? But Ally was right there in her house. She'd know if her problems had blown over. If they had, she wouldn't have sounded scared as she whispered, "Here he comes."

Sam knew what she had to do. Ally would hate her for it, but that didn't matter as much as her safety. Sam dialed the number for Three Ponies Ranch, praying Jake wouldn't answer. He wouldn't ask why she was calling or hint she should tell him why she was asking for his mom, but he'd be curious and Sam couldn't get through this twice.

As the phone rang, Sam pictured Jake's mom. Small, blond, and brainy, she ruled her family of men as easily as she did her history students. Sam was sure Mrs. Ely would know what to do.

Luckily, Mrs. Ely answered, and Sam blurted out everything she knew, starting with her darkroom conversation with Ally on Monday, ending with the creepy end to their talk two minutes ago.

Jake's mom listened in silence, then drew a deep breath.

"This is a pretty serious accusation, Sam," she said.

Didn't Mrs. Ely believe her? Had she heard about Cha Cha Marengo and decided Sam wasn't trustworthy?

No secrets were safe in Darton County. She'd just proven that herself.

"I believe you, of course," Mrs. Ely went on. "But I wish she'd come to me herself."

"She didn't want anyone to know," Sam said. "She said she'd deny it."

"That's not unusual, but the school nurse will want to look for bruises."

Sam groaned.

"Sam, this will sound harsh, but I have to ask. Are you certain this isn't something Ally's doing for attention?"

Sam didn't have to think about that at all.

"I'm positive," Sam said. "She didn't want to tell me. It was almost like she couldn't help it. And she's going to hate me for this."

"That's all I needed to hear," Mrs. Ely said,

sounding sympathetic.

"What will you do next?" Sam asked.

"I'm calling her right now —"

"Don't!" Sam said, feeling a surge of panic.

"I'm going to ask her if she thinks she'll be safe over the weekend," Mrs. Ely said. "If she thinks she is, she'll have time to get mad and cool down, and maybe by Monday she'll realize her dad needs help and so does she."

Then, in a voice so warm Sam imagined Jake's mom hugging her, Mrs. Ely added, "Sam, you're doing the right thing. Some secrets have to be told."

Mrs. Ely's gentle words were no consolation when Ally called back ten minutes later.

"I hate you!" Ally said in a voice that was almost a growl. "You promised you wouldn't tell, but you did. You couldn't wait to ruin my life. I hate you, Sam Forster, and I'm telling everyone you're a liar. You're never going to live this down. Ever!"

Ally slammed the phone down before Sam could say a word. She thought about calling back.

To say what? Sam asked herself. She had told Ally's secret, just as Mrs. Allen had told hers. But it had been the right thing to do.

As Sam put the uneaten cookie back in the jar and threw the one she'd bitten to Blaze, she wondered if Mrs. Allen had felt the same sad sense of rightness when she'd broken her promise.

❖ ❖ ❖

Strangely, Sam had no trouble falling asleep, but Blaze woke her with his barking after midnight.

Cougar yowled and jumped off her bed. Sam heard his claws skittering on the floor, trying to get away as Blaze plopped his paws on the edge of the bed. Dog food breath blasted into Sam's face.

"What?" she complained, pushing at the Border collie. "It's only the wind."

When Blaze didn't accept her explanation, Sam rolled over, looked at the clock, and told herself that she had no choice but to get up and see what was going on. She was the only one home.

This was a down side to being in charge, Sam thought as she rolled out of bed and pulled on a robe.

"There's nothing there," she said, but she was talking to herself. Blaze had already bolted downstairs and stood scratching at the kitchen door.

Then, above the banshee howl of the wind, Sam heard Dark Sunshine scream.

"Oh, no."

Chills covered her arms at the cry she hadn't heard since the buckskin's first days at the ranch. The sound reminded her of Flick, the cruel man who'd popped his whip under the buckskin's nose, refusing to let her join the mustangs he was hauling off for slaughter. He hadn't acted out of kindness. He'd kept the little buckskin to use as bait, over and over again.

Sunny's scream came once more. Sam had a hard

time believing the mare was just frightened by the storm.

Sam opened the kitchen door. Blaze burst through the opening and streaked across the yard as the wind slammed the door in Sam's face. Shouldering it open, she made it outside.

Blaze had vanished in the tossing shadows of cottonwood branches, but a volley of barks told her he had something cornered. Lights flashed on in the bunkhouse, and all three cowboys came stumbling out in stocking feet.

"What is it?" Ross shouted.

Sam thought she heard a yelp, but she wasn't sure.

"Blaze—" she began, but the wind snatched her words away just as it had the dog's sound.

As she started for the barn, Pepper fell into jogging steps beside her. Ross swung a flashlight's beam over the horses in the ten-acre pasture. Their eyes glowed red and surprised, but nothing in their shuffling looked terrified. Dallas walked toward the bridge, glancing all around as he went.

Sunny's screaming had stopped. Sam and Pepper found the mare and Tempest restless but safe inside the barn. Tempest shoved her mother with her muzzle, asking for a snack as long as she was awake.

Sunny's eyes rolled. Her ears twitched in every direction as if she wasn't sure where the sound that had disturbed her had come from. She stumbled away from her foal, then stopped and sniffed her all over.

A pigeon fluttered in the rafters. Dust danced in the bright overhead lights. Then, sucking sounds of the filly nursing filled the barn.

"What do you suppose that was all about?" Pepper asked.

Dallas entered the barn, still bootless, and shook his head.

"That dog's got something going on," Dallas said, bending to pull a sticker out of his sock.

"What do you mean?" Sam asked.

"Don't know. Either he's taken to seeing ghosts—which I doubt—or there's something sniffing around here he don't like. With all his comings and goings and barking in the night, though, there's no doubt about it. Something's up."

Sam felt her fingernails bite into her palms, then purposely opened her fisted hands.

"Everything's okay now, though," Dallas said, trying to reassure her. "Might as well go back to sleep."

Yeah, right, Sam thought as she walked back to the house. *I've got nothing on my mind but a million secrets, including one my dog is keeping.*

She paused on the front porch, putting her hands on her hips.

"Blaze!" she called into the darkness, but she didn't see the dog again until dawn.

❊ ❊ ❊

Sam fell asleep on the living room couch, but woke when she heard Ross leave in the old truck, bound for Alkali. The wind still blew, but she heard geese honking in the early morning, so the gusts must not be as violent as they'd been last night. Geese had to know better than to fly into a gale.

She'd already had hot chocolate and cold cereal and she was washing her dishes, wondering what she should do until Ross returned, when a scratch sounded at the door.

"Blaze!"

The dog bolted past her to his water dish, lapped until it was empty, then threw himself full length on the kitchen floor and closed his eyes.

Guessing he was still thirsty, Sam refilled his water dish.

Even as he drowsed, though, his tongue kept licking out. She bent close enough to see a small cut next to his tender nose.

"Maybe you did have something cornered," Sam said quietly.

It wasn't her voice that startled the dog awake — it was the phone.

The first thing Sam did was look at the kitchen clock. Seven A.M. was pretty early for phone calls.

"Please let Brynna and the baby be all right," she whispered, then picked up the phone.

"Sam." The whisper was so faint, Sam had to wait

for it to come again before she was sure it was Ally. "Sam?"

"Are you all right?" Sam whispered back.

Then, she felt puzzled. If Ally hated her, why was she calling so early? Why did she sound so urgent?

"I'm fine, but I found out what's going on with my dad."

Sam sucked in a breath. Did she want to hear this? What if it was something illegal?

"It's okay that you told Mrs. Ely," Ally said, then, sounding embarrassed, "but, I . . ."

Sam waited.

"Last night when my dad fell asleep—"

"He didn't leave?" Sam asked.

"No, he was here all night, but because it was so windy, he couldn't hear me. I went through all his stuff. Like, where he empties out his pockets on top of his chest of drawers," Ally said, sounding amazed at her own daring. "But that wasn't where I found— wait a second. I've got to call you back."

"Found what?" Sam shouted.

"Right back," Ally promised quietly.

Sam's mind was spinning and she hoped Ally's father hadn't come in and caught her telling whatever it was she'd been about to confide.

Sam grabbed the phone before the first ring ended.

"He went down to the church, just now. A branch fell in the storm and cracked one of the stained glass windows, so—"

"What did you find?" Sam demanded.

"Not drugs or anything," Ally said with a sigh, "but out in his car, under the front seat, there was this flyer about a rooster fight. It was all misspelled and stuff. Mr. Blair would hate it. . . ."

Ally sounded strange. Sam wondered if a person could be quietly hysterical.

"A rooster fight?" Sam repeated.

"Yes, and it had a timetable that said betting starts at ten and fights start at midnight."

It took a few seconds for Ally's information to sink in, but then it made complete sense. People in town were betting on the fighting roosters Darrell had discovered. He'd said some of the faces looked familiar. Although Sam didn't want to believe it, she supposed the church choir director could be one of them.

"Sam?"

"So, you think your dad was using your money for gambling?"

"It makes sense, doesn't it? Maybe he was losing, but then he turned up with all that stuff last night, like maybe he won?"

"It does make sense," Sam confirmed.

"I've read it can be an addiction like drugs, haven't you?" Ally asked.

"Yeah," Sam said. Then, tensing because she was afraid Ally would say everything was okay again, when it clearly wasn't, she asked, "What are you going to do?"

Ally was quiet for a few seconds, but she sounded determined when she said, "I think I should call the sheriff."

"Do it," Sam said. "Right now."

She didn't tell Ally that Sheriff Ballard would be out of the office for much of the day. That might give her an excuse not to call.

"Have you ever heard of anything like this?" Ally asked. Then, in morbid fascination, she read from the flyer, "'Blood Fest of the Year, Saturday at midnight.' Is that gross, or what? My dad doesn't hate animals or anything, Sam. I just . . ."

"You were right, Ally, it's probably an addiction. You're just lucky you found out in time to do something, before he bet your car or house or—" Sam broke off.

Had she gone too far? She was talking about Ally's father, after all. Sam closed her eyes and held her breath, waiting.

"I'll talk to you later. I'm calling Sheriff Ballard right now."

Sam let her breath out in a rush, then she said, "Let me give you his number. It's sad, but I've got it memorized."

Sam's spirits lifted after that.

She helped vaccinate all the horses except Tempest. The filly would have to wait until she was six months old to receive her injection, and Sam couldn't help thinking how unfair it was that Tempest would get her first shot at the same age she'd be taken away from her mother.

Sam tried not to imagine Jen at the parade, watching Linc do whatever skullduggery he was doing, while she was stuck at home. Strawberry helped keep Sam's mind on her work by nipping the seat of her jeans. Hard.

Once all the injections had been given, the cowboys rode out to repair a windmill that had been damaged in the wind. Ross had noticed it when he'd driven back from town, but he hadn't paused to inspect it because he'd been carrying the chilled vaccine.

All alone again, Sam paced and flopped down on the couch to read a mystery novel. It was nice to have the leisure time to read, but Sam hated being grounded. She wanted to be out doing things, not waiting for Jen to call from Apple Mills.

And then, she did.

"I've only got a few minutes," Jen said. "The horses were great during the parade, but the wind has them acting up. I'm not sure Golden Rose will load at all, so I'm staying out of Mom's way."

"Did anyone come meet Linc?" Sam asked.

"No," Jen said.

"Oh, man," Sam moaned. "I thought we'd have the whole horse theft thing wound up and I'd be off the hook with Preston, and—"

"Wait," Jen told her. "It's almost that good."

"Tell me," Sam begged.

"Here's what happened," Jen said, then her tone changed completely. "Yes, ma'am, I'm afraid I am going to be on the phone for a few minutes."

Sam listened to the drone of another voice, but she couldn't make out the words.

"I know," Jen said sympathetically. "That's what people think, but you see, it's a fallacy. Not all teenagers have cell phones. Some of us are at the mercy of the phone company. It's true. We just carry tons of quarters and pray we'll see a pay phone. It is hard to believe, but—you have a nice day, now!" Jen shouted, then drew in a loud breath. "Okay, where was I?"

"About to tell me what happened," Sam reminded her.

"Sheriff Ballard was riding Jinx all around the parade route and Darrell was copying down every license number in the parking lot—"

"Darrell was there, too?" Sam couldn't believe it. Wasn't it bad enough that Jen had been included and she hadn't?

"Don't panic. He was just writing down numbers. You would've hated it, but then he recognized a personalized license plate he'd seen at the rooster fights—"

"You know about them?" Sam gasped. What was going on around here?

"Well, I do now," Jen said, "and I think it's totally

disgusting. So does Sheriff Ballard, but he's got to look up some local statutes or something to see if it's illegal."

"Of course it is," Sam insisted.

"Hmm, usually I'd defer to your legal expertise, but the sheriff's not so sure," Jen teased. "The betting part is illegal."

"I'm calling the Humane Society," Sam muttered.

"Anyway—Sam, I've got to hurry, my mom's looking around for me and I can only hide in this phone booth a little longer. Oxygen deprivation, you know? Plus, it smells like someone—"

"Tell me what else happened," Sam said.

"I saw Karl Mannix! He was dressed like a street sweeper, cleaning up manure behind the horses in the parade. There were these guys in vaquero costumes riding in front of us, and then there he was, just sweeping away."

Talk about hiding in plain sight, Sam thought. He would be invisible, doing that kind of work, but he could also be on the lookout for Linc.

"So, how did Linc and he get together?"

"They didn't," Jen said.

"What?"

"We talked to Linc later, and he told Sheriff Ballard that someone—not Karl Mannix—phoned him and called off the meeting, that they couldn't go through with the transaction because he'd spotted the sheriff. The guy must have been really mad, too, because Linc looked terrified. And then, somehow, Karl slipped away and escaped without moving a vehicle from the parking lot, because they were all there, but—"

"This is terrible," Sam moaned.

"Not really," Jen said, "because the call to Linc was made from a cell phone with a global positioning system, and they're tracking the guy down! How cool is that?"

"And Ballard says police work is nothing like it is on TV."

Sam recognized the scoffing male voice instantly.

"That's Darrell, isn't it? Let me talk to him!"

Sam's heart was pounding and the movie screen in her mind was painted with dripping red letters spelling out BLOOD FEST. If Darrell had already told the sheriff about the rooster fights, he could tell her where they were happening. The roosters could be rescued before they died in awful combat.

"Okay, catch you later," Jen said. "Hey, Darrell! Come here. Some smitten gal wants to talk to you!"

"Hello, darlin'," Darrell said.

He was so sure of himself, Sam wanted to hang up. But she didn't. In fact, she tried her hardest to be nice. After all, he knew something she wanted to find out.

"Hello . . ." Sam bit her lip and managed, "dude."

Darrell laughed at her attempt to be cool.

"I hear you've really been helping the sheriff,"

Sam said, buttering him up. "Jen told me all about it."

"Yeah, he's about to mark this one 'case closed,' all because of me," Darrell bragged, but Sam heard the humor in his voice.

"So, since you told him all about Fluffy's secret, how about letting me in on it?"

"What do you mean?" Darrell asked. "You knew before anybody, except me. And Fluffy."

"Yeah, but you never told me where they were keeping those poor roosters."

"I still won't," Darrell said. "I don't trust you not to go do something stupid."

"Thanks a lot," Sam said. She blew her cheeks full of air. "Just give me a hint, and then if I figure it out, it's not your fault."

Darrell made a considering sound, then he gave a short bark of laughter.

"Okay, I've got it. I'll give you a hint, but this is like a really hard riddle. You'll never figure it out."

"Tell me," Sam said.

"Rusty old school bus," Darrell said.

And then he hung up.

Chapter Seventeen ❧

Sam didn't remember where she'd read that the thing you want to do least was usually the thing you should do first, but she believed it.

She was about to follow that rule, times three.

First, she'd break her word to Dad to stay home, grounded. She really didn't want to do that. There would be consequences and they wouldn't be pretty. That was for sure.

Next, if she wanted to save those roosters, she had to go through Lost Canyon and into a creepy ravine, looking for a bus that was not yellow and not a school bus, despite Darrell's hint. She didn't know what she'd do once she found them, and that was why she had to do the third thing.

She'd made a half promise to Sheriff Ballard, and though she really didn't want to call Preston, she knew he was the best help she could get.

Jake wouldn't ride up there with her because it could be dangerous. Pepper, Dallas, and Ross would be the perfect companions to break up that rooster-killing bunch, but they wouldn't defy Dad, and there'd be no question that helping Sam would be doing just that.

No, she had no choice. The man who disliked and mistrusted her was her best bet.

She couldn't wait for Sheriff Ballard to corner Karl Mannix and start looking for something else to do, and she wasn't foolhardy enough to go alone, but how could she allow something called "Blood Fest" to happen if she could stop it?

When she answered the phone, Mrs. Allen didn't sound cold and distant like she had before.

"Hello, Samantha," she said, surprised. Maybe she wasn't angry anymore. Sam had to admit that she was glad, and maybe that was why Sam apologized again.

Then again, maybe it had something to do with Ally.

"Mrs. Allen, I know I didn't do a very good job of apologizing before, but I understand why you told Preston about the Phantom's lead mare. It was because, well, she belonged to Preston first, right?"

"Yes, dear. That is right. And don't—how do they

put it?—don't beat yourself up over it. I understand how much you love that stallion and I know that even though people will tell you it's too risky to love a wild thing like him, you can't help it."

Sam shivered at Mrs. Allen's words, wondering where that had come from, but all she said was, "Thank you."

"You're welcome." Mrs. Allen cleared her throat. "Now, did you say you were calling for Preston?"

"Yes, ma'am," Sam said.

Then, as Mrs. Allen's voice faded away, Sam could have sworn she heard the old lady summoning the retired policeman with some name like Finny. But that didn't make any sense at all.

Two hours later, Sam and Preston rode Ace and Honey side by side into Lost Canyon.

"She looks great," Sam said, marveling at the palomino's sun-bright coat, her rippling ivory mane and tail and a gait that said she rejoiced in her rider. "I don't see any sign of a limp."

Preston shook his head and clapped the mare on the neck. It was clear to see he loved the horse, but he didn't admit it. Instead, he said, "She can use this exercise. And I've got a little test in mind for her."

"What kind of test?" Sam asked.

"I heard that gray stallion, the one she ran with, haunts this canyon about this time of year."

Sam's mouth turned dry as cotton. It was nice

that Preston had finally accepted her as a horse rescuer instead of a thief, but did he mean he was setting Honey up to choose between him and the Phantom?

"Do you really want to take the chance of her seeing him?" Sam asked. "It's only been a few days and a herd stallion has a lot of control over his family—even the lead mare."

"So I've been told," Preston said, "but if I'm going to ride her in this territory, I'd better find out if I can trust her."

"I don't know," Sam muttered, but she was also wondering how long he planned to stay in this territory. Did he plan to marry Mrs. Allen?

"So, we're checking out a camp of fighting roosters," Preston said, changing the subject. "I left a message for Heck, but he's busy chasing down the man he thinks is Christopher Mudge."

"Why aren't you?" Sam blurted. "I mean, after all this time . . ."

"I know," Preston said, nodding. "I've been asking myself the same question, but your friend Mrs. Allen asked me not to go. She thought it might involve some gunplay—which I doubt—so I decided Heck could handle it on his own, while I helped you out with these chickens. And, after all, I am retired."

"This should be pretty safe," Sam said.

Preston bristled. Did he think she'd called him a coward?

Sam hadn't meant it that way. Before she could

explain, though, Preston gazed into the distance as if a pleasant memory had crossed his mind, and said, "Can't do much but get scratched and pecked, I hear."

Wow, Sam thought, turning her attention to the trail as they passed through Lost Canyon. Preston must have the world's biggest crush on Mrs. Allen if he'd passed up the chance to arrest the thief who'd stolen his horse.

The stony path narrowed, but Sam didn't look off the edge, down to the turquoise ribbon of water in Arroyo Azul. She'd ridden the Phantom for the first time down there.

She didn't search the wide stone benches that made the arroyo look like the Roman coliseum, either. Sometimes the Phantom stood on one of them, watching over his herd as they drank down below.

Sam hoped the stallion was far away from here. Preston's test for his palomino wouldn't make anyone happy.

"Last September, this was a mustang trap," Sam told Preston as they rode through a sunny area overgrown with pinion pine and sagebrush.

Preston took a good look at the broken and bleached boards that had been part of the trap. He allowed Honey to stop and sniff them. Sam wondered how much of the mustangs' story the mare could read there.

"I haven't heard a single rooster," Preston said as they kept riding.

"Me either," Sam said. "My friend said they crow almost constantly. He figured that's why the guys kept them out here, instead of in town."

"We almost there?" Preston asked.

"Almost," Sam said.

Ace's shoulders tensed and his front legs moved stiffly. He threw his forelock back from his eyes and snorted, but he moved on.

Sam knew her worry was telegraphed down the reins to her horse, but she couldn't help it. She felt a jolt of childish fear when she saw the bus.

There was no reason it should give her the creeps. This ravine was obviously deserted. The only sounds were chirring cicadas and sagebrush bobbing in the wind, scraping against the rusted metal of the bus.

The only other time she'd come here, she'd been with Jen and they'd hiked in.

Now, she and Preston rode. If there was trouble, escaping would be easy. They had two instantly responsive mounts. A single touch would send the horses whirling around to gallop out of the canyon.

Except, Sam thought, giving Preston a side glance, that wasn't what cops did when they encountered trouble. They rode toward it, not away from it.

Maybe that was why the sight of the narrow chasm with the faded blue bus jammed into it made her nervous. She didn't want to face down a clutch of criminals in such close quarters.

Not that she planned to go into the bus.

According to Darrell, the roosters were tethered outside by little A-shaped shelters. But where were they? And if they were here, why were they so quiet? Maybe her guess had been wrong.

"Think it rolled down there and just stuck?" Preston asked as he studied the bus. "It's all creased and rusty on this side, like it had a bad crash."

"Maybe," Sam said. "It's stuck tight, I know that. Once you get inside, you can touch the hillside through the windows on the driver's side."

The breeze plucked at tattered cloth inside the bus, pulling it out for them to see.

"Clothes tucked into the windows in place of curtains," Preston observed.

"It was a hideout," Sam told him. "Not a very comfy one, though. Some of the seats are broken loose from the floor and others are split, with stuffing puffed out of them. And it stinks."

In the quiet, both horses lifted their heads and stared at the steep hillside.

Maybe the Phantom was nearby, Sam thought.

But then she reconsidered. Ace wasn't acting like he did when he scented the stallion. He moved rigidly, as if he was only here because Sam had made him come.

"There," Preston said quietly. He nodded instead of pointing, and Sam saw what he'd indicated. Hidden among the waving weeds, roosters were chained to small shelters.

"I wonder why they're being so quiet," Sam mused.

"That's not normal?" Preston asked, and Sam remembered he hadn't worked in a rural area.

"No way," Sam said, and then, as if he'd heard her, a small rooster with black-and-white feathers jumped atop his shelter and released an ear-splitting cock-a-doodle-do.

Sam was laughing when she felt Ace's stockinged hind feet strike with staccato uneasiness.

"You're not afraid of a mouthy little rooster," Sam said, patting the gelding's neck, but then Preston shook his head with a quelling motion.

He lowered his hand from the reins, toward his . . . what? His stirrup?

Sam didn't know what he was doing, but all at once she wished they had walkie-talkies. She wanted to notify Sheriff Ballard what they'd found. They couldn't move the roosters on horseback, and there was no time to waste. Besides, she suddenly felt way too isolated and alone.

If men like Ally's dad were winning enough to buy mandolins and formal dresses, a lot was at stake here. The criminals probably wouldn't give up without a fight.

Except there really didn't seem to be anyone here. That creaking sound she'd just heard had come from the bus door, folded almost closed but hanging from a single hinge so that it stirred in the wind.

"Wonder what it was used for before it crashed?" Preston said, still staring at the bus.

"My friend Jen says it shuttled prisoners between court and jail," Sam suggested.

"Could be," Preston agreed. "Want to take a look inside?"

"You go ahead," Sam said. "I've been in there. It's not just smelly—there are mice and bugs everywhere. Probably snakes, too, there to eat the mice."

"And you don't like that," Preston pointed out, as if that was just what he'd expected.

"I'm not afraid of mice and snakes," Sam said. "Or spiders. But I'd prefer they didn't surprise me."

She remembered the shiny-coated mouse that had run up her leg when she'd been sneaking around inside the bus with Jen.

"Amen to that," Preston said. He glanced at her from the corner of his eyes. "It was never spiders and snakes that kept me from enjoying my female partners, come to think of it."

Sam couldn't tell if he was joking. If he wasn't, she didn't want to talk about Preston's bias against female officers. She'd seen Brynna in action, and no male officer could do better, but the retired policeman seemed determined to tell her why he preferred male cops as partners.

"Naw, the reason I didn't like having a female partner is they get to have all the fun."

Sam hadn't expected him to say that.

"They do?" Sam asked.

"Sure. Most bad guys are stupid. They dismiss the female in uniform as weaker, and focus on the male partner. So, while the bad guys were busy facing off with me, my female partner would slink around behind 'em, take 'em down to the ground, and handcuff 'em."

"And that's fun?" Sam asked.

Preston chuckled, and for the first time Sam found herself liking him.

Her pleasure only lasted a few seconds.

A bullet struck the boulder between the horses, peppering them with shards of granite.

"Go!" Preston shouted.

Sam had already leaned to her right. Ace gathered himself to run, but then a voice cut through the whining sound still hanging in the air from the shot, and that voice stopped her.

"Don't you do it or I'll gut-shoot that mare right out from under you, and nail that bay before he can make two jumps up the trail."

Gathering in her reins, Sam turned.

The man coming through the yellow weeds held a rifle against his shoulder, and though he wasn't sighting down the barrel, he'd only have to lift it an inch to do it.

Tall and broad-shouldered, about Dad's age, he wore piggin' strings, the leather strips used to tie calves, dangling from his belt. Even though he was hatless and walked with a limp, he moved like a seasoned buckaroo. That was how Sam recognized him.

He was Flick.

Curtis Flickinger wasn't carrying his coiled bull-whip this time, but he was the same man who'd taught Dark Sunshine to scream, the same man who'd scarred the Phantom's neck and threatened to leave Sam hog-tied on the hillside over-looking Arroyo Azul.

Who would have thought he'd return to his old hideout? It made sense, though, Sam thought. Only she and Jake had seen him here.

He was Cowboy, too. She just knew it.

Don't no one want to cross Cowboy—isn't that what Bug Boy had told Preston? Sam could see why. And Cowboy had decreed that any stolen horse was a dead horse, because it was safer that way. That would fit Flick, too.

She knew it was him and she wondered if Sheriff Ballard had checked to see if he'd been released from prison. Maybe he'd escaped.

Crowing from the top of his shelter, the black-and-white rooster seemed to be doing his best to act as a watchdog.

Flick gave the rooster an annoyed glance. Then, calm and cocky, Flick kept walking toward them.

"Swear to God I'll shoot that mare right out from under you if you don't stop reaching for your boot," Flick said.

Preston dropped his reins and raised his hands.

"I'm not going for anything in my boot," he assured Flick.

"Get on down off that palomino," Flick said.

He still hadn't glanced at Sam as he crab-stepped down the steep part of the hillside. The agitated roosters rustled and crowed, springing to the ends of their tethers as if they could fly away.

"Get off," Flick repeated.

"I'd rather not," Preston said.

Afoot, she and Preston would lose their advantage, Sam thought.

But then, as casually as most men would hitch up their pants, Flick swung the barrel of the rifle aside and shot the black-and-white rooster.

Oh no, Sam thought. She didn't gasp, and neither horse shied at the sound, but the squawking hadn't stopped, even when the explosion of bright feathers had drifted down to the ground.

Then it was quiet again.

Sam kept watching Flick, but from the corner of her eye she caught Preston's glance. His expression said he wouldn't have dismounted, no matter what, if he'd been alone.

Somehow, though, he wasn't looking at her as a liability. He glanced at her with confidence, but she had no idea why.

"Okay, I'll dismount," Preston said, looking ever more pointedly at Sam, "but you remember what I said about being a good female cop. . . ."

"What's that mean?" Flick guffawed. "Think she's gonna hightail it out of here, screaming for help?

Naw, I'd put a bullet in her nag and sell him to Baldy Harris, if she tried. That'd about break her heart. 'Specially if I lamed him first."

Sam swallowed hard. She'd bet Flick was reminding her how he'd fallen on the canyon's rim and how he'd been hurt. That time, they'd left him while they went for help.

"Getting off," Preston announced, then, and to Sam's amazed eyes, it looked as if he did it with no hands.

"That's better," Flick said. "I been wantin' to stake that mare out as an invite to that gray stud."

Sam's heart shivered in her chest, but she didn't let Flick see her react. He knew the Phantom had been hers. He knew—of course! The letter Linc Slocum had showed the sheriff hadn't been from Karl Mannix at all.

It was Flick who had a standing offer of ten thousand dollars for the capture of the Phantom. Once before he'd tried to catch the stallion and sell him to the millionaire. That time he'd failed, but now he was trying again.

"Used a trip wire and almost had her—"

Each word he said ended a mystery. Honey's leg had been cut by Flick's trip wire.

"—but that stallion rushed me, spiteful as if he remembered me from before. Knocked me down with his shoulder and by the time I got up, they were both gone."

Flick spat on the desert floor, then balanced his rifle with one arm and reached for a piggin' string.

Was he going to tie Preston up? If so, he'd be preoccupied. Sam had to do something to help.

What had Preston said? Bad guys focused on the male partner. It was true.

Flick actually turned his back on her while he tied the retired cop as if he were a calf.

"Yeah, it'll be nice to have this mare," Flick said, glancing up at Honey. "When I thought I couldn't get her, I went after that buckskin of mine. Heard me, didn't ya?"

When he glanced up at Sam, he didn't seem to notice that she'd urged Ace a little closer.

"Yeah, I saw everyone speedin' away from your ranch like their tails were on fire, leaving you alone with those cowhands and I just came on down to take her. Didn't expect the barn to be locked, or for her to remember me, too."

Flick gave a cruel laugh. "And shoot, I've never seen such a commotion over one dumb barking dog."

Don't listen, Sam told herself. *Don't think of Blaze's bleeding lip. Do something.*

He wouldn't be saying all this if he meant to let them get away.

As if someone had touched her on the shoulder and whispered, Sam suddenly knew what she had to do.

She had a rope. Flick didn't.

She was mounted. He wasn't.

He did have a rifle, but Ace could drag him off his feet and all over the ravine if she could only rope him. She didn't think about her remedial roping skills. She only thought of getting her horse into position for the best throw she could make.

Gently, Sam closed her legs against Ace. He took her a step closer to Flick and suddenly the cicadas on the hillside went silent.

Sam heard the thud of a hoof just as Honey and Ace lifted their heads. The palomino nickered in recognition.

No! Sam's mind shouted. *Run!*

The Phantom stood about a quarter mile up the hillside. His lone white form looked down at them.

Preston shifted his attention from Flick to Honey, but he couldn't silence the palomino with his stare. A second neigh floated from her to the silver stallion.

"Okay!" Flick stood up, backed a step away from Preston, and rubbed his palms together. "Now things are gonna get interesting."

Chapter Eighteen ↝

Sam eased Ace a bit closer.

Communicating with Ace was something she knew how to do, but she couldn't read Flick's mind and predict his next move.

Would he use Honey for bait to attract the Phantom? But he didn't have a rope or a corral. Even if the Phantom came close, how would he catch him?

Flick glanced over his shoulder. A frown wrinkled his brow. If he'd noticed Sam was closer, though, he didn't mention it. Instead, he tried to scare her.

"I think I might just put a round between his eyes," he told her. "What do you think? Can I do it from here? And if I acted like I was gonna hurt this mare, or you, would he come snortin' and gallopin' to the rescue?"

He thinks he can control me by scaring me, Sam thought. *He thinks I'll just freeze or do whatever he says.*

Sam tried not to give him that power.

Flick sighted down his rifle barrel at the stallion. She watched him squint one eye closed, then urged Ace forward another step.

Ace obeyed, then planted each hoof and stood firm. She was close enough, he seemed to say. Now it was up to her.

Sam's hands shook as she reached down and unsnapped the leather strap holding her rope. She had to steady her fingers enough to throw a perfect loop.

This was her only chance, and she'd better hurry. Flick had no qualms about shooting the Phantom and the stallion was just standing there.

His mustang instincts must have helped him sense the danger, but even the smartest horse wouldn't know the range of Flick's rifle.

A glance told Sam that Preston was working to free himself. Flick must see it, too.

In case he didn't, though, Sam tried to keep Flick's attention on her.

"Won't Linc pay the ten thousand dollars for that stallion?" Sam croaked.

"Well, now, he might," Flick answered instantly. He lowered the rifle and tilted his head to one side, seeming to consider her reminder. Then he shook his head. "But I'm thinking it might be ten thousand dollars worth of fun, to—"

Enough.

Eyes focused, arm whirling the loop above her head, Sam swung her rope toward Flick. It had to settle over his head and pin his arms to his sides. This time, when an accurate throw really mattered, she had to aim right.

The rope slid through her fingers, singing toward him in what seemed like slow motion. Flick saw the loop coming. He dodged to one side and dropped.

Preston kicked out, slamming both boots into Flick's knee, knocking him off balance.

Sam heard hooves and the Phantom's neigh, but she didn't look at the stallion. Her eyes were fixed on her rope. The loop cleared the outlaw's head, but she hadn't made a clean catch. When the loop closed, one edge sawed against the right side of Flick's neck. The other side was caught under his left arm.

All he had to do was grab the loop and lift it off over his head. But he'd have to drop the rifle he still clutched in his right hand to do that.

"Giddyup!" Preston yelled, reminding Sam and Ace of the desensitization class and his order to her to have Ace drag him.

Sam wheeled Ace. The bay gelding jumped, jerking Flick off his feet.

Was it herd instinct or some desire to help that lured the Phantom down from his safe spot on the hillside? He bolted past Preston and the bus. He galloped past Honey without faltering, and then he was right beside her, tucking in next to Ace.

The stallion wasn't racing for fun. He huffed, but not from exertion. His hooves thundered and ears flattened, disappearing amid torrents of white mane. Head flat and nostrils wide, he ran past Ace, leading him on.

Ace followed. Fighting the reins, his head wrenched from side to side. Sam held on as the bay mustang answered the call of the stallion who'd been his leader and tried to rip the reins from her grip. She tightened them instead, but even the gelding's trot was too fast.

Flick wasn't yelling and thrashing as Preston had when they were pretending, but she couldn't let Ace follow the Phantom. He had to slow down. They were dragging Flick way too fast.

The Phantom stopped a hundred yards ahead and pawed the dirt. A dust cloud surrounded him as he chastised Ace for being so slow, but it gave Sam a chance to pull Ace to a stop.

Sam looked back and saw that Flick still held the rifle. How was that possible?

Panting, he rolled up, onto one knee.

Could he shoot from that position? Sam didn't give him a chance.

"Giddyup!" Sam shouted.

She heard the impact of Flick's chest hitting the dirt as Ace bolted into a lope, headed for the silver stallion.

But then Sam heard Preston shouting, and a glance back showed her the retired policeman was on his feet, running after her.

"Don't drag him to death!" he shouted. Preston knew murder when he saw it, and he was warning her.

Sam jerked her reins. Ace's heels skidded and he squealed in bewilderment.

I know, Sam thought wildly. *Drag him to death or let him shoot us? We can't win.*

"Hang in there!" Preston shouted, but how could she?

This was like a bad dream.

Ace half reared, but she clucked her tongue, calming him, reining him to turn and face Flick.

How could she "hang in there" when the outlaw lay motionless on the desert floor?

Nearly crouching, Preston rushed toward the rifle Flick had finally dropped.

It'll be over when he gets the gun, Sam thought.

Black dots frenzied like a million buzzing bees before Sam's eyes. She felt herself waver in the saddle.

"Stay with me, Sam," Preston called, but it was the Phantom's neigh as he approached Sam and Honey at a majestic trot that helped her stay focused and strong.

Hang in there. The words echoed in Sam's mind. She could do that.

Preston knew she had no experience, so he must be counting on her courage.

Taking a deep breath, Sam wrenched her eyes away from the unconscious man and watched the horses.

Honey lowered her head in submission. Her neck curved like a golden swan's looking back at the stallion as he came closer. And then she straightened. Head held high, she moved to meet him.

Preston had the rifle clamped in one fist, held horizontal to the ground, but he turned away from Flick to watch his horse.

"Honey," Preston said quietly.

Sam sensed the mare stop, but Ace's muscles tensed. He snorted and Sam knew even before she looked that she and Preston had made a mistake.

Flick had lifted her loop soundlessly. Now he ducked out of it.

Preston yelled something at the same time Sam heard her own cry, but Flick had already launched himself at her.

Hadn't Preston said in the desensitization class that posse members would probably never have to face a criminal grappling for their gun? But she had no gun. Was Flick after her horse?

Sam kicked at Flick, but he was too close. Her boot didn't jar him back a single inch.

Instead, she lost her stirrup and he grabbed Ace's near rein, yanking the gelding's head around as his hand grabbed at Sam.

He's trying to drag me from the saddle, Sam thought with sudden clarity. He wanted to use her as a shield between himself and the rifle, and she couldn't let him do it.

Sam leaned away from him, still kicking. If his arm snaked around her waist, his leverage would be too good. She wouldn't have a chance of staying on Ace.

Sam had one more thing to try. It meant dropping her reins and leaning toward her attacker, but she had nothing to lose.

Closing her hand, but not with her fingers inside, Sam felt herself falling as her fist crashed down on Flick's nose.

She heard a sickening crunch and saw a gush of blood as she tumbled past him and slammed shoulder first onto the ground, rolling.

Ace's hooves, dancing nervously, passed her. He joined the Phantom and Honey, but he didn't run away.

Flick howled and reached for his nose with both hands. He was still moaning when Preston jumped on top of him and tied him with his own piggin' strings.

Sam struggled to her feet.

She watched Preston secure Flick with professional efficiency. He probably would have read him his rights, too, if he hadn't been retired, Sam thought; and the roosters . . .

It seemed like there was a congratulatory chorus of crowing roosters as Preston straightened.

"I'd say your shot missed that rooster," Preston said, but he wasn't looking at the roosters. His stare stabbed past Sam and she turned to follow it.

The Phantom's silver head lay across Honey's withers, just in front of the saddle.

Brynna would probably say the stallion was exerting his dominance over his lead mare one last time, but to Sam it looked like a friendly good-bye.

It was, she thought excitedly. The stallion proved it, as he backed up far enough to nibble a wavy clump of Honey's mane.

Whisking his tail and giving a snort, he glanced at Preston. The man stood still and there was a respectful look on his face, but when he merely took a breath, the stallion bolted.

Dirt spun from under his hooves and he soared over yards of desert, putting himself as far from the unfamiliar human as he could. He didn't look back at Honey, Ace, or Sam. Tail streaming silver behind him, the Phantom galloped away.

Sam sighed. Her horse was safe, she thought, and maybe it was the sudden relief that allowed her to realize she was cupping her right hand in her left, blowing her breath on it as if that could somehow ease the pain that accompanied the proper use of the Ely Brothers' hammer fist.

* * *

Exactly a week later, Sam stood on the front porch of her house at River Bend Ranch.

Because Gram had insisted, she wore her bridesmaid dress from Dad and Brynna's wedding and she stood in the quickly-cooling dusk, handing candles to guests as they arrived for Preston and Mrs. Allen's engagement party.

Dad, Brynna, and Gram had already welcomed Sheriff Ballard, Ally, and her father, and the Elys— all except for Jake—with cups of punch and crystal plates piled with six different kinds of cookies.

Now the last guests, the Kenworthys, hurried into the crowded kitchen to loud greetings, but Jen lagged behind.

"What's this for?" Jen asked, holding up the pumpkin-colored candle.

"When Gram and Mrs. Allen were girls," Sam explained, "there was this candle-passing ceremony all their girlfriends did when anyone got engaged. And, since Mrs. Allen eloped, she skipped the tradi-tion of her first engagement—"

"So, she's getting it now," Jen said, smiling. "That's cute."

"I guess," Sam said, but she couldn't shake off the melancholy that came with thinking that the marriage wouldn't last long because Mrs. Allen and Preston were so old.

"I know what you're thinking," Jen whispered, then she touched the book she'd tucked under her arm. "Statistically speaking, they're not that old. I'll show you something later that will cheer you up.

"Right now, though," Jen said, grimacing, "it looks like someone else has something to say to you, and though it probably won't cheer you up, I'm abandoning you to handle it on your own."

Sam glanced back to see Jake striding across the ranch yard.

He wore a long-sleeved white shirt with jeans, and his black hair had grown out enough that he'd had to wet it and brush it back from falling in front of his ears.

The screen door slammed behind Jen, and Sam was facing Jake alone.

"Where'd you come from?" Sam asked. Then, daring him to treat her like a kid, she took a deep breath and said, "I'm too old for you to lecture me, you know."

"I know. I won't. I just have one thing to say."

He looked down at the tips of boots she'd never seen before. They were mahogany brown and smooth and polished so that they glowed under the porch light.

"Go ahead," Sam said.

"Puttin' the whole thing with Flick aside," Jake said, "'cause I know you'll say it was about roosters, not the Phantom—"

"It was!"

"Yeah," Jake said, "but horses were runnin' all through the trouble you got us tangled in."

Sam drew a breath to contradict him, then let it out. As much as she hated to agree with him, Jake was right.

"All I'm sayin' is, quit puttin' your whole heart on the line, Brat. About everything, but especially about the Phantom. The life of a wild horse is dangerous. How long do you think you'll have him?"

"You kids get in here," Gram called from inside the kitchen, but Sam noticed that no one opened the screen door to interrupt.

"Not that you really have him now," Jake said. Then, with a shrug, he added, "Just think about pulling back a little bit, okay?"

And then Jake held the screen door open, so Sam could enter the party before him.

Ally stood in the corner strumming her guitar, introducing the guests to the song they were about to sing together. She smiled at Sam as she came in.

"All right," Gram said, quickly lighting Sam's candle. "Everyone's candle is lighted and those of you who didn't know 'Tell Me Why' have had a chance to look at the lyrics, so here we go."

Gram turned off the kitchen light, and everyone stood in candlelight as they began to sing.

"Tell me why the stars do shine.
Tell me why the ivy twines. . . ."

Ally's voice soared over the others, but no one seemed to care, and Sam hoped their beginning friendship would last.

Ally had thanked her an embarrassing number of

times for revealing her dad's secret. Together, Ally and her dad had already attended meetings for people addicted to gambling and their family members.

Sam thought everything would probably be okay, because Mr. McClintock had admitted his gambling problem and his hatred for the direction it had taken him, saying he hadn't even seen blood and feathers. He'd only thought about the money.

"Tell me why the sky's so blue
And then I'll tell you just why I love you. . . ."

Sam's eyes moved to Mrs. Allen's shining face. She looked up at Preston, who seemed as embarrassed by this ceremony as he had been when his fiancée had told everyone his first name was Phineas and that was why he went by his last name, Preston.

He'd laughed, though, when she said she thought "Finny" was a perfectly lovely nickname and that he had given her just the "darlingest" engagement present—a black-and-white rooster named Lucky.

"Because God made the stars to shine.
Because God made the ivy twine."

Sam noticed Sheriff Ballard fanning himself with the lyric sheet. He wasn't following along, but he wasn't grumping like he had been all week, either. Every time Sam had heard him talking to Dad, he'd been complaining that he didn't have time to be parceling out all the fighting roosters to local ranchers. He kept doing it, though, and Sam thought he was just dissatisfied because even though he'd tracked Flick to Lost Canyon through the cell phone's global positioning system, he still hadn't found Karl Mannix, and Linc Slocum was harassing him relentlessly.

"Because God made the skies so blue.

Because God made you, that's why I love you!"

As everyone clapped and blew out their candles and Gram turned the lights back up, Sam noticed that Dad and Brynna still stood with shoulders touching. Tears ran down Brynna's cheeks and Dad looked so softhearted, Sam thought an outsider wouldn't believe, looking at him now, that he could have been so angry.

She didn't like to think about it. The consequences of his anger were bad enough: she was grounded from everything but school and school events until Halloween. And she'd been lucky that Brynna had helped her negotiate that concession, because Dad had wanted to ground her until Christmas.

Blaze's howl floated to them from outside and everyone laughed, pretending it was a comment on their singing.

His howl sounded sad to Sam, though, and she ducked outside as soon as she got the chance. This was supposed to be a celebration, and she didn't want to ruin it for anyone else.

Blaze rushed across the yard, mouth open and tail wagging, looking much happier than she was, and then the screen door closed quietly and Jen was right beside them.

"Okay, hear the news," Jen announced, flashing the cover of a world almanac. "I've looked it up, and though Preston's projected life expectancy at the time he was born was sixty-five and Mrs. Allen's was sixty-six, with nutritional and medical advancements, they have a lot longer!"

Jen glanced at the book and then at Sam. "It's so cool. Barring accidents and bad guys, he can expect to live an extra twenty-four years and she gets another twenty-three. . . ."

Sam watched her friend's mind click off numbers like a calculator, as she finished, "Given their age difference, they ought to come out about even!"

Morbid as Jen's calculations were, they both laughed.

And when Jake's statement—that the life of a wild horse was risky and she wouldn't have the Phantom long—popped into her mind, Sam wondered if maybe he was as wrong as she'd been.

"Can I look at that for a minute?" Sam asked. "I'm supposed to be helping with refreshments, but—"

"No problem," Jen said. "Take it and I'll go cover for you!"

Alone in the twilight, Sam tilted the book so that she could read the fine print of the index.

"Life expectancy . . . animals . . ." she muttered to Blaze, and then she flipped to the page.

Holding her breath, she read the entry for horses, and though the average life span was only twenty, the world record was fifty years.

She didn't release the shout of joy building inside her chest, but the sight of River Bend's horses — especially Ace — grazing peacefully, filled her with delight.

Sam gazed up into the lavender-pink sky. She ignored the voices, even Jake's, saying, "Don't do it, you're only going to lose him."

Even if a mustang's life was dangerous, she might have him for a long time.

Sam closed her eyes and the voices faded away.

From
Phantom Stallion
↩ 23 ↪
GYPSY GOLD

If there could be such a thing as a second summer, this was it.

Samantha Forster lay on her back in the warm grass and gazed at a cloud Pegasus. Drifts of white cloud made up the mane and tail and gray-edged clumps looked like muscular shoulders. If not for the cloud wings trimmed with sun gold, he'd look like the Phantom.

The mustang stallion could be watching from a nearby ridge or peering through a screen of pinion pines. Sam lay totally still, wishing he'd appear.

Sam's jeans felt hot against her legs. Her head was pillowed on her jacket. Her outspread arms were bare to the green shoots poking up between the brittle autumn grass left uneaten by deer, antelope, or wild horses over the summer.

Why hadn't the cold nighttime temperatures kept the baby grass from pushing up from the warm darkness of the dirt? Why didn't the grass have more sense than to explore where its tender tips would be frozen off any night now?

Sam smiled and closed her eyes. She basked in the sun's warmth and studied the scarlet network of veins crisscrossing the inside of her eyelids. She must be half asleep if she was actually asking herself why grass didn't have the sense to stay underground.

Right now, though, being half asleep was a good thing. She'd promised her best friend, Jen Kenworthy, that she'd play dead for at least an hour.

The two girls had ridden out from River Bend Ranch on Ace and Silly after school the day before.

Armed with a hand-drawn map from Jen's Advanced Biology teacher, the girls had searched for the turkey vultures' roost yesterday on an offshoot of the trail up to Cowkiller Caldera. At dusk, they'd found a tree filled with the black birds.

"Oh, yeah!" Jen had rejoiced and her excitement had electrified her palomino. She'd had to turn the mare in circles to keep her from bolting. Once her mount had settled, Jen had whispered, "We'll be back in the morning."

Grinning without opening her eyes, Sam recalled that Jen hadn't been talking to her. Only her best friend would make a promise to turkey vultures.

They'd turned their horses around, walked back down the hillside and pitched camp far enough away that they wouldn't disturb the birds.

Jen had researched turkey vultures and come to the conclusion that they were totally misunderstood. She'd vowed to do firsthand research for her project so that she didn't repeat any other scientists' mistakes. That firsthand research included luring the birds near enough that she could sketch them.

Now Jen and Sam were lying still as corpses, hoping a curious turkey vulture would actually land beside them and hop close enough to satisfy its curiosity.

"They have such good senses of smell, they'll know we're not dead," Jen whispered beside her.

Sam rolled her eyes as far to the left as she could without moving her head. She saw blond braids and a tanned face, but Jen's lips didn't seem to move.

"Won't smell rotten enough," Sam joked.

"Sam," Jen said patiently, "they only eat freshly dead things."

"I didn't know buzzards were so picky," Sam teased.

"There are no buzzards in the United States," Jen hissed. "Now we have to hush. Any minute, they could fly off for South America. This flock is rare. It could be the one that stays in Nevada through October."

Sam pressed her lips together, telling herself this flock of turkey vultures wasn't the only thing that was rare. She'd bet there weren't two other teenagers in the country getting their pre-Halloween thrills by offering themselves as bird bait.

Still, Sam was glad Jen had coaxed her into sharing these peaceful moments.

Sam's life had been hamster-on-a-wheel crazy since she'd moved back to northern Nevada from San Francisco. She never would have thought of soaking up October sunshine in a meadow that would soon be blasted by winter storms.

This was a great escape after almost a month of being grounded.

For four long weeks she'd done what she was told—morning chores, school, afternoon chores, and homework—over and over again. She'd learned her lesson this time. She wouldn't do anything to make Dad, Gram, and Brynna worry. Although sometimes it was impossible to tell what would set them off.

Her only fun during those long weeks had come from perfecting her bareback riding skills on her bay mustang Ace.

Since she wasn't allowed to leave the ranch on horseback, she'd sat on him in the corral, trying to find a perfect balance that didn't involve squeezing her legs and accidentally sending him forward.

One afternoon Dallas, River Bend's foreman, had finally asked, "You gonna roost on that horse all night?"

It had sounded like heaven to Sam. What could be cozier than spending the night on Ace, leaning forward with her arms around his neck and her cheek leaning against his mane?

She and Ace had come a long way together since she'd returned from San Francisco. She'd come home a totally timid rider. If she was a cowgirl now, Ace got most of the credit. He'd tricked and bullied her until she knew that if she didn't take charge, he would.

He'd never be a push-button horse, but she loved him with all her heart.

Sam sighed. Jen shushed her again.

Sam raised her eyelashes a tenth of a millimeter and saw three turkey vultures riding the air currents above her.

Cross-shaped black bodies circled, mimicking Sam's own position. Except, in place of arms, they had wide, prehistoric-looking wings. Sam wanted to believe they were just as afraid of her as she was of them, but what if the vultures really mistook her for a dead thing?

It could happen. She remembered a Thanksgiving when she was a little kid, when she'd mistaken a plastic grape for the real thing.

Gram had arranged the pretty red plastic grapes in a Thanksgiving cornucopia. Sam had snatched one and chomped down on it before anyone caught her ruining the centerpiece. With the plastic burning her taste buds, Sam had spit it out. Then her sense of betrayal had turned to anger.

What if the vultures swooped in for brunch, discovered she was faking, then grabbed her with their talons and pecked out her eyes?

"Quit freaking out," Jen hissed.

"I'm not," Sam answered.

"Okay," Jen breathed, but those two syllables managed to say Jen was not convinced.

Sam reminded herself she loved animals. All animals.

Vultures just did what they were born to do. Sure they stuck their heads and necks inside dead bodies, but Jen claimed turkey vultures also spent three hours a day cleaning their feathers—preening, she'd called it.

Sam and Jen had agreed that was a lot longer than either of them ever spent trying to look pretty.

Sam forced air from her lungs and tried to lie flatter. She felt the bumps of the herringbone braid Jen had plaited into her hair this morning, and the tickle of what might be ant feet crossing the nape of her neck, but she lay still.

In the quiet, she heard her shirt move with her breath, then listened as a horse blew through his lips.

Down the hillside, Ace and Silly were getting restless.

Jen had packed into the wilderness with horses more often than Sam, so when Jen insisted on feeding the horses hay instead of grain so they wouldn't be pumped up with energy and dig holes at the camp-site, they'd done it. When Jen pointed out that maps and memories could be faulty and they should water the horses every time there was a chance, they'd done that, too.

Only Jen's decision to tie Ace and Silly to a picket line instead of hobbling them made Sam uneasy. She loved Jen's palomino, Silk Stockings, but there was a reason the mare's nickname was Silly.

Still, the horses had stayed tied all night and all morning while Jen cooked a skillet full of biscuits.

Talk about preening! Sam thought. Jen had brought along premade biscuits just in case hers didn't work out, but it turned out she didn't need them.

Using her mom's cast-iron skillet, Jen had cooked up crisp, golden biscuits that were tender in the middle and delicious.

As Sam thought of the extra biscuits they'd wrapped up and saved for lunch, her stomach growled. Apparently that didn't bother the vultures.

A faint coolness made Sam's eyes spring open. One of the turkey vultures had moved closer. It glided near enough that she saw its head tilt.

That bird knew very well she wasn't dead meat, but it wanted to see what she was.

Pop!

At the sound, all three birds rose higher into the sky.

A horse squealed.

Pop! Pop!

Sitting up, Jen gasped, "Were those shots?"

"I don't know." Sam lurched to her feet, heart pounding.

They weren't shots. Of course they weren't.

She wet her lips and stared at Jen. Behind her glasses, Jen's eyes were wide and worried.

"Should we go see?" Jen asked.

Her uncertainty surprised Sam. Jen was a rancher's daughter and a cowgirl to the bone. Still, Jen was sensible. She wanted sufficient information before she made a move.

They both listened hard.

"If it was a gun, going toward it is the last thing we should—" Sam's voice broke off at the thudding of hooves.

Their horses were loose!

Something clattered, rolled, and shattered. Metal rang from impact and then the sound of hoofbeats faded.

"Let's go!" Jen shouted.

Grabbing her jacket, Sam broke into a run and Jen matched her steps.

Beyond the pounding of their feet, the girls could still hear the hooves.

"They're running away," Jen said in a wondering tone.

Sam took longer strides as she yelled in agreement, "And it's a long walk home!"

❊ ❊ ❊

The campsite was weirdly quiet.

The horses were gone. Running after them and shouting for them to stop would only make them gallop farther and faster.

Together, Sam and Jen stood, hands on hips, and looked around the clearing.

It was easy to see what had happened. The carefully strung picket line snaked across the campsite, pulled down by the spooked horses before they trampled the sleeping bags.

Sam bent to retrieve her sleeping bag. Hooves had flung it into the dead campfire.

"Do you know how glad I am we doused the fire before leaving?" Sam muttered. She shook out the sleeping bag and brushed at the smear left by charred sticks and ashes, but then she shuddered.

If they'd left the campfire burning after breakfast, the sleeping bag could have been kicked into the embers by the horses, and blazed into flames. Fire could have spread to Jen's sleeping bag, then to their supplies. The whole hillside might have caught fire.

The handle had shattered off Jen's blue pottery mug, but her mom's skillet was where she'd left it, propped against a rock to dry after she'd washed it. Alongside the skillet were their stacked tin plates.

In fact, only three things—the picket line, sleeping bag, and cup—were out of place. The campsite looked pretty orderly except for the white ooze.

"The biscuits," Jen moaned. She pointed at the

foil-wrapped tubes, which had split open to let sticky dough escape.

"Refrigerated biscuits," Sam corrected, and they both threw their hands up in disbelief.

Why hadn't one of them thought of this before? Kept cool, the dough waited quietly in those tubes. But the morning sun had heated through the cardboard. The dough inside had risen, expanded, and popped the tubes open.

"At least it wasn't gunshots," Jen said.

Sam nodded. Last month's encounter with a rifle was enough to last a lifetime. She'd faced a horse rustler with a gun and she never wanted to do it again.

The memory made her hands tremble. She inhaled a shaky breath and sat down on a boulder.

"Are you okay?" Jen asked, examining her with an analytical stare.

"I will be," Sam said.

She concentrated on the scent of lingering campfire smoke and the herbal freshness of the pinion trees. Gram and her church friends had harvested pinion pine nuts just last weekend. Gram had been toasting them in the oven when Sam had returned home from school the day before yesterday.

The remembered scent made Sam's pulse settle down.

"Sorry," Sam said, looking up at Jen.

Her friend waved the apology away.

"Go ahead and rest." Jen meant it, but she was striding around camp, picking things up and arranging them in her backpack. "I have to go after Silly. I don't know what she'll do out there."

Jen's palomino mare was a ranch horse. Beautiful, strong, and surprisingly sensible in parades, she was used to sharing pastures and corrals with the other Kenworthy palominos—not running wild.

And no matter how much Jen joked about her horse being neurotic, they loved each other.

As soon as Jen had crawled out of her sleeping bag that morning, the mare had fussed for her touch. When Jen had drawn near enough, Silly had rested her head on Jen's shoulder and left it there, eyes peaceful as Jen stoked her.

Now, Jen knelt to roll up her sleeping bag. She wasn't about to wait for the horses to return. She was breaking camp.

"I think—" Sam broke off, shaking her head.

"Yes?" Jen asked, pausing.

"I wonder which one of them will lead." Sam gestured down the trail. "They both know the way home."

As Jen mulled that over, Sam thought about Ace. She didn't blame her horse for taking off when she wasn't there to tell him not to, but really, he'd been through police horse desensitization training and tolerated all kinds of weird stuff. Why would he panic at the sound of popping dough?

She thought of the snort she'd heard earlier. Ace had been ready to move on.

If she'd been standing here, holding his reins, turning him to look toward the sound, allowing him to study its source with both eyes, he would have stayed. But she'd been up the hill, so he'd taken the excuse to flee, leaving her afoot.

Sam shook her head. When you hung around with horses, you never got bored. They came up with something new every single day.

"I think they'll stay together, but we've got to go after them," Jen insisted. Then, wistfully, she added, "I'm pretty sure we've seen the last of the turkey vultures, so we might as well."

Sam had forgotten all about the birds, but Jen's shoulders sagged as she gazed into the blue sky. Except for a few long drifts of clouds, it was empty.

"Did you see enough?" Sam asked.

Jen shrugged.

Sam placed a knee on her sleeping bag to hold it closed while she knotted the strings. She tried to think of something that would cheer Jen up.

"At least the horses are saddled," she said.

After breakfast, they'd saddled up to ride to the roosting tree, but Jen had changed her mind. She'd decided the turkey vultures would be less suspicious of two motionless humans without horses.

"Good point," Jen said, but then she looked

around them. "You know all that gear they carried up the mountain?"

Sam tried not to think about it. "We can do it," she said. "And we'll be walking downhill." Sam was trying to sound upbeat, but then she swallowed, feeling a little thirsty.

"Tell me again why we filled our canteens and left them hanging on our saddles?" she moaned.

"We still have that," Jen said, pointing at their big plastic water jug.

Though it was only half full, the jug would be heavy.

"Want to drink it here? It's not like we're going to die of dehydration," Sam said.

Jen pressed an index finger to the bridge of her glasses and cleared her throat as if Sam's words might come back to haunt them.

Sam rushed on, "All we have to do is take the trail back down to the road. If we don't see the horses by then, someone will drive by."

When Jen didn't agree, Sam grabbed the jug and swished it around. Then, as if to seal a promise, she gulped half the water, and handed the jug to Jen.

"Here's to you, partner," Jen joked.

She drank, wiped her wet lips with the back of her hand, then flattened the empty jug, folded it, and slipped it inside her backpack.

Stomachs sloshing and backs draped with gear, the girls started downhill.

Sam kept her eyes fixed on the trail ahead.

She would not look back. It was melodramatic and stupid to think that the vultures were stalking them.

And if they were, she didn't want to know.

Read all the Phantom Stallion Books!

#1: The Wild One
Pb 0-06-441085-4

#2: Mustang Moon
Pb 0-06-441086-2

#3: Dark Sunshine
Pb 0-06-441087-0

#4: The Renegade
Pb 0-06-441088-9

#5: Free Again
Pb 0-06-441089-7

#6: The Challenger
Pb 0-06-441090-0

#7: Desert Dancer
Pb 0-06-053725-6

#8: Golden Ghost
Pb 0-06-053726-4

#9: Gift Horse
Pb 0-06-056157-2

#10: Red Feather Filly
Pb 0-06-056158-0

www.phantomstallion.com